D0984522

SHADOW
OF THE
JACKAL

NAVI' ROBINS

SHADOW

OF THE

JACKAL

NAV'I ROBINS

Copyright © 2021 by NorthShore Publishing House Inc.

Cover design: Navi' Robins
Typesetting: Navi' Robins

www.nsgraphicstudio.com

For

Ebonee JoDee

Kenitra HM Trey

CHAPTER ONE

"**W**HERE IS HE GOING?!" Miguel yelled in Shadow's face as another man pressed the hot iron rod on his chest. Shadow's flesh sizzled and bubbled under the extreme heat, activating his pain receptors, and he responded by screaming at the top of his lungs.

"We can do this until you talk or you're dead. You decide which one comes first."

Miguel then nodded to the man holding the iron rod on Shadow's chest, and he slowly removed the rod. Shadow's flesh tore as the metal detached itself from his chest, exposing the flesh under his burnt skin. Growling and jumping forward, Shadow tried to reach his antagonizer, but his chained arms were out of reach, and the movement created more discomfort for his tortured and damaged body.

Shaking his head as he watched Shadow grimace in pain from his movement, Miguel chuckled, "You got heart, *cabrone*, but heart won't save you. Only the truth! Where did he go?!"

Looking into Miguel's eyes, Shadow smiled and said, "To ya momma's house, if you hurry, you could get there just in time to watch him put it in her *culo*,"

1

"Funny, how about I have my friend over there shove that hot iron up your *culo* and see if you're still in the mood for comedy, eh?"

Shaking his head, Shadow forced his dying body to push out a coarse chuckle and responded, "You can shove whatever you want up my ass, still won't stop ya momma from getting that dookie love she been begging for!"

"Fuck you!" Miguel yelled in Shadow's face. He then pulled his right fist back and landed a devastating right hook to his mid-section. Shadow began coughing and vomiting blood all over the concrete floor.

"You're not laughing now, are you, *cabrone*!" Miguel screamed as he continued to punish his prisoner's body. Shadow's body became limp as he began to lose consciousness, and Miguel called for his helper to bring him the ammonia so that Shadow can remain alert.

"I want him to feel every fucking burn, razor cut, and broken bone. He will talk, or he will die, but slowly."

His helper handed Miguel a cotton swap saturated in ammonia, and Miguel pressed it under Shadow's nose and then forced some of the liquid up his nostrils. Shadow's eyes sprung open, and he screamed in agony as he hissed and moaned, forcing the burning liquid out of his nose.

"Are you awake?! No sleeping on the job, Shadow! We have so much to do before we're done here. Now, I will ask you again before my assistant starts breaking your fingers and toes. Where did *he* go?!"

CHAPTER TWO

One year earlier

THE STARTLING SOUND OF the television's surround sound system filling the living room with rapid gun fire broke Zahir out of his concentration, and his body jerked violently on the navy blue recliner. The laptop resting on his lap started to slide off his legs, and he reached down quickly to stop it from tumbling to the floor. Looking towards the fireplace, Zahir noticed Kai standing in front of the flat-screen TV mounted over the fireplace's mantle, repeatedly pushing the tv remote's buttons. He seemed determined to turn the surround sound system up to get the full effect of the iconic drive-by shooting scene from his favorite movie, "Menace to Society."

"Kai! What the fuck? You see me trying to study, and you come in here turning up the tv like you crazy!"

Kai refused to acknowledge Zahir and continued to move through the tv's settings menu, looking for the best sound options available. Noticing his little brother wasn't listening to him, Zahir placed his laptop on the black lampstand next to the recliner and stood up.

"Bruh, I'm telling you, if I come over there, I will wrap that fucking remote around your skinny ass neck."

Rolling his eyes, Kai whispered, "Yeah ri–,"

Without warning, Kai felt Zahir snatch the remote control out of his hand. He then placed his right hand on the back of his head and shoved him away from him. The force propelled Kai forward, and Zahir quickly noticed his brother's forehead would collide with the sharp edge of the fireplace mantel. Gasping, he reached forward, grasping a handful of the back of his white t-shirt and pulled him back and away from the fireplace. The push and pull motion caused Kai to lose his balance, and his body tumbled backward onto the mahogany hardwood floor. His body collided with the floor with a loud thump, causing the glass décor scattered throughout the living room to jump and send a sharp sound throughout the house.

"I'm telling momma!" Kai yelled at Zahir as he quickly jumped to his feet.

Shrugging, Zahir chuckled and responded, "I don't care. I told you to turn the tv down, but you like trying people. And after you tried momma last week by coming in the house after nine on a school night, I wouldn't even say shit to her. She told you she was gonna whop yo ass, so being a lil snitch might make her remember she owes you an ass whopping."

"Fuck that! Nah, momma let that slide."

Zahir stared at Kai, smiling brightly and nodding his head.

"Yeah, momma always letting shit slide. Uh-huh. Keep telling yo dumb ass that."

Kai's hazel brown eyes started to move back and forth as his mind tried to recollect how many times their mother let anything go. After discovering he couldn't recall a single time, his mouth turned downwards, and his left nostril lifted while he shook his head.

"Whatever, imma find a way to get you back for that shit."

"Be my guest. Next time I'll just let your head crack on the fireplace. Coffee bean face ass nigga!"

"Zahir, you darker than me, so what you talmbout? California raisin face ass nigga! I heard it through the grapevine, singing face ass nigga. Take your ass outside and camouflage, you pitch black plague on this planet, ass nigga. Fucking tar baby, go fill out a pothole on the Dan Ryan! I know you ain't talking shit, bro!"

Kai was unrivaled in his skill to signify, and Zahir knew if he played his game, Kai would take it too far, and he would have to lay hands on his little brother. At only sixteen, Kai had the uncanny ability to get under anyone's skin and make them lose their self-control. He'd once caused the pastor to kick over a desk at Sunday School and storm out the classroom because he kept asking him, "If God had strong-armed Mary from Joseph, or was it a mutual agreement."

So, to avoid any further confrontations so close to their mother walking through the front door, he decided to concede.

That tar baby almost took me outta here, though, Zahir thought as he waved his little brother off and returned to the recliner and his laptop.

Watching Zahir return his attention to his laptop, Kai scoffed in triumph and picked up the remote from the floor. He pointed the remote towards the tv and then quickly glanced over at his big brother. Zahir's hazel brown eyes stared back at him; the dynamic contrast of his light-colored eyes surrounded by an ultra-dark and muscular exterior made his brother appear like a black panther staring down its prey. Swallowing hard while trying to appear unmoved by his brother's piercing gaze, Kai turned up the volume but to an acceptable level and flopped down on the large navy blue micro suede sectional.

"Bro, put on a shirt! Ain't no bitches around. Always trying to flex and shit because you think you swole." Kai teased while laying down across the sectional.

Whatever, I see you didn't turn that volume all the way up. He knows what's up. Zahir thought as he returned his attention to his laptop.

Suddenly, the sharp melody of the doorbell startled Zahir, and he swore loudly as he slammed his laptop down on the lampstand.

"All right, don't fuck up and break that laptop momma bought you for your birthday; they'll never find the body," Kai teased.

"Whatever! Shit, I have a test tomorrow. I don't have time for this."

"You want me to answer the door?"

"Nope, the last time you did, you fucked around and almost got us evicted, talking shit to the landlady."

"Shit, she finer than a muhfucka! I was trying to shoot my shot!"

"Yeah, alright. Remember what momma did, though, right?"

Kai cringed as the memory of his mother embarrassing him in front of the landlady flashed through his head.

"Nigga, just answer the door. It's probably UPS delivering another one of momma's packages. She's always shopping online and shit."

"Shit, it better be and not one of those voter registration people talking about making America Great Again."

"Trump muthafuckas!" Kai teased as he enacted a Nazi salute.

"Fuck you and that Simply Orange looking muhfucka!"

Kai laughed out loud while nodding in agreement.

6

Zahir reached the door and peered through the peephole. The flash of red and blue glazed across his eyes as he swallowed aggressively when he noticed two police officers standing at the front door of their townhome. Biting his bottom lip, Zahir's mind began to calculate every possible outcome once he opened the front door as he watched the two white police officers sway on their feet at their front door.

One of the officers decided to ring the doorbell again, and as he reached for the circle of light in front of him, Zahir quickly unlocked the door and swung it open.

"Good evening officers, how can I help you? My mother isn't home at the moment."

The officers looked down at the ground and then back at each other. The way they responded when he mentioned his mother caused Zahir's chest to tighten and his heart rate to increase. He knew what was coming next, but he didn't want to hear it. He couldn't.

"I'm sorry young man, but your mother was in an accident about an hour ago."

Is she alright? What hospital? Are you sure? Let me call her to make sure you have the right person.

The questions danced on the edge of Zahir's tongue, but from the way the officers refused to look him in his eyes, he knew none of those questions mattered. Their mother was gone, and nothing would ever be the same again. Fighting back the tears, Zahir tried to close the door behind him so he could speak with the officers without Kai hearing their conversation. He needed answers, and he wanted to know who was responsible for taking their mother from them. But as he tried to close the door, Kai appeared in the doorway.

"Hey, why is "One Time" here?"

Zahir closed his eyes and lowered his head. He didn't have the nerve to face his brother and wanted to protect him from the heartache of hearing their mother was dead from a stranger. But the sudden whimper that escaped his lips revealed Kai already knew. The officers had the worst poker faces as they showed their entire hand to Kai. Kai collapsed to his knees, and his body trembled as he clinched his fists in an attempt to swallow the pain that was building inside of him. Still unable to turn and face his brother, Zahir reached behind him and placed his hand on his brother's shoulder. The electric current of Kai's agony seemed to pulse through Zahir's fingers and travel up his arm, piercing the soft flesh of his heart. Zahir's lips trembled as he inhaled deeply.

Noticing the state to two young men were in, the police officers gestured for them to step inside, away from the flashing lights and sirens.

"We're really sorry to be the ones to bring you this news." One of the officers whispered as he followed the brothers inside.

CHAPTER THREE

One week later

"ZAHIR! KAI! MY RIDE is here. I'll see you boys over at the service!"

The muscles in Zahir's face tensed as the sound of his aunt's voice invaded his ears. The high pitch and forced southern twang were like acrylic fingernails running across a chalkboard. Zahir looked at himself in the cracked and dirty bathroom mirror and longed to hear the aggressive yet sweet tone of his mother's voice one more time. Exhaling, Zahir lowered his head and closed his eyes. He didn't want to see her, lying still and lifeless in a wooden box, covered in make-up and designer clothing, in an attempt to make her body appear at peace. It was all a lie, a lie he didn't want to share with strangers that carried the family name. She was an outcast, labeled bougie, because she wanted better for herself and her sons. Moving them out of the south side of Chicago and into the suburbs was the final straw, and many family members decided to cut her off completely. Including Zahir's loud mouth Aunt Juanita.

Juanita was a mid to late-fifties overweight woman with an acute case of diabetes and high blood pressure. Over the last five years, her health deteriorated until she could not walk independently and moved around her apartment in a motorized wheelchair. The doctors warned that she didn't have much longer to live, and despite her knocking on the devil's door, Aunt Juanita was the most vocal when it came to passing judgment on her younger sister and what she decided to do with her life. So, when his aunt Juanita volunteered to take Zahir and Kai in, he knew that it was all about a social security check and nothing more. From the moment they stepped into her filthy, roach-infested apartment, Juanita reveled in every second to use his mother's tragedy as validation of her righteousness. She ran a virtual victory lap each day leading up to the funeral and, at the same time, anticipating when the first Social Security payments would come in so she can benefit herself while doing the bare minimum for them.

The thought of Juanita shopping on his mother's dime caused him to grasp the edges of the bathroom sink, holding on so tightly his arms began to tremble.

Whatever I have to do, I will do it, but I be damned if I let that bitch ball out on my mother's dime while she talks shit about her and feeds us shit and grits every day.

Glaring around the bathroom and nearly gagging at the soiled bathtub and toilet seat, the severity of their new reality hit Zahir's mental stability like a ton of bricks. Although only living in the suburbs for a little over four years, the change of environment had a lasting effect on him. He'd become relaxed, the stress of the hood no longer affecting how he viewed his future. But as he took in his new surroundings, he understood that the drastic changes would need to be met with drastic solutions.

Standing upright and adjusting his lavender tie that hung down the front of his grey collared shirt, Zahir nodded at his uneven image in the cracked mirror and quickly left the bathroom. Turning towards the living room, he watched in silent disgust as two medical personnel helped Juanita roll herself and her wheelchair in the white van that came to transport her to his mother's funeral. Unfortunately, due to his auntie's deteriorating medical and financial condition, Zahir and Kai would have to take the bus. He watched until the van pulled off before calling out to Kai to let him know it was time to go.

Two hours later

Zahir's forehead oozed liquid rage as he watched one by one, family and so-called friends stand in front of his mother's casket and pretend her passing was a heartache they couldn't bear. Kai's sobbing made it more difficult to hold back his emotions, but he wasn't going to give anyone in the cheap storefront church the satisfaction.

Look at this shit. They got my momma laid up in that cheap ass casket in this musty and dirty ass church. Their bathroom was even nastier than Juanita's bathroom, and they had the nerve to have a sign over the bathroom sink that read, "Cleanliness is next to Godliness." If that's true, then this is the Church of Our Savior Satan the Anti-Christ. My momma deserves better than this.

Zahir looked over at his brother, slumped over, overcome with grief, and wrapped his arm around him.

I got us, bro. Whatever I gotta do, I got us.

Suddenly the sound of Juanita's motorized wheelchair drew Zahir and Kai's attention to the center aisle. They both watched as she rolled up to her sister's casket. She looked down at her sister's lifeless body for a few seconds, emotionless, examining the body with a manufactured concern that the brothers noticed immediately.

I bet you don't think your shit don't stink now, huh bitch? Juanita thought as a gush of air escaped her nostrils. The room gasped for air as everyone noticed Juanita's silently taunting her deceased sister, and Kai's patience was spent.

Awe hell nawl, Kai thought as he attempted to get up with the intentions of flipping Juanita over in her wheelchair and stomp her face into the dirty carpet until she stopped breathing. But Zahir quickly held onto his brother, using every ounce of strength to keep his brother seated. Leaning over, Zahir whispered into his brother's ear,

"Don't you disrespect momma like this. Not here, not now. Don't worry; she'll get hers soon enough. Be patient." Zahir said, attempting to comfort his brother. But realistically, he didn't have a plan of action, just the determined intention to make her suffer.

Nodding, Kai gritted his teeth and turned away. Refusing to look at Juanita triumphantly stare down at his mother like a victorious gladiator watching the life leave her opponent's eyes. After hearing the scuffle behind her, Juanita turned and glared at the two brothers with a grin that made Zahir's blood boil. From the look in her eyes, he could tell she had plans for them, devious and full of indignities that would leave a lasting scar for the rest of their lives. She continued to look directly into Zahir's eyes, attempting to intimidate him, but he refused to turn away, sending a clear message that he wasn't afraid of her.

Fuck you, bitch. I ain't scared of you.

Suddenly, a deep masculine voice bellowed out, ending their silent standoff.

"Move, woman! Other people would like to pay their respect, and you're holding up the line messing with those boys. You should be ashamed of yourself for acting like this at your sister's funeral. Now roll your *ignant* fat ass out the way."

The voice came from the mouth of Will "Cain" Johnson, a skeleton from their mother's closet she fought hard to keep hidden but always seemed to fall out when no one was expecting. He earned the moniker "Cain" because he ran an inconspicuous sixty million a year network that moved more weight than any other African American in Chicago. Like the biblical Cain, he seemed to have the mark of God himself, protecting him from law enforcement or anyone else from touching him or his empire. He was the OG, the original gangster, the only OG in the game that remained on top for over twenty years and never spent a single night in jail or a second in any Illinois courtroom. No one knew who worked for him, how he moved his weight, but it was certain no one in the "hood" had access to purchase his product. He didn't "employ" anyone from the hood or spent much time there, which made him very unpopular with the other gang leaders in the city, especially David Pierce, aka King David, the head of the largest street gang in Chicago. But Cain was connected in ways most gang leaders could only dream of, and they didn't dare make a move on his operation for fear of stepping on some very powerful and unforgiving toes.

He was the last person anyone expected to show up at the funeral, and people began to whisper as they watched Cain stand over the casket, staring at Sharon's body in silent reverence. As Cain stood over her casket with his hands interlocked in front of him, Zahir and Kai watched him closely.

Man, I hope this muhfucka don't say or do anything stupid, Zahir thought as he continued to watch Cain closely. He began sizing the six-foot-three giant and calculating his chances of taking him if he was forced to defend his mother's honor. After about five minutes, Cain placed two fingers on his lips, kissed them, and put them on Sharon's forehead. Her cold and coarse skin chilled his fingers, the sensation of feeling a woman so full of life, now frigid and lifeless, moved him, and he inhaled deeply, attempting to fight back his emotions. Looking up at the church's ceiling, Cain nodded his head and whispered,

"Rest in peace, Baby Girl."

He then adjusted his black Armani suit jacket and strolled over towards the mourning brothers. Kneeling in front of them, ignoring how the soiled carpet could ruin the pants of his three-piece suit, Cain looked into their eyes and said,

"Your mother was an incredible woman, and I am truly sorry for your loss. I know neither of you know me beyond what you've heard in these streets, but I give you my word that if you need anything, anything at all, Get at me. I got you."

Shaking their hands, Cain rose to his feet with ease, taking Zahir off guard.

Damn, this nigga over forty and got up like he was around thirty. Yeah, I would have a hard time taking this nigga if it came to it. Them knees didn't even pop when he stood back up.

Kai looked up at the dark-skinned giant and rolled his eyes, unmoved by his show of remorse. Looking away, he mumbled something that Zahir couldn't quite make out, but from the look on Cain's face, he could, and he shook his head and walked away. Kai watched Cain as he walked out of the church and thought, *bitch ass nigga. Just cause you used to fuck with our moms don't mean you are invited to her funeral.*

Zahir watched his brother's reaction and shook his head. He considered warning him to slow his roll with the most powerful drug distributor in the city, but he didn't want to set his brother off. After the night their mother died, Kai became unhinged and unable to contain his anger, and the last thing he needed was for him to have to whop his ass at their mother's funeral.

Several hours later, the brothers said their final farewells to their beloved mother as they watched her casket lowered into the earth. Looking around, the brothers watched as family members quickly made their way to their vehicles, no one offering the boys a ride home. Before long, the two brothers stood by the hole that held their mother's body, contemplating their next moves as a new chapter opened in their lives without the guidance and protection of their mother. An engulfing burn of hatred seared through Kai as he watched people pull away in their vehicles, pretending they didn't see the two of them standing by themselves at their mother's gravesite.

My family ain't shit, Kai thought. Looking over at his brother for answers, Kai watched Zahir look down at the ground, motionless. He appeared in a trance, possessed by his thoughts. Zahir was constantly calculating and solving problems. He possessed an incredibly gifted mind and leadership qualities that allowed him to influence others easily. Even at a young age, he would delegate tasks to his little brother and cousins when they needed to raid the kitchen of snacks without his mother knowing. He was rarely caught with evidence, and his plans always worked if carried out the way he planned them. It was the reason why their mother gave him the nickname "Shadow," because he continuously operated behind the scenes as a night alpha predator, providing orders to his pack and never revealing himself unless absolutely necessary. Other people mistakenly believed it was because of Zahir's dark, ebony skin tone, but she adored his skin tone and would never make fun of it. So, Kai depended on his brother to come up with a plan, anything that would result in the two of them not having to live with their aunt Juanita.

After about ten minutes, Kai became impatient and tapped his brother on the shoulder. Slowly looking up, Zahir glanced at his brother and said, "Let's go, bro. Gotta catch the bus before they stop running out here."

Kai lowered his head, and his shoulders slouched in defeat. Noticing his brother's response, Zahir said, "We'll be good, bro. I just need time to put some shit together. I need you to be patient. I got us."

Nodding, Kai started walking towards the graveyard's exit. Watching his brother's defeated demeanor, Zahir exhaled forcefully and whispered, "Mom, if you can hear me, we need a miracle, fast."

CHAPTER FOUR

THE EVENING SLOWLY BEGAN to take over the day as Zahir and Kai sat on the bench at the bus stop located a few blocks from the graveyard. They'd been sitting at the bus stop for over an hour, and Zahir feared they missed the last bus that ran in the lightly populated suburb. They were at least thirty-five miles away from their aunt's house, so walking home was out of the question, and he didn't have a single penny in his pocket. He gritted his teeth as he concluded that he might have to pan handle for bus fare. Begging was something he wasn't used to because their mother did whatever she had to do to take care of her boys. Now without a mother and no idea who either of their fathers was, Zahir had no other option but to walk over to the grocery store down the street and start asking people for money to get home.

He remembered before they moved out to the plush suburbs, every time they would be out shopping or running errands with their mother, no matter how the person looked, she would always give beggars a few dollars. Zahir hated it but kept his thoughts to himself. On the other hand, Kai would voice his disgust at the idea of people begging for money instead of working for it. Their mother would scold him and would always reply,

"Feed your Karma by paying your blessings forward, baby. You never know when you'll need to ask someone for help."

Feed your Karma. Zahir never quite understood the point of it. But when Cain pulled up at the bus stop in his black Mercedes S63 AMG, offering them a ride home, the concept became clearer. Kai hesitated to accept Cain's invitation, but noticing it was completely dark with no bus in sight, he understood he had no other option. Climbing in the back seat, the intoxicating scent of a new car filled their nostrils, causing the two boys to relax in their seats. The interior of Cain's car was like something out of a dream. The supple black leather seats seemed to embrace their bodies while the center council offered a plush arm rest and state-of-the-art technology at their fingertips. The neon blue ambient lighting made the car appear like a nightclub, while the bass-heavy dancehall music blaring through the speakers excited their senses.

Impressive, Zahir thought as he watched the automatic seatbelts wrap around his upper torso securely. Cain watched the two of them in his rearview mirror and began to drive once he was confident they were situated.

"You're staying with your aunt Juanita, right?"

"Yeah," Zahir responded. Still in a trance at how amazing it felt to ride in a Mercedes for the first time.

"Cool. Again, I want to offer my condolences for losing your momma."

"Thank you," Zahir responded.

Looking in the rearview mirror, Cain glanced over at Kai, who appeared preoccupied with the world outside the car, detached and frigid.

"Hey, have you boys eaten yet?"

"No," Zahir responded, now intrigued by Cain's concern and willingness to want to help.

No one out in these streets does anything for free. What is this nigga on?

"There's an Old Country Buffet on the way to your aunt's, and if you don't mind, I would like to take you boys out to get something to eat. Is that cool?"

Curious to where this was going, Zahir agreed. But Kai wasn't enthused and quickly snapped,

"Nah, we good."

"You good?"

"No, we *both* could use something to eat. We haven't eaten since this morning." Zahir interjected while staring at Kai, sending him a clear yet silent message to "shut the fuck up."

"Shit, your aunt can't cook for shit, so I'm sure what you ate wasn't really a meal anyway. Ok, Old Country Buffet it is."

What the fuck is this nigga doing? I hope this nigga ain't on no weirdo shit cause my brother being stupid right now. I don't like this nigga. There's something grimey about this muhfucka, and I'm starting to see why King David and the rest of the niggas in the hood don't fuck with this nigga. But imma roll with it until this nigga show his hand, and then imma snap off. Fucking Old Country Buffet. Cheap ass nigga. This muthafucka out here driving two hundred-thousand-dollar cars and want to take us to Old Country Buffet. What kind of fuck boy shit is that? Kai thought while he continued to look outside the window.

After making sure Kai would keep his mouth shut, Zahir relaxed in his seat, inhaling the adrenaline of luxury while allowing his mind to navigate through all the possibilities a dinner with Cain could mean.

A half-hour later, Cain's Mercedes pulled into the Old Country Buffet parking lot located at the Ford City Mall on Cicero Ave. The parking lot was teeming with activity as numerous families were exciting or entering their vehicles. The high beam headlights of the Mercedes seemed to freeze everyone in their illumination, causing people to stop and stare as the sizeable black behemoth slowly rolled past them. Zahir noticed their reaction, and at that moment, a burning ambition was set ablaze inside him.

The looks of awe and jealousy intrigued and excited him, and when the three of them stepped out of the vehicle, Zahir made sure to look back at them to let them know he knew they were staring. He then turned to make his way inside the restaurant. As he walked towards the front doors, Zahir began to imagine the onlooker's conversations on their way home, filled with desire and questions. Inspired by the desire to acquire something they believed he had, money and power.

Walking through the glass doors leading into the restaurant, Zahir's eyes glanced around the overcrowded buffet-style restaurant, looking for an empty table. The off-white walls with red accents made the restaurant feel cheap, and he swallowed hard, worrying if he would get sick by eating food that so many people were given free access to handle. Cain left the brothers by the front door and strolled over to the greeter. The greeter looked up, and his eyes widened, and he hurried to lead Cain to his usual table in a secluded corner of the restaurant. Cain turned and called out to the brothers to follow him to the table.

Kai hesitated to follow his brother, looking around the restaurant with disgust.

This nigga thinks he's a big shot cause he got a table at a buffet joint. I swear this nigga is a clown. Why is Zahir so impressed by this fuck nigga?

Zahir, noticing Kai wasn't beside him, turned around and aggressively gestured him to follow him. Throwing his hands up, Kai shook his head and made his way over to the table with Zahir and Cain. Kai flopped down on the worn red faux leather covered bench seat and stared into Cain's face. Cain noticed Kai staring at him and smirked while nodding his head.

"What's up? You got a problem with me, lil nigga?"

"Nah, he don't have a prob–," Zahir tried to interject, but Cain raised his left hand in Zahir's direction.

"Let the lil nigga speak for himself. He's been eye jacking me since he climbed his ass in my ride. So, what's up, lil nigga? You got a problem with me?"

I know this muhfucka don't think he's intimidating me by trying to call me out? Fuck, I should tell him exactly what my problem with his ass is. The streets don't respect you, my nigga, and I don't either.

Kai turned and looked at his brother, who continued to keep his eyes on Cain. Kai could sense that his brother kept his eye on their host, just in case he tried something. Looking at his brother's tense jawline and determined stare, Kai knew that saying what was on his mind could jeopardize more than a free meal. So after a few seconds, he decided to keep his thoughts to himself.

"Nothing personal, Cain, I just buried my mom, so I'm not in a friendly mood," Kai lied. Kai's stomach muscles churned and twisted as he forced down his disgust for the man sitting directly across from him.

"Ahh, I feel you. Yeah, losing a mother isn't an easy thing to do. Especially a woman like your mother. She was a *special* kind of lady."

Zahir's calculating mind began to race with each passing second and words that came out of Cain's mouth. He felt Cain was about to put the two of them through a series of tests that would push their emotional thresholds.

"When I first met your mother years ago, it was during the summer at Rainbow Beach. Man, let me tell you. She was the finest muhfucka out there, rocking a two-piece thong bikini. Ass just spilling all over the place." Cain continued as he sat back and made himself more comfortable on the bench.

Ok, what exactly is this nigga on? Today is not the day to be talking about our mom in a thong and her ass. What is he trying to do? Start a fight in Old Country Buffet? And the way Kai is breathing and mean-mugging this nigga, he's about to get exactly what he wants.

"I mean no disrespect, but you lil niggas are old enough to recognize when a bitch is finer than a muhfucka, right? I mean, I just had to have that ass sitting on my face." Cain thundered while making hand gestures of himself hosting up something over his face.

Cain needs to stop because Kai is two seconds from swinging on his ass. I want to fuck his ass up too, but this shit ain't adding up. Here is a man who runs an illegal drug operation that makes over sixty million a year. He has never been locked up and has the entire city shook. Muhfuckas talk mad shit about his nigga behind his back. Mad disrespectful, but when this nigga comes around, crickets. No clown ass nigga could pull that off. Not the type of sucka ass punk that's sitting across from me. Talking shit about how he couldn't wait to fuck our mom. Either he's the luckiest bitch nigga on planet earth, or this is an interview, and he's testing us to see our reaction to fuck shit.

Zahir placed his hands on the table and interlocked his fingers while he continued to listen to Cain disrespect their mother on the day they buried her. The more Cain carried on, the hotter the room became, and his hands began to tremble as he clinched them together in an attempt to keep his anger in check.

Meanwhile, Kai felt the sweat slide down the middle of his back, and the sound of the loud crowd slowly faded away. The sharp sound of plates and silverware colliding vanished, the exciting splash of steam escaping a grill top as cooks threw more meat on hot metal cooktops became a whisper. The only thing he could hear, assaulting the thin skin of his inner eardrums, was Cain, describing in every detail his first sexual encounter with their mother. His descriptions were vulgar, filling the fifteen-year-old grieving son's mind with images of his mother doing things that he only saw in pornographic videos. Cain's assault on his mother's untainted memory was tearing him to pieces, causing an unbridled rage to grow inside his chest.

"I had no idea your mother could do the things she could do with her mouth. I mean, she used to make a nigga wanna scream. I damn near had a heart attack the first time she swallowed a nigga's kids. And after she took my full load, she kept on sucking and then hopped on this dick and rode me like she hadn't been fucked in years. Oh, my Gawd, Yo momma! Yeah, that bitch was a freak!"

Cain yelled cheerfully while looking off into the distance as if entranced in his sexual memories of their recently deceased mother. Kai's trembling body was a prisoner, ready to break free.

Imma kill this nigga, Imma kill this nigga, IMMA KILL THIS NIGGA!

Kai's lunged forward, his fist clenched and pulled back, ready to strike Cain in his mouth, hoping to tear his front teeth from their gums. Zahir reached up as his arm extended forward and, in one swift motion, interlocked his inner right arm in

Zahir's swinging arm, stopping his forward momentum. Pushing Kai back down on the bench, Zahir placed his left arm across Kai's chest, preventing him from trying to hit Cain again. Zahir stared at Cain, refusing to take his eyes off of him while he struggled to hold his brother at bay.

Cain watched the exchange between the two brothers attentively, his face emotionless and calm.

"Muthafucka, I should kill you for talking that shit about my momma!" Kai snapped at Cain, still fighting with his brother to get free.

Noticing Cain's relaxed demeanor, Zahir knew the entire exchange was a test, and Kai may have fucked it up for the both of them. Still determined to see what Cain had planned, Zahir looked over at his brother and whispered, "Go to the dessert bar and stay there until I call you back over here. Let me handle this. Kai turned and looked into his brother's eyes for answers. The pain of betrayal infecting him as he looked at his brother in disbelief.

"You gone handle it? Did you hear this muthafucka? The way he talked about our mom? Our mom! The dead one? The one that we just laid to rest after that lame-ass funeral? You gone let that shit ride?"

"Go over to the dessert bar and calm the fuck down. What do you think is going to happen after you hit this man in the face?"

"The nigga gone go to sleep!"

"Wrong, one of the muhfuckas that's been watching us the entire time over by the window is gonna put a bullet in both of us. Then this nigga will walk outta here like ain't shit happened."

Cain's eyebrows lifted when he realized how attentive Zahir was. The teenager never looked in the direction of his

24

backup squad, yet he noticed them without alerting Cain he knew they were being watched.

"They probably have a silencer on their guns, right?"

Cain remained silent, listening to Zahir break down exactly how things would've played out had Kai's punch been allowed to connect with his face.

"Now, take your stupid ass over to the dessert bar, and let me make sure we get outta here alive."

Kai looked down at the floor and nodded. Making sure his brother fully understood their situation, Zahir moved out of Kai's way to allow him to leave.

Still watching his brother walk over to the dessert bar, Zahir asked, "What do you want, Cain?"

"I want fresh blood, and I was hoping I could recruit the both of you, but after that display, Kai can't roll with me. But you, Zahir, you are the muh-fucking truth, lil nigga. I have recruited many a nigga, and not one of them could point out my backup. You got the eye. You got the eye for this life."

"Why the disrespect? Why push us by bringing our dead mother into this shit?"

"Because how I run my operation, I need runners that won't take shit personally. I need workers that are about the money and not about settling scores, like bitches. There's a reason I don't fuck with hood niggas or sell product in the hood. Every nigga in the hood is marked. Every dollar those niggas spend is accounted for by the Feds; every ounce of product they move is logged as evidence. So when they hem a nigga up, and they always hem a nigga up, they have everything they need to send your black ass to prison or turn you into a snitch. No nigga in the hood will ever get away clean, and if you want to rule this city, you need to remove yourself from the streets. What niggas refuse to realize is the same muthafucka they buy product from is the same muthafucka that sends their black asses to jail. So, I don't get money with street-hustling niggas, because Kings don't hunt with pheasants."

"So, where do you move your product?"

"Slow down, lil nigga. I haven't even given you a job yet, and you are already asking for the operation manual." Cain responded with an uncomfortable chuckle while looking around the restaurant.

"Well, I want in."

"Just like that, huh?"

"I'm not here to play games with you, Cain. I know you're a brilliant man and run an operation that gets all kinds of money, and the way I see it if I'm going to get myself and my brother out of the situation we're in, you are my best option. I can't have us staying with my aunt for too much longer."

"Yeah, and you need to get your brother out of the hood before one of those niggas pop his ass. He's a hot head and doesn't like to listen. If he let niggas fuck his head, one day they will put a bullet in it." Cain responded while looking over at Kai. He had a look of genuine concern for Kai which momentarily puzzled Zahir.

"I won't ever let that happen."

"You can't talk to them niggas in the hood. Back in the day, we used to be able to at least reason with them. But this new breed of nigga…shit, you can only remove him from that environment to keep him safe."

"Then you're my ticket out of that environment."

Inhaling deeply, Cain leaned closer to Zahir and grunted, "Once you commit to this, your ass belongs to me. There is a reason why I run this fucking city, and it's because everyone

26

that works for me understands precisely who I am and what I'm capable of. They know I don't give second chances, and excuses are for dead men.

Now, if you can deal with that, then I can use you on my team. If not...well, enjoy the dinner; it's on me, and have a nice life."

Leaning back into the bench seat and shrugging his shoulders, Cain adjusted his white collared shirt and stared at Zahir, waiting for his response.

Being that close to Cain was an intimidating experience. He was a huge man, not simply because of his build and height but also because of his aura. His midnight-colored skin, chiseled features, and deep voice were only the backdrop to a man who secretes fear-inducing chemicals from his pores. Cain had hood niggas shook, and being this close to him gave Zahir an idea why.

But fear wasn't an option for him. He needed a way out of their current predicament, and Zahir believed this meeting was no coincidence. Life had given him an opportunity, and he was determined to take it.

"I can deal with that," Zahir responded confidently.

CHAPTER FIVE

One week later

ZAHIR STOOD IN LINE, waiting to get inside the school, shifting his weight from one leg to another. Leaning to his right, he glanced ahead and swore loudly once he noticed the line wasn't moving. A student behind him, seeing his impatience, chuckled and said,

"You'll get inside that zoo soon enough, bruh. They have to go through everyone's bag like TSA in this muthafucka."

Turning around, Zahir responded,

"They should have more than two metal detectors by now."

"Where you think you at, nigga? The burbs? Yeah, I know who you are, Zahir, and you got a little brother named Kai that goes here too, right? Y'all thought y'all was getting away from the hood when your moms took y'all asses out to the burbs. Now you're back and think the hood has progressed. Nah, nigga. The hood ain't changed, only how many niggas die every day in this bitch. You never know; you could be next."

"Fuck you say to me nigga?" Zahir snapped while stepping closer to his nameless antagonist.

"Look at this nigga, acting hard and shit," the student chuckled while pointing at Zahir. "Nigga, you better relax yo'self before you get blasted."

The student then started to reach inside his jacket pocket. Zahir looked the student up and down and shook his head.

"Nigga, you ain't got shit standing in line for a metal detector. You fronting because you know without a gun, I would beat the brakes off yo ass. Yeah, you heard about me, right? So, you must've heard *everything* about me. So, you know, even if you had a gun, you still might get your ass beat. Matter of fact–"

Zahir then grasped a handful of the student's jacket collar and pushed him out of line.

"Get yo punk ass to the end of the line."

The student attempted to push his way back in line but noticed the larger and muscular Zahir wasn't backing down, so he reluctantly back away and walked towards the back of the line. As Zahir watched the would-be bully head towards the end of the line, he noticed a pair of eyes looking back at him. Seeing he caught her staring did not stop her from continuing to study Zahir. She'd heard the Jones brothers were back in the neighborhood but didn't pay them any attention until now. Looking over the unblemished and smooth dark skin on his face, high cheek bones, leading down to a perfectly chiseled chin, his piercing hazel eyes, and full lips, she understood why the brothers were the only thing on the girl's lips around the school. Even in a fall leather jacket, she could see his muscular arms pressing against his jacket's sleeves. He was a delight to look at, and to see him man handle a bully was the icing on the cake for Zaya.

The last time I saw this nigga he was skinny and ugly as hell. Now, this nigga is fine and still hood as fuck. That suburb life didn't soften this nigga one bit.

"Zaya, what's up, girl?!" Zahir called out to her while he stepped out of line and joined her.

"Excuse me?!" You stepped out of line, and you need to take your ass to the back!"

Rolling his eyes, Zahir looked at the girl standing next to Zaya and huffed, "What's up, Peaches?"

"Don't what's up me, nigga!" We have been waiting in line just like yo ass. Take your ass to the back."

"Why don't you take my spot up front since you so pressed to get in school?!"

"Nuh-uh, nawl nigga. You ain't slick. You trying to talk to my girl, and she already got a nigga. So, I'm not going anywhere."

"Damn, Peaches, take your high yellow ass somewhere. I'm just trying to catch up with my girl."

Brushing her blond hair back, Peaches snapped, "Yo black ass ain't the one to talk. You wish you had a beautiful redbone bitch like me, nigga."

Zahir's left nostril twitched, and corners of his mouth retreated downward at the thought of having Peaches touch any part of his body. Going back and forth with Peaches wasn't going to get Zahir any alone time with Zaya, but he wasn't going to be run off by her either. So he decided to manipulate Peaches' self-absorbed behavior to his advantage.

"Peaches, I'm trying to hook *you* up. They said it's gonna rain this morning, and from the way this line is moving, we might be out here when that shit comes down. That's gonna fuck up your hair real quick. Then you're gonna wish you took my spot in front of the line."

Peaches looked up and stared uncomfortably at the grey sky while twisting her mouth to the side of her face. Looking at Zahir and then his spot in line and back at the sky again, Peaches sucked her teeth and said, "Whatever nigga. I guess you got a point. A bitch can't be out here looking like a blond poodle, so I'll take your little spot in line. But…I'm watching your sneaking ass "Shadow." As I said, Zee got a man, and just because your names go together, don't mean *y'all* do."

Zaya watched Zahir and Peaches exchange in amusement, fighting back the laughter that was dangerously close to exploding out of her mouth and expose how easy it was for Zahir to manipulate her.

"Bye, girl. I'll see you inside." Peaches said while hugging Zaya.

"Cool. I'll see you later, girl."

"Bye, Shadow!" Peaches snapped before prancing towards Zahir's spot in line. Within a few seconds, Peaches' loud mouth could be heard telling a student she was taking Zahir's place in line.

"Same ole Shadow, huh?" Zaya laughed while giving him a pound and then wrapping her arms around him. As their bodies embraced, the two of them could feel an energy flow through them. It was a different feeling from the many times before when they played as little kids on the block. Running through the water gushing out of the fire hydrants during the hot summer months or flipping on old mattresses thrown out on empty lots. This embrace meant more, and neither of them wanted to let go, but eventually, Zahir released his embrace and stepped back to look Zaya over.

"Damn, girl. You got thick than a muhfucka!"

Turning around while rolling her hips, Zaya giggled.

"Yep, I'm not that skinny, no ass lil girl y'all used to tease on the block."

"Ha, shit, you was a toothpick out this muhfucka."

"Whatever, Shadow! Yo ass wasn't a catch either, and the way your mom used to come out and whop y'all ass when you were down the street at my house was funny as hell."

The smile quickly vanished from Zahir's face as the memory of his mother flashed through his mind. Noticing the change, Zaya reached down and held his hand in hers, and whispered,

"I'm so sorry about your mom, Zahir. She was a wonderful mother and woman."

Remaining silent, Zahir nodded and turned towards the front of the line. He needed a moment to regroup and not allow his emotions to take over. Zaya knew she needed to change the subject, so she tapped him on the shoulder and asked,

"Where's Kai's crazy ass?"

"He had an earlier start. You know he's into the whole technology side of the game, so he goes to that special class for that, and they start around seven."

"Is he still talking about people?"

Zahir immediately started smiling, turned to Zaya, and nodded,

"Yep, and he got reeeal good at it, too. They gone hate him up here cause he's gonna be shattering egos all day. If he could get paid for it, we'd be rich."

"These niggas up here are too sensitive. So I hope he can fight just as well as he can talk about somebody."

"Oh, Kai can hold his own for sure."

33

"So you were giving him training while you were out in the burbs knocking them white boys out in them boxing and MMA tournaments?"

"Yeah, that's the only time he listens to me. He got hands, but you know his temper be fucking up how he thinks."

"Yeah, but he'll get better, right? He got the golden gloves champion watching his back." Zaya teased.

"Hands don't stop no bullets, though."

"That part," Zaya said solemnly.

"Hey, how's your dad?"

"Still crazy and still hate your ass," Zaya responded. A frown suddenly formed on her face before it disappeared as quickly as it appeared.

Sighing, Zahir shook his head. With him agreeing to work for Cain, he was sure that hate would only get worse. Zaya's father, "King David," was Cain's biggest rival in the "game." So, if he wanted to remain Zaya's friend, he would have to keep his relationship with Cain under lock and key.

Suddenly, the line started moving, and the two friends braced themselves for another day of High School in one of the most violent neighborhoods in the city.

CHAPTER SIX

Two weeks later

ZAHIR LOOKED DOWN AT the slop on his plate and then at his brother's plate. The smell was painful to accept inside his nostrils, and his stomach muscles tightened and flipped each time he inhaled. Juanita sat on the opposite side of the table, staring at the brothers with a look of malicious satisfaction on her face. She was waiting for them to take their first bite of her meal which she purposefully ruined to make them suffer. Every time she looked into their faces, it reminded her of her "perfect little sister." The one that everyone said would make it out of the hood. The pretty one. Even after having two kids out of wedlock by two different men, she was still the favorite. She never had a chance to make her sister suffer until now.

Watch from hell, bitch. I'm gonna ruin these two lil niggas.

Kai looked up and noticed his aunt grinning at him, and his eyelids lowered halfway over his eyes.

"Did you purposefully make this food nasty?"

"Excuse me?"

"I'm just saying cause this doesn't even look like food fit for a dog."

35

"Well, bow wow and eat up. Cause neither one of you will get up from that table until you finish your food."

Kai leaned forward and sniffed his food, and yelled, "Ugh, this smell like you cooked it in ammonia."

"You can eat or get out of my house!"

Zahir looked at his aunt, pointed his finger, and grunted, "We ain't going nowhere."

"What the fuck you say to me, boy?!"

"I said, we ain't going nowhere, and we are not eating this food either. You cashing checks because we live here, and I know you can't survive without those checks. I know they cut your benefits in half before we moved in here."

"You been going through my mail?"

"That's not the point. The point is, if you don't want DCFS to come in here and see all this filth and the slop you keep trying to feed us and pass it off as food, I would suggest you stop threatening to put us out."

"This is my house!"

"Nah, bitch. This is *our* house now!' Kai yelled.

"Get the fuck out of my house right now before I shoot both of you muthafuckas and claim self-defense! You know they are killing black muhfuckas like you in the street every day. What's two less black ass niggas to a cop?" Juanita screamed while reaching for her handgun hidden on the side of her wheelchair. Pulling it out and aiming it at the two of them, Juanita snickered, "Oh, I bet I get some respect now, huh?"

Zahir and Kai slowly got up from the table and backed away.

"I want the both of you out of my house, now! You can sleep in the street for a couple of days until you learn some respect. Your momma never taught you not to bite the hand that feeds you? Stupid ass niggas! Get out!"

"Come on, Kai, let's get out of here."

Kai looked his aunt up and down and followed his brother out of the house. Outside, the night air met them with a frigid embrace that caught the two of them off guard. But Zahir didn't let that deter him as he continued to walk to the corner. He needed to make a call, but his service was disconnected a week prior since his aunt decided he didn't need a cellphone. There was only one person he felt he could turn to for help.

"Come on, bro."

"Where we going?"

"To Zaya's."

"Wait, hold on, bro. I'd rather walk back in that muthafucka than go to that crazy nigga's house. I know Zaya is fine and all, but bruh, her daddy is crazy, and all dem niggas that stand guard outside his crib can't wait to shoot a nigga."

"I know, but who else can we call? Cain hasn't contacted me, and I'm sure you don't want to see him again, do you?"

Nodding, Kai responded,

"Point taken. Let's roll."

Kai then started walking ahead of his brother in the direction of Zaya's house.

An hour later, Zahir walked up to a large two-story Greystone. Once a massive home for the rich during the Chicago Renaissance era and then converted into a two-unit apartment building. When King David made it his house, he decided to return it to its original purpose of being a single-family home. Zahir looked up at the massive windows that covered the front of the Greystone and noticed other improvements Zaya's father made to the house since the last time he was allowed ten feet within its front steps. The windows were slightly tinted, but you could see completely through to the back when all the lights were on. A ballsy move in Zahir's mind being that King David had many enemies that would have loved to snipe him while he ate dinner or watched TV.

Once he noticed his presence was detected, he stopped his brother and whispered,

"Fall back, bro. I'll take it from here."

"Bruh! You're gonna need me if shit gets real!"

"If that happens, there's nothing our fists can do to stop us from getting merced. Neither of us is strapped, and I'm sure every one of those niggas is packing. So, fall back. Please, bro. Listen to me for once."

"Ok, but if anything happens, you know what I'm gonna do."

"Yeah, I do. That's why I need for you to trust me on this one."

Nodding, Kai reluctantly hung back and watched his brother stroll up to the home everyone considered the den of wolves. The cold breeze played around his head and fingertips, enhancing his anxiety as he watched his brother stop at the concrete staircase leading up to the Greystone.

Zahir took a deep breath as he was immediately surrounded by twelve men, all of them reaching behind them, waiting for him to give them any reason to cut him down in the street. Holding his hands up, he exhaled,

"I'm here to see Zaya."

One of the men, the largest of them all with his head wrapped in a blue and black scarf, stepped forward and hissed, "Zaya ain't seeing no body tonight, my nigga. Who are you anyway?"

"Zahir Jones, people call me Shadow."

Without warning, all the men bellowed in unison, "Awwww shit!" and started laughing loudly.

"What's up, Shadow?" the bandana-wearing man gleefully greeted Zahir while slapping fives. "Nigga you got big. I didn't even recognize you with cho black ass. Nigga, you almost got your wig split. But if Zaya's dad finds out you out here looking for her, you just might."

"What's up, Malik. Listen, I really need a solid from you. Can you call her so I can talk to her?"

"Nigga, you trying to get me killed?"

"No, it's not like that. On my momma, I'm not on that. This is on some life and death shit, Malik. You know I wouldn't come here if it wasn't."

Sighing, Malik pulled Zahir to the side of the Greystone and placed a call. Once he heard Zaya's voice, he lifted the receiver to his ear and whispered, "Hey Zee, are you alone?"

Zahir immediately heard Zaya yell through the phone's earpiece, "What the fuck? Am I alone? Nigga, what kind of weirdo shit you on tonight!"

This nigga walked right into that. Zahir thought, smiling.

"Shhhhh, shut da fuck up! I ain't on that kind of shit girl. Your boy Shadow out here, and he said he twisted up real bad. Now you know I could get bent for doing this. So, don't fuck me. Now, can you talk to your boy?"

"Oh shit! I'm sorry, Malik. My bad. Yeah, it's cool. Put him on."

Looking at Zahir, Malik handed him the phone, pointed at him, and said, "You owe me, nigga!'

"Big-time, Malik. Good looking out."

Malik then returned to the front of the Greystone to give Zahir some privacy. Once he was sure Malik wasn't in hearing distance, he lifted the phone to his ear.

"Hello, Shadow, what's going on? Nigga you brave like a muhfucka coming over here."

"Fuck all that. Listen, I need you to call Cain for me and tell him I need him to get at me."

"Nigga what?!?" How many niggas are you trying to get killed tonight? You know my dad hates him more than he hates you! Da fuq?! Are you working for that nigga now?"

"Not yet, but my aunt just put us out, and I need him to put me on ASAP. Now I know I can trust you to hold this down for me, right?"

"Shadow, nigga you be asking for too much, I swear. But you know I got you. Hold on; I'll use my burner. Give Malik the phone."

"Ok."

Zahir got Malik's attention and called him over to him.

"What's up?"

"She wants to holla at you."

"Sup Zee?"

Malik nodded his head a few times and replied, "I got you, Zee. Consider it taken care of."

Malik quickly hung up the phone and put it in his back pocket.

"Hey, Malik, I wasn't finished talking to her!"

"Yeah, but she was finished talking to you. She told me to tell you she will take care of that for you. She also wants me to take you to the hotel in Hyde Park and set you and your brother up there for a couple of months. You're underage, so they not gonna rent you a room. She also told me to break you off some bread to hold you over until you get right."

Zahir looked down at the ground, speechless. Malik chuckled and patted him on the back and said,

"The streets got you, Shadow. Regardless of whatever beef you have with King David, your mom was family. Most of us know you not that kind of grimey nigga. But you know how dat nigga King David is. He's stubborn, and once he believes some shit, nobody can convince him otherwise. Plus, if Zee is rocking with you after that shit, then I'm rocking with you. So, let's roll."

"Thanks, Malik; let me get my brother so we can roll."

"Wait, Kai out here with you?"

"Yeah."

"Ha, your lil brother is one funny nigga, I swear! Get him so we can roll. I wanna hear him roast a few muhfuckas on the way over there." Malik laughed loudly.

An hour later, Zahir stood over his sleeping brother in a two-bedroom suite at the Hyatt, leaned against the wall, and allowed his emotions to flow.

Just this once. No more tears after tonight. It's about money or mayhem.

CHAPTER SEVEN

Twenty-four hours later

ZAHIR SAT IN THE living area of their hotel room, staring down at the burner phone on the walnut living room table he bought with the ten thousand dollars Malik gave him on behalf of Zaya. For her to dish out that kind of cash to him made him wonder if she really had a man or if her man was about to get sent down to the D league. Being friends aside, Zahir was certain after everything that happened between them and the time they've been apart; their friendship was not on the ten-grand level at the moment. So, there was something else. But, Zahir had to focus on more important matters, and despite the fact he could soon be dating the girl he's had a crush on since he was six, getting that call from Cain was more critical.

To avoid any more confrontations that could ruin his chances of getting things started, Zahir sent Kai out to watch a movie and get something to eat. But he knew Kai was going to take the money he gave him to find some weed and holla at the Hyde Park girls as they strolled by on the busy 52nd street strip. It was known that Hyde Park had some of the finest girls on the south side, and Kai was eager to snatch him up a "bougie bitch" and ruin her life.

The minutes seemed to crawl as the cream-colored walls in the hotel suite appeared to close in around him. The large living area felt smaller and smaller the longer he waited for his phone's clock to read 6:30 pm.

6:25…shit!

Zahir stood up and began shadow boxing to relax his nerves, pivoting his body with each air-splitting blow, twisting and turning, and then ducking while moving his body to the right and landing an uppercut to his invisible opponent. His moves were fluid and precise. He jabbed at the air, ducked, and moved his body around his opponent, landing a right hook to their kidney. With each strike, he exhaled forcefully, then inhaled as he moved out of harm's way. His hands moved with swiftness and determination that would be devastating to an actual opponent, unable to see when a punch was thrown or where it would land. He was a champion, and his body was trained to move like one.

Suddenly, the phone began to vibrate on the tabletop, and Zahir rushed over to pick it up. Relaxing his breathing, Zahir received the call.

"This is Zahir."

"I'm out front."

Zahir hung up, grabbed his jacket, and rushed out the door.

Zahir strolled out of the hotel lobby and looked around for Cain's Mercedes. A loud horn grabbed his attention, and he noticed Cain sitting in a black newer model Chrysler 300. It was a jarring change from the luxurious S63 he was driving a couple of weeks ago. Zahir started to climb in the back seat, but Cain gestured to join him in the front. As soon as he sat down, Cain pulled off, heading towards Lake Shore Drive.

As he joined the bustling traffic on Lake Shore Drive, Cain reached down into the driver-side door pocket and pulled out a brick of cash. The bills were bright and unblemished as if printed a few hours ago. Cain tossed the brick of money in Zahir's lap and said,

"See how that feels."

"Oh, shit! How much money is this?"

"Ten stacks! Clean and ready for circulation. Feels good in the hands, doesn't it?"

"Hell yeah! Thank you so much, Cain. I don't know what to say."

"Huh? Thank you?"

"Yeah, for the money. I really appreciate this. This is gonna help my brother and me out."

"Nigga, if you don't give me my money back! I didn't say you could keep it."

What the fuck?

"I said see how that feels. Not, here hold this, or this is for you. Did you do any work to earn that money?"

His excitement sucked out of him; Zahir bowed his head while still holding on to the brick of cash and responded, "No."

"When you go apply for a job at McDonald's or Chick Fil A, those muhfuckas don't hand you a week's worth of pay on the first day you start without you doing a second of work, do they?"

"No, but they don't toss a check in your lap either and say, see how this feels."

Ha, Touché. I walked right into that one.

Clearing his throat and adjusting himself in the driver's seat, Cain nodded his head in agreement and responded,

"Well, this ain't McDonald's."

"If it were, I wouldn't be here."

"Is that right?"

"I'm not about to live my life flipping burgers and taking orders from cheap people who believe their 3.99 entitles them to abuse me. I'm not about that life."

"Fuck you right, lil nigga! So what life are you about?"

"Real money, plain and simple. All the other bullshit has to take a back seat."

"That's what I wanna hear. I love me an ambitious nigga. I'm not afraid of a nigga wanting more as long as he understands who he works for. I will never fuck you over, Zahir. Ever. I'm hard, but I'm fair. I won't turn on you, and as long as you are loyal and follow the rules, we cooler than a fan. However, I was a lil nervous when King David's daughter Zaya called me. But I got a feeling she's more loyal to your black ass than her daddy. Plus, I know she was the one that set you and your lil brother up at that nice hotel in Hyde Park. Although she is dating dat nigga Midas, I feel like she would do anything for your broke ass instead of a young boss nigga like Midas. So, I'm sure you two will be sharing shit, and I'm cool with that, but I want you to know that if I have to question her loyalty to keep who you work for a secret-"

Cain didn't say another word, but Zahir understood precisely what he was saying without saying it aloud.

Midas, the up-and-coming rising hood star that worked for King David. He had the golden touch when it came to moving "work." He was a natural-born salesman and kept his crew focused. He wasn't flashy or loud, and he made sure his thirty "runners" followed his example. He was young, intelligent, and ambitious. All the qualities that make a young hustler a "star" in the hood. So, it was no surprise that Zaya was dating him and that her father admired him enough to allow it. And by the way Cain spoke of him, Zahir could tell

46

King David wasn't the only one that admired Midas and probably wouldn't mind him joining his organization one day.

"Are we clear, Zahir?" Cain continued, snapping Zahir out of his concentration.

"Shadow."

"What?"

"If I'm going to be out here in these streets working for you. I want to be called Shadow. Everyone on the block calls me Shadow."

"Oh, that's tight…but no. I'm not calling you Shadow out in this muhfucka. I told you before; we don't fuck with the streets. So, you will be known as Zahir Jones when you are working with me. Now, when you take your black ass back on the block or hang with your lil friends, then they can call you Shadow, Shazaam, or Sharkeisha. I don't give a fuck."

Shaking his head, Zahir glanced outside the window and noticed they were pulling into the Montrose Lake Front parking area. The park was deserted, and he slowly sat up, trying to make sure there wasn't someone waiting in the dark, ready to take him out at a moment's notice. Noticing Zahir's nervousness, Cain chuckled and said,

"Relax, lil nigga. You good. Now give me back my money."

Handing Cain the brick of money, Zahir asked, "Can I really pull ten stacks a week with you?"

"Oh, you were paying attention."

"Always."

"Good shit! Ten stacks is a slow week. But yeah, ten stacks is easy money when you fuck with me."

"Fuuuuck! I can feel that. On the real, I can feel that."

Cain pulled into a parking space and turned the car off. Unbuckling his seat belt, Cain turned to Zahir and clapped his hands loudly.

"Ah ight. Let's get down to business. I need you to pay attention and no questions until after I'm done. Understood?"

"Yes, sir."

"Cool. Now, you wanted to know how could a man like myself move so much weight in this city and never get hemmed up. Well, that's because I don't cater to the 99%. I cater to the 1%. The elite of the fucking city. Mayors, Governors, movie stars, singers, actors, government officials, foreign delegates, etc. I supply product for very powerful and connected people, and discretion is paramount in this business. And for our attention to detail, we are paid better than anyone else and protected. As long as we keep the product flowing and the shit discreet, we never have to worry about one time kicking our doors in and seizing everything we are grinding out here for.

So no street shit, no beefs, no shootouts on public streets. We operate behind the scenes, and my runners are inconspicuous. And that's the job you'll be doing. Delivering product to people who are worth millions of dollars. But don't get it twisted, these muthafuckas may be doing business with niggas, but they still don't like niggas. So, at the restaurant, I had to test the both of you on how you handle shit when a muhfucka says some off-the-wall shit to you. I can't have my runners taking shit personally and capping a customer when they open the door and yell out, "My nigga!" These people do not want to be embarrassed by their habits of drugs, hoes, and other crazy shit that you don't want to know about.

So, your job is to carry product to a specified location which will more than likely be a home in the North Shore area or a high rise in downtown Chicago. You must not, I repeat, you must not go dressed like a hood nigga. When you're on the clock, your attire will be from them square ass spots like Abercrombie and Bitch or some other plain and bland clothing line store these white muhfuckas love."

It's Abercrombie and Fitch…but whatever. Zahir thought while shaking his head.

"You need to blend in as much as possible with the square crowd. So, no Jordans either."

Zahir's eyes bolted open, and just before he was about to protest verbally, Cain pointed at him and roared,

"Shut up! Shut the fuck up! If you want to pull a brick or more a week, nigga you got to make sacrifices, and not wearing Jordans when you're on the clock is a very small price to pay. This job isn't about flossing while you're working. It's about flossing when you're not. I don't need you carrying around thousands of dollars of my product, rocking three hundred-dollar shoes. You just scream, rob, or arrest me. You can't be rolling like that while you are walking down a street lined with multi-million-dollar homes in the middle of the night. You won't be a bum, but you won't be dripping either. And your "kissed by midnight" black ass need as much camouflage as you can get, rolling through these rich white folk's neighborhoods.

And if you're wondering, nope. You will not be driving to your destinations either. All movements will be with a designated Uber driver. If the driver isn't available, you are to take the Metra train. You are to avoid, at all costs, the Chicago El trains. Catch a bus to the Metra station and then use pace buses. El trains have canine units, and they will sniff out the product, and you'll become a liability. And in this business, liabilities are eliminated. I need you to understand what you're getting yourself involved in fully. This is that next-level shit, and I need that next-level commitment. At this moment, you are at the point of no return, so you really don't have a choice in the matter. You wanted in, well you're in.

You start next week, so just like any other company, you need a uniform. So, here's some money. Go get you some corduroy trousers and duck shoes," he teased.

Cain then pulled a half-inch worth of bills from the money brick and handed it to Zahir. A long uncomfortable silence followed as Zahir stared at the money that Cain had just given him.

I have to play my cards right because if not, I could put Kai in danger. But I'm already here, and there's no going back now. So, Shadow, suck this shit up and get this paper. But there are a few unanswered questions that I need for this nigga to make clear. So...

"Is it time for me to speak?" Zahir said, breaking the silence in the car.

"Yeah, you have the floor."

"How am I supposed to keep my involvement with you a secret from people like King David and other people from the block?"

"Besides keeping your mouth shut, my other runners no longer live on *the* block. They move out the hood and set up shop somewhere that no one knows who they are. Since it's been a winning formula, I would suggest following that same pattern. Listen, Zahir, I know this is a new kind of hustle from what you're used to seeing, but I know you're going to do great things in this business. You are smart, you can hold your own, and you have an eye for this shit. Just what I need to help keep this shit running smoothly."

"What about my brother?"

"What about him? Oh, that crazy lil nigga can't work for me. Oh, he's loyal, but he has zero control and gives zero fucks.

50

That's a great trait out in these streets, but with me, that's a recipe for disaster. So, I can't use him."

"I understand. But is he allowed to know what I'm doing?"

"The nigga already knows. As long as he keeps his mouth shut, you good. *Keeping* his mouth shut, now that's *your* problem. But if it becomes *my* problem...."

Again, Cain went silent, and Zahir cringed at the idea of losing so many people he cared about if he was unable to keep them quiet.

"Now you know I'm ex-military, right?"

"No, I didn't know that."

"Now you do. So, I will be training you on some fundamentals of gun usage and other tactics in the coming weeks. I can't have you out here not knowing how to use a gun."

"So, I will have a gun?"

"Of course! It's better to have one and not need it than to need it and not have it. The gangs won't dare touch *me*, but they don't know who my runners are, so if they step to you, you have to be able to hold your own. But I don't want you shooting up innocent people on the corner because you don't know how to aim down your target. I need you sharp and precise when you have to regulate a muhfucka."

"Wait, I don't know if I could actually kill someone. I mean, I know it comes with the territory, but I would rather avoid taking someone's life *if* I had that option."

Cain leaned back while a sly smirk formed on his face. There was a glow in his eyes that puzzled Zahir.

Why is he looking at me like that? Zahir thought, watching his soon-to-be employer closely.

"Damn, nigga. You the shit. You really are made for this shit."

Noticing the confusion on Zahir's face, Cain tapped the young man on his shoulder and said,

"You not a trigger-happy nigga, and that's what makes you perfect for this shit! Violence downgrades productivity because once a misunderstanding gets physical, most or all of your resources are now allocated to war. It brings unnecessary attention to your operation, and it creates enemies where there wasn't any. You have law enforcement, politicians, the hood, everybody watching your every move, and that's when niggas slip up. Making dumb ass moves because they are operating on emotions and revenge-type shit. They do not give the money and movement of product the attention it needs and start making too many mistakes. It's always the same ole shit, you kill one of theirs's, they kill two of yours, and it keeps going on and on and while niggas is out here doing all this killing–"

"Ain't a nigga out here making money," Zahir interjected.

"And there it is," Cain responded while pointing at Zahir. "That's why I said you are made for this shit! And I'm not talking about the street corner game cause anyone can apply and make money doing that shit. Nah, I'm talking about this high-level shit. The kind of level that gets you into places a street nigga could never get in. Protection that a regular street corner nigga don't even know exists. You where you belong, lil nigga. Had you gone and fucked with King David and his band of trigger-happy hustlers, you would come up too quickly, and they would merc yo ass and make it look like rivals did it.

It's too much hate out in them streets."

Nodding his head, Zahir took it all in, gathering invaluable insights into Cain's operation and expectations.

CHAPTER EIGHT

Z AYA'S BARE FEET SLAPPED loudly on the black heated floor tiles as she strolled past her father sitting on the couch in the living room. The echo of her feet colliding with the tile caused her father's eyes to squint as his jawline tightened. Looking up from the laptop sitting on his lap, King David shook his head in annoyance.

Returning his attention to his laptop screen, his eyes suddenly widened, and a low growl moved up his throat.

"Zaya! Let me holla at you!"

Zaya inhaled deeply as she closed her eyes once her father's dreaded phrase, "let me holla at you," invaded her ears. In all of her seventeen years of being his only child, never has that phrase meant anything other than trouble.

Let me see what this crazy man wants now.

Jogging back into the living room, Zaya flopped down on the couch next to her father in an attempt to cause his laptop to turn towards her line of sight, giving her a glance at his screen and maybe a heads up on why she was in trouble. What she saw on the screen made her cringe, and suddenly the usually warm and cozy house felt frigid and uncomfortable.

Shit, she thought as she lowered her head.

"Zaya, can you tell me why you took fifteen thousand dollars out of your savings account last month?"

"I gave it to Shadow." She whispered.

"What did you say?"

"I gave it to Shadow," this time louder but still timid.

"You gave fifteen stacks to Zahir Jones?! Why would *you* do that?!"

"Because his aunt kicked him and his lil brother out, and they needed a place to stay and some cash until he could figure things out."

"There's all kinds of niggas out here getting kicked out, and no one slides them fifteen stacks, so what's so special about this nigga, Zee?"

"Daddy, you know why he's special."

"What tha f?!?!"

King David suddenly balled his fists and ran them across his cleanly shaved head. Zaya could see the beads of sweat forming on the bridge of his nose. A clear sign that his anger was quickly turning to rage. King David slowly placed his laptop on the coffee table in front of him and closed it. His full lips retreated into his mouth as he looked up at the ceiling, breathing deeply. He didn't want to continue the conversation in the emotional state he was in because he knew the only response he would get from his daughter was sarcasm and anger, which would make matters worse.

"Zee, why do you continue to associate with him after knowing what he did to you?"

Zaya remained silent, her eyes moving back and forth as she tried to figure out what to say to her father. There were so many things she wanted to tell him, but she knew the moment she did, her father's life would be over. She hated being cornered, but she loved her father, and she would do anything to keep him as far away from death as possible, even if that meant keeping him far away from the truth.

Shrugging her shoulders, Zaya responded, "I don't know, daddy. We go way back, and people change. I know you don't see it, but I know he's changed."

"You right; grimy niggas do change. They get worse because they get better at being the worse and hiding it."

"Daddy, come on, you're not being fair,"

"I'm not being fair? You can't be serious, Zee. That nigga deserves to have his eyes shut permanently for what he did to you, but I let it slide, for you! Now, the nigga back and he got you out here peeling him off fifteen thousand dollars, why? Are you fucking this nigga!?"

"Daddy?!?"

Zaya's eyes began to water as she looked into her father's eyes, heartbroken that he would think of her as the type of woman that would pay a man to fuck her.

My daddy tripping like a muhfucka. I need to set him straight right now cause this shit has gotten outta hand.

"First of all, you broke the "no cussing in the house" rule, so you know what you gotta do, hit that swear jar with a "Benji". But more importantly, unless you consider yourself a failure since you've taught me the game *and* how to finesse these niggas, there's no way you could believe I'm sleeping with Shadow and paying him for it. We not finna do *that*. You know me well enough to know I could never date a nigga like Shadow while he down and out like that. I'll help a nigga out, but I'm not about to sleep or date any man I have to take care of. He's a friend; I already got a man.

I saw my boy needed a solid, and I extended a helping hand. Something I know if the shoe were on the other foot, he would do the same for me. I don't expect you to understand our bond, but I do expect you to respect the woman you raised. I don't do struggle love from the jump. It's one thing for him to be on when I met him and then fall off once we deep in it together. Of course, I'm not gonna leave him cause he's shown his pedigree at the beginning by being the kind of nigga that could be "on". And if he was on once, he can be on again and imma be that woman to help him do it. That's what *you* taught me, daddy, and I've never forgotten that lesson.

So, with all due respect, don't come at me like I'm some fucking weak ass trick out here breaking niggas off for some dick. And yeah, I know, I gotta drop a two-piece in the swear jar."

King David looked down and the floor and smiled. Hearing her stand up to him made him proud, but it still didn't fix his problem with her friendship with Zahir. So, he decided to take matters into his own hands.

"You know what, Zee, you're right. I was outta pocket. I apologize. I should not have asked you if you were sleeping with Zahir."

"It's cool, daddy. I get it. Just don't let it happen again."

"Oh, really? So, you making demands?" King David responded while rising to his feet and standing over her.

"I don't make demands; I set standards," She responded, slamming both hands down on the plush leather coach and then standing up to face her father.

The both of them stood in front of each other, only allowing a few inches of air to separate them. Holding their breath, the father and daughter glared into each other's eyes, faces cold and still like stone. Suddenly a grin began to form on King David's face, and within a few seconds, he and his daughter were laughing hysterically, holding each other up from falling over. After nearly a minute, King David wiped the tears from his eyes and held his daughter close to him.

"Zee, baby girl, you know your daddy loves you, right?"

Closing her eyes, Zaya nodded and whispered, "Yes, daddy, I know."

"So, you know my concern comes from a place of love and not jealousy or my need to be an overbearing father, right?"

"Yeah."

"So, listen to me. Stay away from Shadow. He can't be trusted, and he ain't plugged out here, and you know what happens to niggas who ain't plugged? They get their lights blown out, and I don't want you hanging with that nigga at the right place and at the wrong time when that shit happens. Cause if anything happens to you...I will burn Englewood to the ground to find the muthafuckas responsible. So, please...do it for me...stay away from Shadow."

Zaya held her father close to her as she tried to purge her thoughts of every reason she shouldn't listen to her father. She knew Zahir would be joining Cain, her father's nemesis, as his new runner. She knew that because of Zahir's ambition and intellect, eventually, Zahir would rise through Cain's ranks and become either one of his top lieutenants or his second in command, and ultimately one day take over his empire. She knew that his rise could mean her father's fall, but despite all of the reasons she should listen to her father, she chose a single reason why she shouldn't...Love.

So, she did something she'd never done before. She decided to lie. She'd never looked her father in his eyes and lie to him. She'd withheld information and let her father come to his own conclusions, but she'd never used his love against him and lead him to believe her lie was his truth. But for Zahir Jones, she was prepared to do anything, even betraying her own father's trust.

"Ok, daddy, I'll fall back."

Kissing her on her forehead, her father smiled and said, "That's my Zee."

As he held her in his arms, he closed his eyes and thought,

I can't believe she lied to me to my face. What the fuck this lil nigga got over my baby? I got to handle this shit before he gets my baby killed.

After watching his daughter head upstairs after their talk, King David reached for one of the multiple burner phones spread out across the glass top coffee table and placed a call.

"Malik."

"What's up?"

"Come inside, let me holla at you."

King David quickly ended the call and waited for Malik to join him in his living room.

Malik stared down at his phone and exhaled so forcefully, his full lips vibrated in the cool night air. He knew something was wrong, and whenever King David said, "let me holla at you," he knew he was going to have to put in some "work" or commission one of the foot soldiers to put in work.

"Shit!" Malik hissed.

Which one of these niggas done fucked up now?

As Malik walked through the front door, King David called for him to join him in the living room. Malik walked into the living room and was greeted warmly. Exchanging their gang handshake, King David tapped Malik on the shoulder and gestured for him to follow him into the basement.

Fuck, I knew it. Dis nigga never have me go in that basement unless he needs me to handle some murder shit.

Malik followed King David down the carpeted stairs leading into the full finished lower level of King David's luxurious Greystone. Once his feet met the mahogany hardwood floor at the bottom of the steps, both men took a sharp left and headed towards the double doors leading into the custom home theater. Malik's eyes began to glow as he looked around the red, black, and gold elegantly appointed theater room. King David spent over three hundred thousand dollars to recreate a home theater system that resembled a 1920's movie house. Walking through the doors into the theater was like traveling back in time, and Malik enjoyed watching movies and getting high with the rest of the crew whenever King David would host fight night or movie premier parties. Because he was a wanted man by rival gangs and dirty cops, King David rarely left the confines of his home, so he paid thousands of dollars to have new movies delivered to him as if he ran a commercial Multiplex Theater.

The only time King David would leave his home is when it was time to re-up for the crew or if a matter needed his "personal" touch.

"Have a seat."

"Thanks," Malik said while plopping down his six-four, two hundred and sixty-five-pound muscular frame on the red velvet theater seat.

King David reached for the large touch screen remote, turned on the sound system, and increased the volume. Malik moved closer to King David, and the two men began to converse.

"Listen, I need you to handle something for me."

"What's up?"

"That lil nigga Shadow, I need him gone."

"Wait, what?! Zahir Jones, that Shadow?"

"What other nigga out in these streets people call Shadow?"

King David noticed the immediate look of regret and confusion on Malik's face, and his response made him want to pull out his gun and blow Malik's head off. But Malik was his most skilled and trusted lieutenant, and losing him over some emotional shit wasn't something King David was willing to do. So, despite his urge to murder him, King David decided to inquire why his lieutenant felt remorse for the job he was giving him.

"Nigga, what's that face for?"

"Listen, Rock; I ain't in the position to tell you how to run your empire and who to merc and who to let live."

"Nigga, I asked you a question."

"I think killing Shadow will be a huge mistake."

"Why?"

"Zaya."

"Zaya? What about Zaya?"

"She will suspect you did it or had me do it."

"Niggas die every day in these streets!"

"Yeah, but this is *Zaya* we are talking about. That's your daughter, and you already know how you peep shit. You don't think she'll peep that shit?"

"I don't give a fuck; she'll get over it!"

"KD, she won't."

"Fuck! This nigga took fifteen thousand dollars from her! I don't even know how she did that without me knowing! That nigga and his brother been laid up at that hotel in Hyde Park for almost a month, and she just took that money out the other day! Usually, I keep a close eye on her accounts, but you know we just had to re-up, so I'm not logging into shit but these streets. She knows this, so she waited until I wasn't checking her shit to pull those funds. That means someone may have loaned her the money until she could repay them. I wonder if they gave her the money or they gave Zahir the money? Because neither of them is old enough to rent a hotel room on their own. So that means one of these grown niggas out here fucked around and loaned her that bread. Which is a fucking betrayal cause every nigga in this city knows how I feel about that nigga Shadow! Let me find out who did that shit, and they gone have a really bad day. Fuck!!"

Malik swallowed hard as he prayed to himself that King David never found out that he was the "someone" that loaned her the money. He didn't think it was a betrayal at the time, just a favor to Zaya, who he cared for like the little sister he lost, so he didn't have it in him to tell her no. Also, Malik prided himself in reading people, and no matter how closely he watched Zahir, there was nothing in his character that would indicate he was what King David believed him to be. So, he didn't feel like helping him would ultimately come back to haunt him. Still, as he stood in front of one of the most ruthless killers he's ever known, Malik's mind worked overtime trying to figure out how to distract King David from his investigation into the loaner of the fifteen thousand.

"What nigga out here getting paper that could lace my baby with fifteen thousand like it ain't nothing, yet old enough to secure a hotel room in Hyde Park?"

Bingo!

Unbeknown to King David, through his rantings, he'd just offered the perfect scapegoat, and Malik began to attentively wait for the right moment to lay the sacrificial lamb at King David's feet.

"The only nigga I know that is close enough to Zaya that's getting that kind of paper is Midas."

"Get the fuck outta here, Midas?!"

"Yeah, why is that so hard to believe?"

"Because that nigga would never cross me while I continue to allow him to date, my daughter. I made that nigga! Now every nigga that run with him thinks he an OG or he a made man cause they think he fucking my daughter with *my* permission."

Malik scoffed at the idea of Zaya allowing the quiet and reserved Midas anywhere close to fucking her.

"Exactly, that lil nigga may be able to make a lot of money on these streets, but he's easy prey for someone like Zaya to finesse. So, I don't think the nigga even knows about your beef with Shadow. The nigga only been living around here for a couple of years."

Rubbing his hand through his full beard, King David shook his head and growled, "She played this nigga right into her hands. He probably thought she asked him to get the room for the both of them, not knowing it was for that nigga Shadow. Fuck, she good!"

"That's your daughter."

"Da fuq nigga?!"

"I don't mean no disrespect, KD, but you taught her everything she knows. Of course, she's gonna figure out how to get around your rules and shit."

"So, you think I should make an example of Midas?"

"Nah, the nigga may be gullible when it comes to Zaya, but he ain't disloyal. How about you let the nigga handle it for you?"

"Send Midas to kill that nigga Shadow? That shit brilliant, Malik! Use the jealous boyfriend angle."

"Nah, no, no, no! Besides the fact that if Midas kills Shadow, we could lose one of our top hustlers *and* his crew because he's going to have to lay low for a while, I still think killing Shadow would be a huge mistake. Let him go whop Shadow's ass instead."

"Hmmm...I want the nigga dead, but I would let the nigga live if Midas and a few of his crew could whop his ass. I mean, *really* dig in that nigga's ass. Even a good pistol whipping till the nigga piss and shits on himself. I need it done publically, so everyone can see him go down like the bitch ass nigga he is."

Shit, this nigga hates Shadow like a muhfucka.

"So, what do you need me to do to facilitate this ass whooping?"

"I need you to get at Midas tonight and whisper some shit in his ear that will get him riled all the way up. Then give him some key advice on how to handle it and let everything else unfold. I know Midas ain't a Rottweiler or a Pit, he's more like a Doberman, but a Doberman can be dangerous when aggravated."

Nodding, Malik agreed and quickly excused himself to go about the task given to him.

Yeah, a Doberman can be dangerous unless you're sending it to fight a wolf, Malik thought as he walked out the front door of King David's Greystone mansion.

Walking up to a group of teenagers standing in the middle of the street, Malik called out to one of them.

"Aye, Brian you seen Midas?"

"Yeah, he was posted up on 63rd and Green not too long ago."

"Aight, bet," Malik responded before hopping into his black newer model Mercedes E-class and sped up the block towards 63rd street. Within a few minutes, Malik slowed his car down to a crawl as he watched Midas and his crew work the four corners of 63rd and Green Street. Bryson, aka Midas, was like a general, commanding a masterful street symphony of the hustle and grind. He earned the moniker Midas for his uncanny ability to turn any corner or block into a goldmine.

Malik watched them and admired their drive and attention to detail, ensuring the block was protected and monitored every second of the day. There were spotters on the roofs and inside key apartments on the outskirts of the block; they were working in every direction. Midas also had some of his spotters equipped with police radio scanners and night vision goggles, and laptops with internet access to hack into the CPD cameras for added security.

Because of his extreme surveillance measures, his pushers didn't have to worry about hiding from the cops or rival gangs, so they focused all of their energy on moving the product. It was a beautiful thing to observe in action.

These niggas are official out here, Malik thought as he parked his car a few houses away from where Midas and a couple of his boys were standing, watching everything going on around them. Midas heard Malik's car door close and quickly looked in the direction of the sound. His eyelids lowered halfway over his eyes as he strained to recognize the sizeable six-four frame strolling towards him in the failing light of the evening. Still unable to figure out who was walking towards him, he quickly reached behind him to pull out his gun while hissing at his two companions and nudging his head towards the direction of the intruder. Malik noticed their reaction to him and chuckled.

"Calm down. You know who it is," Malik said, his unique roaring voice announcing the arrival of the dark mocha giant of Englewood.

"Oh shit, Malik. You almost got—"

Stepping directly in front of one of Midas's companions, Malik towered over him, allowing his massive frame to cast a shadow of terror over the three of them.

"I almost got what, lil nigga?"

Swallowing hard while taking a few steps back, Midas's companion replied, "Nothing bro, shit, you just scared me, that's all."

"Scared money don't make money," Malik scoffed

Midas watched their exchange, smiling while shaking his head.

"What's up, Malik? What brings you to the hottest block in the "Wood"?

"Shit, I was on my way up to Ashland to get something to eat, and when I drove by, I saw the block was lit, so I stopped just to kick it for a split second!"

"Shit, every block we hit is lit," Midas responded while gesturing for his two companions to give them some space. He knew something was up because King David rarely let Malik leave his post in front of his house, and when he did, he didn't have a lot of time to shoot the shit.

"Facts!" Looking around for a few seconds, Malik gave Midas a puzzling look and asked, "Yo, where's Zee?"

"At home, studying, and shit."

"But she's usually out here kicking it with the crew."

"Yeah, I know, but lately, she's been staying home hitting the books and shit."

"Hmmm," Malik said while twisting his mouth to one side of his face and slightly turning his body away from Midas's view.

"Aye, Malik, what's up. You act like you know something!"

"Iono shit, bruh. Listen, imma head up to Ashland. Y'all keep hustling out here and protect yo neck. You know these streets are wild, bro."

"Nah nigga, I know you know something." Midas protested while trying to move in front of Malik.

"Midas, you cool with me nigga, and I respect your hustle, but you don't want these problems."

Throwing his hands up, Midas moved out of the way and responded, "My bad, bro. I meant no disrespect. I just thought we were cool enough for you to keep it one hundred with me."

Exhaling forcefully, Malik turned to face Midas and growled, "Nigga, if I tell you what's up and this shit gets back to me, I don't care how much money you make, I will bury yo ass."

Malik could tell Midas had accepted his terms without saying a word, so he gestured for him to follow him in the alley across the street. Before following Malik, Midas turned to one of his soldiers, placed his index finger under his right eye, and then pointed at him. His soldier nodded his head and moved closer to the curb so that he could get a better view inside the dimly lit alleyway just in case the impromptu meeting with one of the most vicious killers in Englewood went south.

The smells of urine, rotten food, and urban decay invaded Malik's nose, the mist of ammonia from the urine caused his eyes to water, and he swore loudly as he grew impatient with Midas's casual stroll as he crossed the street to join him. Midas walked into the alley, seemingly unbothered by the rancid odors that were making Malik dizzy.

I'm so glad I'm not out in these streets having to deal with this shit. Malik thought as he watched in awe at Midas's lack of reaction to the smell of the alley. *These niggas are numb to this shit. I remember I was the same way. The only smell that concerned me was the smell of cash.*

"Ok, Malik, what's up? It's that Shadow nigga, ain't it?"

"Nigga! If you knew, why da fuck you have me come in this funky ass alley?"

66

"Nah, I didn't know for sure, but I've noticed that she's been pulling away from me ever since that nigga came back. I am just putting shit together. That bitch fucking that nigga, ain't she?"

"Midas, don't get yo wig split talking crazy, bruh."

"My bad, fuck!"

"I don't think she fucking the nigga, but I do know she laced him with fifteen stacks."

"Fifteen sta—, Nah bruh you lying! Nigga, ain't no way she gave that broke ass nigga fifteen stacks. No way!"

"Yeah, she did."

Looking around and swearing under his breath, Midas shook his head and asked, "Who else knows?"

Got him.

The defeated tone in Midas's voice assured Malik that he was on the right track, so he decided to push the envelope to derail Midas's ego.

"Right now, just me. The streets ain't up on it yet, but once it gets out, you know niggas. Even though I know, she ain't fucking that nigga, yet. Most niggas will think she is or that fifteen stacks was a down payment on some fucking in the near future."

"A down pay—" Midas whispered while covering his mouth.

"If this shit gets out nigga, yo crew gone start clowning yo ass, and you know once your soldiers feel comfortable enough to start clowning you, you know what comes next."

"The disrespect."

"Yep, the disrespect."

"But, what can I do? The money probably already spent, so I can't go make her get it back."

Malik chuckled and said, "Nigga, you know damn well you ain't gone be able to tell her to give nothing back. Fuck wrong with you?"

"Yeah, you right. So, what can I do?"

"Shit, go handle that nigga, so by the time it goes viral in the streets, it's already a dead issue."

"Yeah, I should merc that nigga."

This nigga stupid as fuck.

"Nah, fuck you mean merc the nigga? Whop that nigga's ass. Make sure you get his ass up at that school so everyone can watch. Killing that nigga ain't gone do shit but stop yo money and end the relationship with Zee. Think my nigga. There's no way you're gonna be able to stop this from getting out in these streets, so you deal with that nigga on some real nigga shit. It's easy to shoot a nigga. You don't get any points with Zee or King David by just popping him. You need to make it personal and public. The only thing you should be using the heat for is to pistol-whip that nigga. Make him submit to you and let everyone see that shit.

Shooting that nigga will make you look weak. Like you scared to square up with that nigga."

"Ain't nobody scared of his broke ass. I don't need a gun to whop his ass."

Yeah, whatever nigga. Everybody in the hood knows that Shadow got hands. Malik thought while nodding in agreement with Midas.

"A'ight, cool. But let me ask you, can you fight, tho?" Malik asked while lightly tapping Midas on the chest.

"Huh? Nigga, what kind of question is that?"

"A question you ain't answered yet, *nigga*! You know what, I'm not gone ask you again cause I don't want to be disappointed. Listen, take a couple of your soldiers with you. You know, to help stomp him after you knock his ass out."

"You don't think I can beat his ass?"

"Nawl nigga! I know niggas that can fight, and anytime you ask them, they don't answer a question with a question. Look, it's cool; not every muhfucka out here got hands, but you got a squad, and that nigga Shadow is rolling "solo dolo." So, you and a couple of your squad should be able to handle him without issues."

Malik paused as his eyes began moving back and forth.

"You know what, take three with you. That's four total, with you included. I think that should be enough. Yeah, you should be good."

Shaking his head, Midas scoffed and began to walk back to his post. When he was halfway across the street, he heard Malik call out to him and say, "On second thought, take four, my nigga."

In response, Midas threw up the piece sign and continued walking.

Shit, Shadow gone beat they ass, Malik thought as he headed for his car.

CHAPTER NINE

A couple of days later

ZAYA SAT IN THE front passenger seat side-eyeing Midas as he slowed his black 2019 Lincoln Continental to a crawl in front of her school. He'd been behaving strangely the entire morning, and the three members of his squad riding in the back seat made her skin crawl. He'd never let anyone from his squad ride with them when he dropped her off at school, so when she opened the car door and noticed the three goons sitting in the back, her internal alarms went off.

During the entire ride to school, she monitored their movements behind her, each of them with looks of determination on their faces, eyes bloodshot red from being insanely high and intoxicated.

These niggas about to ride down on somebody at my school.

"Midas?"

"Sup."

"I hope you and your niggas ain't about to roll up on my school and start shooting and shit. If so, let me out before we get to the front door. I don't want to be associated with dumb shit."

"Zee, ain't nobody gone shoot nobody."

71

"Then what these niggas doing here?" She asked, pointing at the three passengers in the back. "I know they not here for moral support."

"Oh, we got some shit to handle, but no gun play…this time." Midas chuckled while he maneuvered around a car, unloading students at the front of the school.

Zaya began to calculate who at her school would've offended Midas and his crew to the point they were willing to risk getting arrested just to prove a point. Before she could conclude, a smile grew on her face when she noticed Zahir standing out front, standing in line to get inside the school. She rolled down her window and nearly leaned her entire upper torso out of the window, yelling Zahir's street moniker.

"What's up, Zee?!" He yelled back.

"You know what it is! Money over everything!" she playfully yelled back.

"Bitch! Da fuq you doing yelling at that buster ass nigga!"

Bitch?!

The three passengers in the back cringed when they heard Midas call Zaya a bitch, the image of King David beating him to death with one of his sixty-pound chains flashing through their heads. Something he was notorious for when anyone crossed him or his daughter. Zaya's eyes suddenly looked upward while she tilted her head to the side.

"Wait? Did you just call me a bitch?"

"Fuq, you mean? You heard me, *bitch*! You fucking that nigga?"

"Midas…imma give you an opportunity to slow your roll, bruh."

"Nah, fuck all dat! You gave this nigga fifteen stacks. No bitch out here giving niggas that kind of bread if they ain't fucking. I don't care what kind of friendship y'all got."

How did he find out about that? Who this fool been talking to? Zaya thought.

"Yo Midas, let us out bro!" One of the passengers pleaded.

Midas spun around in the driver's seat and spat," What you say nigga?!"

"Look, Midas. We ready to ride with you to beat this nigga's ass. But the shit you on right now with Zaya, ain't it, bruh. We ain't trying to see King David for you disrespecting his daughter! You know how dat nigga get down about Zaya. We came to move on that nigga, Shadow. Not all this extra shit you on. Pull over and let us out, bruh."

"Fuck you hoe ass niggas! See if you get money with me again. Fuck niggas! Get the fuck out, my whip!"

The three passengers didn't wait for the car to come to a complete stop as they rushed out the back doors. As the last one got out of the vehicle, he mumbled, "Shit, nigga you ain't gone get no money period after this hoe shit you on. Peace."

Zaya kept her eyes on Midas until the last passenger left the vehicle, and then she decided it was time to let Midas know precisely who she was.

"Let me tell you something. You think just because we talking; you have ownership of me? That fifteen thousand I gave Shadow was *my* fucking money. Not yours, not my daddy's or anyone of your lame ass niggas you got working out on these corners. My money and I will give it to whomever I want. Same thing with this pussy, nigga; *pussy* nigga. If I want to give it to Shadow, imma give it to him. I haven't given it to you, no matter how many lame-ass lies and lines you tried to lay on me. I ain't one of these weak hoes you and your crew be fucking at your chill spot. Oh, you didn't think I knew about Tamara, Kiesha, Julissa, and Angela? Those raggedy "for the

73

streets" bitches you be fucking with that community dick, and you think you can flow with me?

Nigga please, you dry as fuck when it comes to me. You'd have better luck fucking a bucket of sand than thinking you gone get inside this pussy. And I wish you would jump yo monkey ass out of this car and try and beat my homeboy's ass. Shadow will drag yo ass all over this street, and you know it. That's why you brought three other niggas to help you. Now, they gone, and you sitting here alone and gone pull the fuck off as soon as I get out of this car cause you ain't trying to get at my boy, Shadow. I don't even need my dad to fuck you up for calling me a bitch. My boy will do it for me."

"Ain't nobody scared of that broke ass nigga. I'll beat his punk ass!"

"Oh, really? Bet!"

Zaya then got out of the car, slammed the door, and screamed, "Yo, Shadow! This nigga Midas called me a bitch and just told me he came up here to beat yo ass!"

Shadow was already on alert when he heard Zaya screaming in the car, and hearing that Midas called her bitch and had intentions of a confrontation with him set him off, but he knew that if he caused any street beef, Cain would cut ties with him. He had to remain clean, and to do so; word would have to be that Midas started the confrontation. So, he hesitated and waited for Zaya's need to embarrass Midas and Midas's need to save face to give him the desired outcome. Before long, the front sidewalk of the school filled up with students, watching the yelling match between Midas and Zaya. Zaya's words cut deep as she used degrading and foul descriptions of Midas, causing his embarrassment to cloud his judgment momentarily, and Shadow observed him, like a scientist watching virus cultures in a Petri dish.

Look at this fool. He knows he doesn't want no smoke with me, but the way Zaya calling him out in front of all these kids, he has no choice but to step up. And the more he goes back and forth with her, the more trouble he gone get into with King David. It's like this emotional nigga can't help himself. He just pissed away all his street cred in a matter of minutes, and I know King David is going to cut him off immediately. But I may have use for him later, so when he steps up to get his jaw rocked, I won't prolong his ass whipping. I'll make it quick, not to embarrass him too much. Oh, look. Any moment now...

A look of senseless rage flashed in Midas's eyes right before he rushed up the pavement towards Zahir and Zaya.

Here we go.

"What nigga? What you running up on the sidewalk for?!" Zaya yelled at Midas, tormenting him to madness. "You ain't gone do shit but get yo ass whopped."

Midas was determined to regain his dignity, so he lunged forward at Zahir, swinging wilding, but missing. His arms flailed from left to right, and Zahir stepped out of their reach, appearing more annoyed than threatened by Midas's attacks. Suddenly, Midas closed the distance between him and Zahir and attempted an uppercut towards Zahir's chin. Zahir calmly stepped to the side. Midas's missed uppercut exposed his chin. Zahir connected a devastating left hook that violently shook his entire skull, instantly rendering him unconscious and sending his limp body crumbling to the cold concrete.

"DAAAAAAAAAAMN!!"

The observing crowd yelled in unison, and then a massive eruption of laughter followed as many of the students begin jumping around and into each other. They pointed down at Midas's unconscious body, covering their mouths and repeating, "You got knocked the fuck out!"

Through the chaos, Zaya stood over Midas, a look of satisfaction on her face as she whispered, "Dumb ass."

A strong pull at her arm jolted Zaya backward as Zahir pulled her away from the celebrating crowd and towards the front doors of the school building. Because of the fight, the line leading into the school dissipated, allowing Zahir and Zaya to stroll right into the front doors, past the metal detectors and armed security. Once inside the building, Zahir led Zaya by her arm into the school's gym. Zaya tried pulling away, but Zahir had such a firm grip around her arm that she felt if she pulled too hard, he would snatch her arm out of the socket.

I know he ain't mad at me for what happened outside. I swear to God, if he starts talking shit to me, we gone have a real problem.

Once inside the gym, Zahir led her under the bleachers and pushed her against one of the metal bars. Zaya's eyes widened, and her mouth dropped as she felt the cold steel collide with her back.

"Hold up, Zahir! Why are you mad at me?! I had your bac—"

Without warning, Zahir forcefully took her face into his hands and kissed her passionately. Zaya felt his tongue invading her mouth; the cooling sensation of the peppermint candy he'd been keeping in his mouth seemed to enhance the moment. Zahir's passion for her was electrifying as he pressed his body against her's, holding one hand on her cheek and the other on her throat. Feeling his hand on her throat and the firmness of his excitement made her eyes roll into the back of her head, causing her to gasp from excitement.

Oh my God! She thought as she accepted the rush of emotions flowing through her. It was a moment long overdue, and as much as she tried to ignore it, she knew this day was coming, and to her, it was a perfect beginning. Zahir suddenly took her tongue into his mouth and began sucking on it while forcefully inhaling the air out of her lungs. Her knees buckled as a soft moan escaped her lips.

Shit, this boy got me open, and I ain't even gave him the pussy yet. How is this even possible?

Zahir slowly toned down the passion while gently kissing her on the lips. He then opened his eyes and whispered, "You could've taken him."

Still, under his spell, Zaya's eyes remained closed as she moaned, "Huh?"

"You could've taken him…Midas. You didn't need me to whip his ass," he responded this time with more volume and urgency.

Completely snapped out of her bliss, Zaya smacked her lips and said, "Why should I? I got you and my daddy. I shouldn't have to beat Midas's ass. If that's the case, what do I need any of you for? Yeah, I can fight; I got hands, but if you say you got love for me, then I shouldn't have to use them unless necessary and today wasn't one of those moments. Plus, he came to whop yo ass, not mine's."

Chuckling, Zahir responded, "Facts."

Zaya suddenly noticed a worried look in his eyes and placed her hand on his face, and asked, "What's wrong? No matter what, I want this. I want us. Shit, I thought it would sound weird saying that out loud, but it doesn't. Wow, I'm not even scared of what this could mean with the way my daddy hates you. Does that make me crazy or stupid?"

"No, that makes *both* of us crazy and stupid, but fuck it, you're worth it."

"So, why you stressing?"

"Midas."

"Midas? Man, fuck that clown ass nigga. If he tries to retaliate, we gone deal with his ass together."

"If he does, I got it. I don't want you involved with that nigga going forward. But that ain't it. You know who I'm about to start working for, and if I start having beef on these streets, that could fuck up a whole lotta money for me."

"Shit, you're right. Cain, don't fuck with that street shit. What you gone do, cause you know my dad gone out that nigga Midas, and that's gone make his crew bounce on his ass. That shit gone make him very hostile towards you *and* desperate."

"I gotta get to him before he gets to me then."

"Damn, Zahir. I didn't know you had it in you."

"What? Wait, what are you talking about? Oh, nah. I'm not gonna do *that*. That would be reckless as fuck. Nah, I'm gonna deal with him another way. Hopefully, if I pull this off, it doesn't come to that."

Grinning mischievously after looking at her surroundings, she responded, "You think you slick, bringing me in here knowing it would be empty this early in the morning. At first, I thought you were mad at me or something."

"I was."

"For what?"

"Wasting your time with Midas, knowing you wanted to be with me the whole time. But that's a dead issue now. Let's go before someone comes in here and see us. The last thing we need is for one of these snitches to run tell your dad about us."

"Mad at me about Midas?! Zahir, please, you got a lot of nerve. You could've said something."

"I could've, but it would've come off as me playa hating on ole boy, and that ain't it."

"Facts, you would've come off lame as fuck."

"Exactly. So, you coming by the hotel later?"

"For what? Don't think you gone get some pussy now that we together."

"It's mines; you gone give it to me regardless. Check it; I bet if I stuck my hands down your pants right now, my shit would come up glazed like Crispy Cream in this bih."

If he sticks his hands down my pants, we fucking right here, PERIOD.

Rolling her eyes, she scoffed, "Whatever, Zahir."

"Yeah, ok. But you ain't said no."

Facts

Pushing him away from her, Zaya pretended to be angry and left Zahir by himself under the bleachers. Zahir watched her leave, admiring her amazing ass sashay from side to side. Licking his lips and smiling, Zahir adjusted the growing excitement in his pants while imagining all the things he would do to her the moment he got her alone.

I can't wait to slide that; he thought as he escaped from the gym in the opposite direction.

The rest of the day, Zaya watched Zahir, in constant thought, his eyes staring off in the distance. He was disconnected from the world around him, and she knew why. He had to figure out how to keep Midas under control without having to kill him. Although Midas wasn't half the man that Zahir was, Zaya recognized that he wasn't a punk either. He ran a tight crew for a reason. He just ran into the immovable object that was Shadow. There wasn't anyone like Shadow, and she accepted Midas for not measuring up, and she respected his hustle and ingenuity when it came to moving product for her father. So, she understood that Midas wouldn't take losing everything laying down, and he would be planning his revenge and killing Zahir would kill two birds with one stone.

She just prayed that Zahir figured it out because she didn't want him to become a killer out of desperation. If taking someone's life became a reality, she wanted Zahir to be a man that chose to do it and had the power to decide when and where. Most street hustlers didn't have that option, and she wanted her man to be one of the few that did.

They exchanged text messages throughout the day, but Zaya didn't want to overdo it because she knew he had a lot on his mind. After exchanging digital goodbyes, Zaya waited out front for her ride home as she watched Zahir and his brother walk towards the CTA bus stop. He seemed determined and at ease when they made eye contact, which meant his brilliant mind had devised a solution, and he was confident in its success. She closed her eyes and exhaled as she relaxed, trusting that her man had it all under control.

Three nights later

Malik walked into the VIP entrance of the Pink Pony strip club while inhaling deeply on a half-smoked blunt filled with marijuana laced with Codeine. He devised a custom mixture for himself to deal with migraines he constantly suffered from due to a head wound caused by a bullet at close range. Pink neon lights illuminated his pathway to the main floor of the club. As soon as he and his entourage entered the main area, everyone's attention shifted from the beautiful women dancing on the stage to the massive man and his entourage standing near the bar. The club's DJ threw a peace sign and nod of respect in Malik's direction, and he returned the gesture.

No gang signs.

King David hated the idea of his soldiers flashing gang signs when it wasn't necessary, especially in a club or restaurant. Kind David would constantly say, "There's a time and place for everything, and when we're out having a good time, flashing the set only ruins that good time." He didn't subscribe to representing the set anytime and any place because he understood that sometimes even soldiers needed a little peace once in a while. So, when they were out on the town for R&R, he made it clear, no gang signs whatsoever. Leave that shit on the set.

King David prided himself as a businessman, and he ran his organization like it. His product just happens to be illegal.

Because of their brutal reputation, everyone in Chicago and the surrounding suburbs knew that greeting anyone that worked for King David with a gang sign when they were out relaxing was a violation that could lead to their swift and untimely death. Malik, a man with a reputation that turned even the bravest men's blood cold, recently became David's second in command when Da Rottweiler, King David's best friend and Zaya's godfather, was sentenced to four years for statutory rape for getting a sixteen-year-old stripper pregnant. He contended she lied about her age and possessed a fake ID, but the courts didn't care and convicted him anyway. So, Malik was the most obvious choice as his successor, and tonight he was celebrating coming into his own. Even if it was only temporary, he was determined to prove himself. He knew he could never replace Da Rottweiler, but he hoped his contribution while he was down would let King David know he was more than just an enforcer.

"Hey, Malik, what yall drinking tonight?" The beautiful bartender asked while wiping down the bar in front of her. Malik leaned on the bar and looked her over while licking his lips. Her firm breast protruded out from her skin-tight top; the deep cut V-neck of her shirt allowed her cleavage to become the centerpiece of her appearance.

"You know how we do it, Cherish. Keep them bottles coming all night!"

"Shit, I know that's right, baby. I got you, sweetie. Gone out there and get yo dick rubbed on, baby. I'll have my girls bring the bottles over."

Cherish then turned around and walked towards the other side of the bar. Malik quickly noticed the thong she wore, exposing assets that nearly made him drool on top of the bar.

"Gad damn, Cherish! Shit, all that ass and you ain't gone let a nigga swipe you down?"

Cherish smiled, bent over, and made her ass bounce, causing a tidal wave of flesh to vibrate and her butt cheeks to collide, making sharp clapping sounds.

"Malik, unless you ready to stop fucking with these simple bitches out on that floor, you not gone be able to slide *this* ass, baby."

Malik ran his hand down his face and swore loudly when he imagined experiencing Cherish's fantastic body. But he knew he wouldn't be able to give up his addiction to fucking strippers. He had a problem, but he didn't care. There was nothing quite like fucking a stripper. Especially one that was experienced and didn't care what she had to do to get his money. As much as he wanted to fuck Cherish, he didn't feel she was worth giving up his addiction only to find out the pussy might be trash.

"You ain't right, Cherish. You know you want to give me that pussy."

Cherish slapped herself on her left butt cheek and kept walking, refusing to respond to Malik's last statement.

One of Malik's closest companions, Torrey, leaned closer to Malik and tapped his shoulder to redirect his attention to the stage.

"Leek, check it, bruh. I think she's new!"

Malik's eyes reluctantly moved away from Cherish's ass to the main stage, and his eyes instantly celebrated what they beheld.

"Oh shit!" He yelled as he moved closer to the stage as if entranced by the spell of her caramel-colored skin, reflecting the pink neon lights. Her body was flawless, possessing attributes that made Cherish's body seem obsolete.

"Nigga, that bitch is bad as fuck!" Torrey said while reaching into a leather backpack and pulling out a brick of cash.

Malik nodded in agreement and observed her as she wrapped her legs around the pole and slid down to the floor. She lifted her legs in the air into a handstand and then flipped over into a split. She then began to seductively look into Malik's eyes while gyrating her hips slowly.

"Gad damn, nigga!" Torrey laughed as he noticed her attention on Malik. "She fucking with you, bruh."

"I know, this bitch gone get all my money tonight."

Malik then walked towards her and snapped his fingers. Torrey immediately handed him a brick of cash. Malik looked her in the eyes while peeling away one-hundred-dollar bills and letting them fall all over her body. It only took him a couple of minutes to toss ten thousand dollars on the stage at her. She could barely contain her excitement the more money rained down on her naked body, but once the money brick had disappeared, Malik turned and walked towards one of the VIP rooms. Torrey stayed behind to watch her, and he smiled when he noticed she was making sure she knew what VIP room Malik would be in.

Got her. That shit works every time.

Torrey shook his head and joined the rest of the crew in a separate VIP room to give Malik and the stripper some privacy.

Malik sat back on the leather couch in the dimly lit VIP room and waited patiently for the mystery girl. He'd already told the security guard standing outside his VIP room to prevent any other stripper from coming into the room. He was known for spending close to one hundred thousand dollars a night at the club, but he'd already experienced all the strippers that were down to fuck at the club, and he wanted the new girl to be his next experience.

Within a couple of minutes, the security guard pulled the room's curtain to the side and let "her" in. She was completely naked, her body glistening with sweat and glitter from the sweet-smelling lotion that covered her body. Her smile was infectious as she moved closer to him.

"Why you leave like that, sweetie? You weren't enjoying our chemistry?"

"I was enjoying every second of it. That's why I dropped that brick on you."

"I appreciate it, baby."

She then placed her arms around his neck, climbed on top of him, and began to grind on him slowly. Even with his pants still on, she knew exactly where and how to increase his excitement with her sensual movement. Being that close to her, inhaling her scent made his heart rate increase and his high vanish. She leaned in closer to him until their lips were almost touching. Grabbing ahold of his ears, she began to massage them while she increased the intensity of her grinding, allowing him to feel the contours of her pussy.

"Oh, fuck." He exhaled as he reached behind her and helped himself to two handfuls of her ass.

"MMMM, baby, I like that. Squeeze this ass, baby. Do you feel that? You like how that feels in your hands?"

She then leaned forward and ran her tongue along the side of his neck and whispered, "I can feel dat dick throbbing, baby. You want this pussy, don't you? You want my mouth to swallow that monster, don't you?"

"Fuck yeah!"

"Mmmmmm, can I pull that muthafucka out, so Serenity can hold it in her hands, baby?"

"Mmmmm, hmmmm."

Serenity licked her lips and began to unbuckle his pants. She then reached down inside and pulled out a throbbing ten-inch shaft of hardening flesh and veins.

Shit, this nigga dick pretty as fuck.

Serenity licked her hand and then wrapped it around his dick, slowly stroking it up and down while twisting her hand. She made sure her grip was light, just enough to excite, but not enough to finish him. She refused to put it in her mouth, although she was already on her knees until Malik came correct. Malik knew what she was waiting for, and he didn't hesitate to reach into the leather backpack sitting next to him and threw out two bricks of cash on the floor next to her. Her eyes widened as she watched them topple on the floor. Both bricks only consisted of hundred-dollar bills, and adding up their totals made her juices flow out of her like a river.

Moaning while licking the tip of his dick and making his body jump, she whispered, "You're gonna need to pull your pants around your ankles, baby, cause this shit gonna be sloppy and wet, and I don't want to mess up those nice pants and boxer briefs you got on."

Malik quickly pulled his pants down to his ankles and guided her head down his shaft. Feeling her warm and over-saturated mouth taking all of him down her throat made him moan loudly, forcing the security guard to move in front of the room's door to block anyone from seeing what was going on inside.

As she slowly pulled his dick out of her throat, she ran her tongue along the bottom of his shaft while moaning softly.

Fuck, I don't think imma last this entire song if she keeps sucking my dick like that, he thought, as he gripped onto the leather couch, trying to brace himself.

Twenty minutes later, Malik stumbled into the men's bathroom, his pants unbuckled and his dick glistening wet. Walking over to the urinals, Malik shook his head in shame.

I didn't even last a full ten minutes the first time, and then when she got me going again, and I slid in that pussy, I came in like ten pumps. Gad damn that bitch got that "Kill Bill." If she weren't in this club selling pussy, I'd wife the fuck outta that bitch. Who I'm fooling, I might wife her even with her selling pussy.

Chuckling at his admission, Malik was preparing to relieve himself at the urinal until the bathroom lights suddenly went out and before he could turn around, a familiar voice behind him commanded,

"Don't move, nigga. Keep your hands on your dick, or I will blow that muhfucka off."

"Shadow?! What the fuck?! How the fuck you get in this muhfucka, you ain't old enough to be in this bitch!"

"Fuck all dat. Why Malik? I thought we were solid, my nigga."

Malik knew exactly what Shadow was referring to, and the cold steel pressing against his back was more than enough incentive for Malik to not play games with him.

"Listen, King David wanted me to merc you nigga! But I convinced him to let you live, but somebody had to teach you a lesson for taking that fifteen stacks from Zee. So, I fucked with Midas's head so he could get at you. No gunplay, tho. I saved yo life nigga, and this is how you repay me?!"

"How da fuck am I supposed to know that's what went down between you and King David? All I know is Midas came at Zaya and me about that fifteen stacks she loaned me."

"Nah nigga, she gave you that bread; that wasn't no damn loan."

Pressing the nozzle of his gun harder into Malik's back, Zahir growled, "Shut yo ass up, nigga. It's a loan; imma give that bread back to her."

"Aight, nigga damn. It's a loan, fuck!" Malik responded, still holding his dick in his hand. The darkness and Shadow's voice sent chills through his body, and his urge to piss vanished as fast as the lights in the bathroom. It's been years since Malik felt the cold bite of fear, and he never thought anyone could awaken it inside of him again until now.

"So, what now, Shadow?"

"I know you just got a promotion, so I need your discretion on that Midas situation."

"Huh?" Malik responded and almost forgot he was supposed to remain still and tried to turn around and face Shadow until he reminded him with another push of the gun's nozzle in his back.

"Malik, listen, I will blast your back and intestines out the front of your body, nigga. Don't play with me."

"My bad, my bad! Ok, what are you talking about discretion concerning Midas?"

"King David set dat nigga lose, didn't he? Well, I know that nigga is fuming right now and planning on retaliating, and there's only one muhfucka in the hood he mad at, me. His name is trash out in these streets now, but maybe we can avoid any bloodshed if I can offer him an alternative. Cause if I have to eighty-six that nigga, that's gone permanently fuck up my bread."

"Wait a minute, you trying to recruit that nigga to work for Cain? Aww, you a slick ass nigga, Shadow."

"Fuck you talking about, Cain?"

"Nigga, I knew he was recruiting you when you came to King David's house and asked to use my phone to speak with Zee. I just never said anything to anyone because I got mad love and respect for you, Shadow. Well, maybe just respect now, cause that love part might be dwindling with you having that gun in my back, my nigga."

"Would you have been open to talking to me about this without the gun?"

Chuckling but making sure he kept both hands on his dick, Malik responded, "Nah, you right. I would've beat yo ass, lil nigga."

"You would've tried, but yeah, this was the only way I could get your attention long enough to listen. I need Midas to roll with me."

"And you think that nigga gone roll with the man that knocked his ass out and strong-armed his girl?

"That nigga love money more than anything else, so if I give him another way to make even more money than what he was making on that corner, Midas gone be with it. Otherwise...

So, I need you to look the other way when I make this move cause if not, Midas is gonna blow up the spot and bring unwanted attention to your operations. With you just taking over for Conrad—"

"Da Rottweiler or The Rock lil nigga, show some respect!" Malik interrupted.

"Nah, dat nigga just bitch ass Conrad to me. I be damned if I call him Da Rottweiler. Now with *Conrad* being down and you taking over his position, you don't need any unnecessary conflicts."

"I see you got this all figured out, don't you?"

"Yeah, pretty much. I just need your blessing on this, Malik."

"Nigga, that means you gone owe me again!"

"What the fuck you mean I owe you. You sent Midas after me. I should be regulating your ass right now for that shit. So, the way I see it, you owe me."

"Nah, nigga. You got this shit all twisted. If I had let King David have his way, it would be another funeral in the hood, and I don't want that. Your lil brother needs you, and y'all just buried your moms. Plus, I know you not guilty of what King David has accused you of for all these years."

"How do you know that?"

"I know grimey niggas that would do some fucked up shit like that, and you ain't it. So, there was no way I would let you get merced over some shit you ain't do. So, I intervened. So, the way I see it, you owe *me,* and now you're asking for another favor while you got that "gad dammit" pointed at my back? Nigga, you got balls the size of that fucking silver bean downtown."

"You know what, cool. I'll owe you, ok. Now, can you do this for me?"

"Yeah, take that nigga with you; he'll be better off over there anyway. Now can I take my hands off my dick, nigga? I have been touching myself for so long; I'm about to Me Too my own gad damn self."

Suddenly, the lights came back on, and Malik quickly spun around to find himself alone in the bathroom. After quickly shoving his dick inside his pants, he quickly checked all the stalls in the bathroom before rushing out the bathroom door, asking the security guards had they seen someone coming out of the men's room. Being that the men's bathroom didn't have a window, the only way out was the bathroom door, and he became more and more confused as to why no one saw Shadow leave.

This nigga take that Shadow shit too far.

Malik rushed into the other VIP rooms where his boys were hanging, and he quickly ordered them to pack it up so they could leave. Without hesitation, they jumped up and rushed out of the room. As he walked out the club's back door, he heard Serenity's soft voice behind him.

"Hey, baby. You leaving so soon?"

"Yeah, we gotta roll, ma."

"Well, here, take my number. Hit me up sometimes. Maybe we can hang, just you and me."

"Bet, I'm with that," he responded.

After exchanging numbers, Serenity kissed him on his cheek and walked to her car. Malik watched her, confused, and called after her before jogging to join her by her car.

"Seems like I'm not the only one calling it an early night."

"Oh, baby, I'm calling it an early career, this was my first night here, and after meeting you, I'm not gonna work in that profession again."

"Oh, so you think you got it like that?"

"You tell me, baby. Do I need to go back in there and keep shaking this ass, or are you willing to *keep* this ass for yourself?"

"Shit, I want that ass for myself."

90

"Well, there it is. So, call me next week so we can get up, ok baby?"

"Cool."

Malik watched Serenity pull out of the parking lot before joining his entourage at their fleet of black Cadillac Escalades.

Torrey looked down at the ground and then back at Malik, grinning.

"Nigga, what you grinning about?"

"You, that must've been some VIP session for you to exchange numbers with her."

"Nigga, you have no idea."

"She a bad muhfucka bro. I would've given her my number too, shit, and been tricking off just like you about to do."

Malik's face went cold as he stared at Torrey without saying a word. Torrey looked at Malik with raised eyebrows while shrugging his shoulders. Torrey was the only man in his crew that wasn't afraid of Malik, and he spoke his mind whenever it suited him. Their stare-off lasted a few more seconds before the both of them erupted in laughter while dabbing each other before climbing into their vehicles to head back to the block.

Across the street, from a dimly lit alleyway, a hooded Zahir stared at the motorcade of Escalades race eastward on 147th. He watched the parking lot a little longer to make sure Malik didn't leave anyone behind before he decided to leave the alleyway and head back to the hotel. He tried to will his feet to move, but the only thing they did was tremble. His chest muscles tightened as the air in his lungs felt encumbered and thick. Without warning, his legs betrayed him, and he stumbled backward against the brick wall behind him. Snatching the hood from his head, Zahir forcefully expelled the stagnant air in his chest, holding his head in his hands. His heart raced, and he felt the adrenaline rush through his veins, heightening his senses. As he regained his footing, an unfamiliar feeling came over him, causing every nerve in his body to vibrate, but it wasn't fear or anger. Fear and anger made him feel powerless, unable to control an outcome or his emotions.

This new feeling made him feel invincible, and as he made his way down the alleyway, he knew it was a feeling he would want to experience constantly, but the only way he would get his fix was to make sure he remained ten steps ahead of everyone, including Cain.

Twenty-four hours later

These niggas think I'm a game out here. Imma light this nigga's ass up and any other nigga that talks shit to me. Ain't no way I'm gonna let any nigga slide going forward. I lost everything fucking with that bitch and then her bitch ass daddy gone take my corner and my crew from me. Ain't no way I'm going out like that. I may not be able to get at that nigga King David or Zaya, but Shadow gone feel my wrath.

Midas took a long pull on his blunt as he continued to load ammunition into his assault rifle in the front seat of his car. Leaning back, he looked at his driver-side mirror, making sure no one watched him or approached his vehicle. The ordinarily busy Harper Court was uncannily quiet, which aggravated him to madness.

Fuck, ain't hardly anybody out here to see this nigga go down.

But he was determined to face Shadow on the street and kill him in front of the hotel he stayed in, no matter who was around. He didn't care that the area was teeming with the CPD and the Secret Service due to the President's Chicago home being no more than a mile from where he was parked. King David made sure no one would give him "work", so he was dead out in the streets, making him desperate and poisoned with the need for revenge.

Flicking ash from his blunt into the center console's ashtray, Midas growled,

"Da fuck this nigga at?"

"Right here."

Shadow's voice coming from the back seat made Midas swear loudly while his entire body jumped, causing his blunt to fly in the air and fall onto the tan leather. He quickly reached over towards the passenger seat, but Shadow's warning of the gun's nozzle pressed against his temple made him stop immediately.

"Fuck!" Midas whimpered while he closed his eyes, waiting for the loud pop of Shadow's gun to go off, sending a bullet into his brain.

"Is all that for me? Aww, Midas, you shouldn't have." Shadow teased while he used one hand to move Midas's gun onto the back seat next to him while keeping his gun pressed against Midas's temple.

"How long you been back there?" Midas asked while slowly lifting his hands in the air.

"I was back here before you got in the car. Fuck wrong with you, nigga? Why would you try this shit here? In Hyde Park?! Are you trying to get merced by the pigs, nigga? Oh, I see, you want to send a message to the streets. Nigga, the streets ain't listening to you no more."

"That's all because of that bitch, Zaya!"

"Nigga, don't mistake the fact you're still breathing as if you still ain't gone get yo brains exposed to that front windshield. So, calm that hostility and bitch calling down. Now, you have two choices: either you can get this bullet from me or get this money *with* me. You decide, but either way, tonight, this beef ends."

"Nigga! Yo, broke-ass ain't getting no money! That bitch is the only reason you and your punk ass brother got a roof over your head!"

Midas's head immediately erupted in excruciating pain after Shadow hit him across the head with his gun.

"Ahhh! Fuck!"

"What was that?"

Midas leaned forward while holding the side of his head to prevent the blood from his newly acquired gash from running into his eyes.

"Nothing." He whispered.

"Now, I'm going to share something with you, and although you are in front of this hotel about to do some extremely dumb shit, I still believe you're smart enough to see the value in it and will keep your fucking mouth shut. Or am I mistaken?"

"You got it, playa."

"I work for Cain and—"

Midas's eyes widen as his body straightened up.

"Say less, my nigga. If you are rocking with dat nigga Cain, and you can get me in, not only will I squash this beef, nigga, I'll rock with you like a muhfucka."

"Getting you in isn't the problem. Can you remove yourself from this street shit and not look back?"

94

"Nigga, I heard how Cain moves weight. Whatever I'm required to do, it will get done with no argument from me. Even if I got to fill a nigga up with some hot shit, I'm with it."

Still keeping his gun to Midas's temple, Zahir tapped him on the shoulder and responded, "That won't be necessary. Only the utmost discretion and loyalty."

"Consider it done."

"Good shit, my nigga. I will get at you in a few days, but I need you to be patient though. Don't make me come back because you can't control your emotions. So, whatever you were feeling about Zaya and me, let that shit go. Otherwise, the next time you hear my voice...."

"Understood, bruh. M O —"

Seeing the look of "I dare you to finish that statement" on Zahir's face in his rearview mirror made Midas close his mouth and simply nod his head in agreement.

"Midas, you can be a solid nigga. I wouldn't have let you live and offered you a way out if I didn't think so. Don't disappoint me."

"You got my word, Shadow. I won't fuck this up."

"I believe you won't. I'll be in touch."

Zahir quickly exited the vehicle, and before Midas could turn around to watch him leave, Zahir was gone.

Where da fuck that nigga go?

With a trembling hand, he retrieved his blunt and relit it. Examing his surroundings, Midas took an aggressive pull on his blunt, held in the purple smoke, before exhaling forcefully. Allowing the drug's euphoric effect to help calm his nerves. He then started his car to leave before someone else suddenly appeared in his back seat.

CHAPTER TEN

THE NEXT AFTERNOON ZAHIR hesitated outside Union Station for a few seconds before inhaling deeply and pushing the revolving doors to let himself inside the massive Metra Train station. The building was teeming with travelers rushing to get to their departing trains. His senses were instantly greeted with the sweet smells of pastries and the undeniable aroma of Garrett's world-famous popcorn. On a typical day, Zahir would rush towards the intoxicating scent of popcorn, but today wasn't a typical day, and he had to stay focused to see his first drop through successfully.

He quickly moved towards the lockers on the far end of the first floor, moving through the crowded corridor and avoiding eye contact with any security guards or police officers posted throughout the building.

1984

He repeated the locker number in his head as he moved through the rows of lockers until he found locker number 1984. As he reached into the pocket of his skinny jeans, his heart began to pound against his chest at a speed that almost made him turn and run in the opposite direction. Something felt off about this pickup, but he knew he had no choice but to see it through. His first drop was his coming-out party, and he wanted to leave a lasting impression on Cain so that he could trust him with more important tasks that would have a larger payout. Zahir took a final assessment of his surroundings before he proceeded to open the locker. The locker's door protested loudly as its door hinges were forced to work as Zahir opened it slowly and peered inside. A large black backpack lay inside, and without hesitation, Zahir snatched it out of its dark hiding place, slid it on his back, quickly closed the locker door, and made his way out of the train station.

As soon as he stepped outside, the Chicago hawk slapped Zahir across the face with a ferocity that immediately made his eyes water. Swearing loudly, he noticed a navy blue compact car pulling up to the curbside in front of him. The driver rolled down the window and said, "You called for a Uber?" The driver quickly took three fingers and tapped on the steering wheel three times. A call sign that he was a part of Cain's organization. Nodding, Zahir promptly climbed in the car's back seat, and the driver pulled into the busy downtown traffic.

"It's colder than a muhfucka, ain't it?" the driver said, looking back at Zahir in his rearview mirror.

Rolling his eyes, Zahir nodded and quickly turned his attention outside the window next to him. Understanding his silent message that he didn't want to be bothered, the driver nodded and returned his attention to the road. Zahir watched the busy city outside his window and wondered how many people rushing back and forth were potential or current customers of the highly valued yet illegal substance in the backpack he carried.

Anyone of these motherfuckas could be a customer; all it takes is to find out what's their preferred poison of choice. And Cain supplied all of it. From drugs, sex, information, and everything in between. Cain was a connoisseur of all things humans desired. Zahir watched as men and women in corporate attire moved through the frigid streets of downtown Chicago and calculated just how much each one of them would be willing to spend on pleasures deemed illegal or immoral.

It's so much paper out here, and I'm going to make sure I get all of it.

Suddenly, the driver swore loudly as the spine-chilling sound of a police car's siren blared behind them. The red and blues quickly engulfed the vehicle's interior, and the driver slowly pulled the car over.

Zahir looked at the driver and then back at the squad car. His eyes searched the driver's facial expression as he refused to look at Zahir through the rearview mirror.

I knew this fucking drop felt wrong. Look at his ass refusing to look at me, and he's constantly texting on his phone. He hasn't reached for his wallet or anything to prepare to greet the officer with his driver's license and insurance. Either this nigga about to sing like a canary, or he about to bolt on me.

Without warning, the driver pushed open his door and sprinted across the street and down an alley. The officer in the car seemed uninterested in the fleeing man, and Zahir immediately recognized the setup.

On my first day, I get picked up by a fucking rat. Fuck!

The officer slowly walked to the car, pulled his gun out, and pointed at the vehicle.

"Passenger, roll down the window and toss out the backpack."

Shaking his head, Zahir grabbed the backpack and tossed it out the window.

Fuck! This is not how I thought this day would go.

A few minutes later, Zahir felt the officer clamp the handcuffs around his wrist as his face was pressed against the trunk of the car. As the cold winds violated his face, Zahir watched as people walked past, looking on with disgust.

Pretend all you want. Most of you would buy what I'm selling if you had the chance to get away with it.

A couple of hours later, Zahir was ushered inside an interrogation room and left alone for several hours. The room's temperature was so cold; he could see the mist of his breath as he exhaled. The room's deadly grey walls were discolored with dark splotches of what Zahir assumed was the blood of previous detainees that refused to answer the famously violent Chicago police's questions.

The room's door slowly opened, and a large man walked into the room, smiling triumphantly. As he moved towards the chair on the opposite side of the table, his egg-shaped body jiggled and bounced. The detective ran his hand through his light brown straight hair and sat down with a lazy flop. Grunting, the detective began opening up a large manila folder and spreading out photos across the metal table. His peach-colored skin seemed to redden the more pictures he pulled out of the folder. He was clearly excited by his handy work.

"I'm Detective Patrick O'Neil, and I'm sure by looking at these photos I have spread out on this table, you can see just how much trouble you are in Zahir Jones. We have you on multiple counts of distribution of an illegal substance, and with the amount of shit you were hauling in that car, you could be facing at least twenty years without the possibility of parole. Now, we understand that you're just a tiny piece of the massive machine that makes up Will Johnson's drug organization. We are determined to bring his empire down, one drug-dealing degenerate at a time until he's the last criminal standing. Now, you can help yourself, or you can cover for him, but make no mistakes; he will not come to rescue you.

We have several of his former employees languishing in County right now, awaiting trial, and they are all using public defenders. Now, we know that you are new, so you don't have much information about his inner workings, who his suppliers and customers are, but we do know that he has taken a liking to you, judging by how much shit he gave you for your first drop."

Exhaling forcefully, Zahir grunted, "So, you want me to become a snitch?"

Patrick's eyes moved back and forth while shrugging his shoulders before replying, "Wow, you're pretty bright, huh?"

The detective's sarcasm was meant to upset Zahir, but he noticed the teenager was unmoved.

"You can either be a snitch or someone's bitch. Because we know you have some very powerful enemies in Englewood. A certain man named after a biblical King?" Patrick teased while winking in Zahir's direction. "He has so many of his guys locked up; all he would have to do is send word that you are to be welcomed with opened arms, and then that's when the real party begins. We know he wants you dead, but he would much enjoy that you die slowly. You're a handsome young man, despite how overcooked your black ass is. Usually, the light-skinned guys are popular, but I'm sure they will make an exception for a young man as attractive as you. Those faggot niggers in County will take real good care of you. Is that what you want, or do you want to help me get a monster and that poison off the streets of my city?"

Zahir grinned and leaned back in his chair and calmly responded, "Lawyer."

"Excuse me?"

"Lawyer. I want a lawyer."

"Oh, you want to play games?"

"I've already said what I said."

"You're willing to take your chances with a public defender, be my guest. I can tell you, with all the evidence we have against you, by the time you get out, your little brother, Kai, will either be a grown man or dead from fending for himself in those streets. And that black bitch Zaya will have about five kids by six different "baby daddies" by the time you get out. But judging by all the fucking you'll be doing in jail; you won't have the same sexual appetite you had before going in. Now, I can make life really hard or easy for you. This is my final offer before I let the chips fall where I want them. Are you in?

It was difficult for Zahir to ignore the reality that Kai would suffer while he was away, and the idea of losing Zaya tore him to pieces, but he knew there was no way he could put their lives in jeopardy just to stay out of jail. He would be trading one prison for another and out in these streets; once you've been labeled a rat, it's only a matter of time before someone sets the trap. So, no matter how terrifying twenty years seemed inside a prison with men loyal to King David, Zahir decided to accept his current situation and not bring those he loved into it. Mustering all the remaining confidence he had left inside of him, he grinned and responded,

"Lawyer"

Swearing loudly, Patrick snatched up all the photos on the table and stood up, shaking his head.

"I thought you were smarter than this. You animals love being locked in cages. So be it. I'll get you your lil lawyer. But I'm telling you right now; I will make sure the DA prosecutes you to the fullest extent of the law. You won't get out until you need a walker."

Detective O'Neil then walked towards the door. Before walking out, he looked back at Zahir and growled, "stupid nigger" and slammed the door behind him.

As soon as he was alone, Zahir exhaled and began to breathe aggressively. He'd been holding his breath in an attempt to keep himself from losing his composure. From his racist rants and threats to those he cared for, the detective pushed his emotional control to its limits. As he tried to steady his breathing, Zahir could hear the echo of a familiar laugh outside the interrogation room's door.

Wait a minute, ain't no fucking way!

The door swung open, and Cain walked through the door smiling, followed by Detective O'Neil and the police superintendent Brian Brown. They all seemed to be enjoying each other's company as if they were "day ones" having a good laugh at Zahir's expense.

What the fuck?

Looking at Zahir with pride, Cain said, "I told you this one was special."

Nodding in agreement, the superintendent responded, "Yeah, you were right. Cause Patrick laid it on thick, didn't he?"

Suddenly, Cain seemed to be searching his memory as his eyes moved back and forth. Without warning, he reached for Patrick's head and forcefully slammed his head on the metal desk. He then placed his forearm on his neck and leaned all of his weight on the detective's neck. Patrick squealed in pain as he felt himself suffocating as his neck gave way to Cain's weight. Zahir looked on in shock as he watched the violent exchange between Cain and the detective. As the detective groaned from Cain's weight, slowly cutting off his circulation, the superintendent did nothing to stop a known drug dealer from assaulting a detective in his presence.

Cain leaned down closer to Patrick's ear and growled, "If I ever hear you call Zahir a nigger again, I will severe your head from your fat greasy Irish body, understood?"

Forcing himself to respond before he passed out, Patrick whined, "Yes, sir."

Getting up while shoving the detective head across the table, Cain responded, "Good boy."

Cain adjusted his peacoat jacket, pointed at Zahir, and ordered, "Get them cuffs off my boy!"

The superintendent quickly sprung into action and hurried over to remove the cuffs from Zahir's wrist. A few minutes later, while continuously apologizing for the inconvenience of his arrest, the superintendent and Patrick informed Zahir that the substance in his bag was, in fact, blue M&M candies instead of the suspected designer drug Xstacy. After handing the backpack to Zahir, the superintendent quickly escorted Cain and Zahir outside of the police station.

A blacked-out Lincoln Navigator limousine was waiting for Cain and Zahir in front of the police station, and Cain gestured for Shadow to get inside. Cain climbed into the limo after Zahir and sat in the seat directly across from him. An uncomfortable silence followed as the two men stared at each other, both of their minds processing the events in the police station from different perspectives. Zahir knew Cain was connected, but what he saw in the police station was beyond anything he could fathom. The amount of power Cain wielded was godlike, and Zahir yearned to learn how to wield that kind of power himself, and at that moment, he dedicated himself to learn as much as he could from Cain.

"Now that we both understand each other, we can get to work, cool?"

"Yes, sir. Let's get this money."

Nodding proudly, Cain leaned forward and shook Zahir's hand. There was a look of pride in Cain's eyes, and Zahir knew he had bigger plans for him and today was a test to see if he had the pedigree to be more than a simple delivery boy. Excited at the possibilities his display of loyalty afforded him, Zahir relaxed in his seat and listened to the music blaring through the limo's sound system.

I'm going to love this life.

CHAPTER ELEVEN

A FEW DAYS LATER, Zahir was being transported to his first drop by an actual employee of Cain's organization posing as an Uber driver. The customer was the CEO of one of the world's leading software developers who had a home in the northern suburb of Highland Park. This time, Zahir was relaxed and confident. Zahir began to reflect on the days leading up to his first official delivery; Cain took time to take Zahir to the shooting range and share keys to the "game" he would need to complete his first drop successfully. Cain made sure his runners had the complete profiles of their drops to communicate in their preferred language. Zahir's first drop was a man who wore two faces. One face was a brilliant philanthropist who wanted to make the world a better place for all.

He was a noble peace prize nominee and the fifth richest man in the world. His contributions saved millions of lives worldwide. He was a beloved advocate for poor people, especially the African American community, of which he gave millions of his wealth through donations to HBCU's and other educational programs to improve the lives of black people in the United States. He was a great man in all accounts, but this was not the man Zahir would be delivering to. He would be delivering to the man who wore face number two.

This man wore the face of a drug and sex-addicted racist who despised anyone that wasn't rich and white. He has used dark channels to donate more money to white supremacy groups than he donated to black people and medical advancements combined. It was rumored that he had financed over sixty percent of all domestic terrorist activity over the last two decades. With countless government officials in his pockets, he used them to further his white supremacist ideals by pushing them to pass archaic laws and amendments to the constitution. Cain wanted Zahir to understand that he must be aware of who was greeting him and govern himself accordingly when he opened his door. The CEO was known for saying things to his runners that would get anyone else put to sleep, but money was the goal, so self-control and discretion were necessary.

After the two of them finished their fifth round of target practice, Cain and Zahir sat down for a few minutes to reflect on everything Cain shared with him about his first drop.

"You look like I just told you another nigga fucked your girl!" Cain chuckled.

Shaking his head, Zahir responded, "Man, listen, if this information came from anyone else, I would've said they were capping hard as fuck."

Placing his hand on Zahir's shoulder, Cain responded, "In this business, you're gonna have to accept that most powerful people wear two faces, some more than that. Some of them are considered heroes, and others in positions of power make some extremely problematic faces. But what we provide, these drugs are inhibitors that prevent these crazy ass people from going completely insane. Without these life-numbing products, these muthafuckas would burn the world to ash. It's men like your drop that keep us above the law. So, if we want to keep getting this money, we have to accept every single one of those faces no matter how fucked up they are."

"So, I take it when I get there he gone be flinging nigger with the hard "er" recklessly."

"Yeah, he's a piece of work, but I'm confident you can handle it."

"I got you."

"I know you do, and I have no doubt."

"I need to talk to you about something, though."

"I hope you ain't bout to ask me for no advance."

"No, I wanted to talk to you about bringing someone else into the fold."

Nodding, Cain smiled and responded, "You want to bring Midas into my organization. You promised him you could get him in knowing if you could, you would squash the beef between you two."

"Wow."

"Surprised I knew about that?"

"After what you pulled at the police station, not really."

"What I'm tripping on is how the fuck you promise employment to someone in *my* shit? You can't just tell someone you gone get them into something you don't fucking own. How you figured that was the move?"

"Because I know you wanted him to join your team. When you picked me up from the hotel to discuss me working for you, I could tell he was someone you wouldn't hesitate to bring on board, but he was part of the opposition. Now that he isn't, I figured I could solve two problems at once. My beef and your need to have a nigga like Midas on the team."

Damn, this lil nigga peeping shit like a pro.

Cain looked over at Zahir and nodded in agreement.

"I like how you handled yourself in that situation. You made a mistake, but you quickly found a solution that benefited you and the bottom line because Midas is definitely *that* nigga. But he's a street superstar; he ain't built to run a crew on this level, so I'm going to allow it, but he's going to be your responsibility. So, he's going to be your designated Uber driver."

Zahir started to protest, but Cain raised his index finger and continued, "As your driver, he will still make more money than he was making on those cold corners for King David, but he needs to be trained and reprogrammed. He has been out in them streets too long to trust he knows how to handle this business on this level. Now, it's up to you to keep him in line and happy with his new position as your driver. If not..."

Understanding he didn't have a choice in the matter, Zahir nodded in agreement.

"Good shit! Now let's get back to this target practice. You've caught on pretty quickly cause you have great eyesight and a steady hand. So, I think it's time to teach you how to aim down a moving target. Let's get it!"

Now, sitting in the backseat of his Uber with Midas driving and attentively watching the road, Zahir reflected on Cain's warning about not getting Midas in line, so he needed to make sure he was entirely on board with his new reality. When Zahir first came to Midas and gave him the news, the initial shock of what he would be doing threw Midas into a rage, but once Zahir told him what he would be paid for being his driver and the lack of stress and danger that came with the position his anger subsided. Zahir could tell that under all the big shit talk, Midas, like many of the street dealers, was growing tired of the street corners. The danger, the stress of getting arrested or being gunned down by a rival gang or set up by a jealous member of the same gang was constantly weighing them down. There were too many variables on the street, and the idea of eliminating those variables and still making more money was an opportunity that Midas couldn't pass up.

But Zahir knew that Midas's ambition would eventually start to rekindle, so he needed to make sure Midas proved himself to Cain for him to be given something else to do. Something that would increase his money and his position in the organization. He would rather sit in silence, but he needed to bond with Midas to build his own mental profile of who he was and what made him tick. Similar to what Cain did for his drops. Money was the motivator for Midas, so anytime you get him the opportunity to talk about how much money he was making on the streets and what he bought with it, he wouldn't shut up. And Zahir needed him to talk. A lot.

"Hey, tell me something, Midas; what were the most you made working for King David?"

"Nigga! One weekend me and the crew sold three hundred and fifty thousand worth of product!"

"Damn, that's a lot of fucking money!"

"You damn right! We were out there from 3 am Friday till Sunday night. Only bathroom breaks, nigga. We ate on our feet in shifts to keep the product moving. Seventy-two hours of non-stop savagery, my nigga!"

"I bet you and your niggas were tired as fuck!"

"Fuck yeah, and we had to get back out there Monday night!"

"Damn, that's dedication, bruh!"

"That's how I got King David's attention, and they started calling me Midas because that corner was dead as fuck because it was a few blocks from a police station!"

"Nigga! You made almost half a million dollars moving weight right down the street from One Time?!"

"Yep! After that, King David put me on to other corners and gave me a larger percentage of our sales because of how well we moved weight."

Zahir could tell Midas was relishing in his past triumphs, and he hated to do it to him, but he needed to take the veil off of his previous situation so that he could understand just how sweet his current situation was. Inhaling deeply, Zahir asked, "how much of that three fifty did you get back?"

"I got three stacks, and my crew got about a stack a piece."

"So, you made about forty-two bucks an hour, and your crew made about fourteen an hour."

"Yeah, what's your point?" Midas snapped, annoyed by Shadow's calculating his earnings, and hearing them said out loud made him feel uneasy.

"With all the risk a nigga take out in them streets, forty bucks an hour ain't it. And your crew clocking fourteen bucks an hour is even worse, and it's no secret why they left you hanging so quickly."

"Nigga, you gone rub this in my face, now? Fuck wrong with you?"

"Midas, I mean no disrespect, my nigga. If I didn't respect you, that night in the back of your car would've ended differently. You feel me?"

"I can respect that."

"What I'm trying to point out here is, you are driving me. Simply driving me from point A to point B, and you are making three times that much, each fucking drop! Imagine how much more paper you and me can get together if we prove the two of us can ace this shit?! Nigga, if you follow my lead, bruh, I will make you fucking rich!"

"Oh, so you talmbout taking over this shit from Cain?"

"Hell nawl, nigga! That's crazy talk! I'm talking about helping Cain grow this shit! Pushing his current customers to spend twice as much and referring more customers. Even more connected, muhfuckas! You are a salesman, my nigga. You can talk a nigga with a quarter to spend a dollar. Now I'm not gonna, "today I'm on the lettuce and tomorrow I'm on the fries" you, but what I am saying, there's too much potential out here, and we can bring in twice as much! Think about that for a second!"

Midas remained silent as he listened to Zahir.

This nigga makes sense like a muhfucka! Ain't none of those GD niggas ever came at me like that, offering to really put a nigga on to some real money.

"Ok, ok, let's say I'm with you on this. Do you think Cain would want to increase his output? Wouldn't that bring more heat on this nigga?"

"Nigga? What heat? Do you see who we sell to? Who gone bring heat on Cain and expose themselves? Not a single one of these rich and famous junkies!"

"Facts!"

"I just need you to trust me and ride with me on this. I promised you I'd put you on, right? And did I not deliver, despite you being outside my hotel attempting to murder me?"

"Yeah, about that, my bad, bruh! Now that I think about it, that shit was wack as fuck. I knew Zaya wasn't really into me, and truth be told, I wasn't really into her either. I was really enjoying the clout a nigga was getting from dating King

David's daughter. Plus, them hoes on the block had a nigga hypnotized."

"Well, now you can fuck and get sucked as much as you want by them hoes and not have to answer to anyone for it. And with the kind of paper we about to get, you gone be able to pull some quality bitches. I'm talking about them downtown bitches."

"Oh, I can feel that. Them high society hoes."

"Exactly! So, what you wanna do?"

"Shadow, I fucks with you. No cap. Whatever you need me to do, I will do it!"

"Good shit, my nigga, now pay attention to the road before these pigs pull a nigga over out here in these rich people's neighborhood."

About twenty minutes later, Midas came to a stop at a giant black rod iron fence. Rolling down the window, he pulled the car up to the intercom and pressed the call button. Within a few seconds, a voice came through the speaker, asking him to identify himself.

"Three times three," Midas replied, and within seconds the gate began to open.

Midas slowly drove up the long driveway that led to a massive Meditteranean-style mansion. His mouth slowly hung open as he pulled into the circular driveway to the front door. Zahir grabbed his backpack and tapped Midas on his shoulder.

"Keep it running."

"Cool. Let me know if anything pops off!"

"Nigga! Do you see this house? Ain't no shit popping but maybe some pussy inside this muhfucka!"

"Oh, shit! Let a nigga roll with you then!"

"Nigga, you know better!"

"Yeah, just thought I try!"

Zahir chuckled, stepped out of the back seat, and walked up to the massive three-story mahogany front doors.

Once he got to the front doors, he rang the doorbell expecting security personnel to open the door, but to his surprised, the drop himself met him at the door smelling of sex and alcohol. He wore an expensive white bathrobe that was soiled with what Zahir could only assume was body fluids of whomever he was cheating on his wife with. Without his glasses that made him seem benevolent and approachable, the CEO's eyes seemed to burn with the darkness that Cain exposed about him.

Looking Zahir up and down, the CEO sucked his teeth, rolled his eyes, and opened the door wider so he could let him inside his mansion.

"The last guy wasn't so...melanated," the CEO teased as he led Zahir through his foyer towards a flight of stairs that led down to a basement. As he reached the basement entrance, the rancid odors of sex, drugs, and alcohol burned the inside of his nostrils, causing his eyes to water.

Fuck! It smells like hell down there.

Instinctively, Zahir wanted to cover his nose and mouth in an attempt to keep the infection of the putrid smells from invading his body, but he noticed the client watching him closely, so he fought back the urge and walked down the stairs behind the CEO.

The basement was dark, only illuminated by a red light that only slightly penetrated the engulfing darkness. But the red light was bright enough for Zahir to see the details of the mayhem that was happening around him. There were naked bodies sprawled out over the floor that seemed to be covered in sheets and mattresses. Momentarily distracted, Zahir watched two women devour each other in the sixty-nine position. Their silhouettes were stunning, each curvature of their bodies exciting Zahir.

Shit! It's lit as fuck down here!

Suddenly the sharp sound of the CEO snapping his fingers pulled Shadow away from watching the two women and back on the task at hand.

"Can we get this shit over with?"

"Yes, sir, apologies."

"Oh, you're an educated nigger! I didn't expect that from someone so...dark. It's usually the lighter ones that are well-spoken."

Refusing to address his racist comments, Zahir waited for the CEO to continue leading the way. Noticing Zahir waiting on him, the CEO flashed an aggravating grin and continued to lead him past the numerous bodies moving like snakes along the floor. They finally reached a door towards the back of the basement. As the CEO opened the door, the light exposed the sensual scene in the basement, and Zahir forced himself not to turn around and take a glance. He wanted to get in and out as soon as possible. Closing the door behind him, the CEO pointed to a large circular white table in the middle of the room, and Zahir opened his backpack and emptied the contents on the surface of the table.

After his backpack was emptied, the CEO looked over his bounty before nodding in agreement that his one hundred thousand dollar order was delivered complete.

"Thank you for your business, sir," Zahir said.

Noticing Zahir was waiting on something, the CEO asked, "I paid, didn't I?"

"Yes, sir."

"So, why are you just standing there looking like a fucking idiot?"

"Aren't you gonna escort me out?"

"Fuck no! Find your own way out. I'm busy!"

Shrugging, Zahir turned and left the room, leaving the CEO sitting at the table filling his nostrils with mounds of cocaine.

On his way out, Zahir decided to take his time and take in the sites before eventually making his way up the stairs and out the front door.

As he climbed into the back seat of the car, Midas yelled, "Gad damn, nigga! What's that smell?! Nigga is that you smelling like pussy and Patron?"

"Nigga, drive!"

"Ok, boss," Midas teased as he began to drive away from the mansion's front door.

"Nigga roll down the windows or something, cause that shit is all up in this muhfucka!"

Laughing, Shadow snapped, "Fuck you, nigga!"

"Real talk, you gotta tell me what was going on in that muhfucka cause it smells like you walked in my kind of party."

Shaking his head, Shadow sat back in the seat and closed his eyes for a few seconds.

As wild as that drop was, I have a feeling that one is gonna be lightweight compared to what's to come.

In the coming months, Zahir's drops became more frequent as his prompt and professional demeanor put the clients at ease, and before long, they would specifically request he deliver their orders. The more deliveries Zahir and Midas did together, the closer they became until Midas, although a few years older than Zahir, looked up to him as a mentor, and he did whatever he asked without question. Spring was quickly approaching, and the warmer weather would mean more parties for the clients, and more parties meant more deliveries and more money to be made. Averaging seventy thousand dollars a week, Zahir was confident in making some upgrades to him and his little brother's life.

Kai heard a key card slide in the hotel's room's door, and he quickly grabbed his gun to meet whoever was coming through it. Noticing it was his big brother, Kai breathed a sigh of relief and stuffed his gun in the back of his jeans.

"Sup!"

"Shit! At home as usual." Kai replied, annoyance lacing his tone and delivery.

"Listen, I know it's been a strange few months, but you know what I'm doing for us."

"I know, but damn. Can you spend some time with your little brother some time? I mean, what's the point of making all that paper saying it's for us, but there isn't an *us*. You all I got, and it ain't like I can go outside and roam because this block is hotter than hell. And you told me to lay low because King David might try to get at you through me."

"You're right, and that's my bad. But I have some great news!"

"What?"

"We getting the fuck outta this hood!"

"Wait! Are you serious?"

"Like a heart attack! WE OUT THIS BITCH!"

"But wait, how long is it gonna take for you to find a spot?"

"Man, the spot is paid for, furnished and everything! Grab your shit; we out of here!"

Unable to contain his excitement, Kai wrapped his arms around his brother and held him close. After a few moments, he released his grip and rushed through the hotel, grabbing his belongings. As Kai gathered his things, Zahir began picking up his belongings as well. After an hour, Zahir started to walk out of the hotel and paused for a moment to take a final look at the place they called home for the past few months. The beautiful and radiant smile of Zaya flashed through his mind, reminiscing on everything she'd done for them and the sacrifices she made for him.

Time to get my baby right.

Kai followed Zahir outside the hotel and looked around for their usual ride with Midas at the wheel. Noticing his eyes searching for Midas, Zahir smiled and said, "Not today, lil bro. We riding in that." Kai followed Zahir's pointing finger, revealing a new black Audi A8 parked in front of the hotel with the flashing hazard lights.

"Wait, this you?!"

"Yep, and as soon as you get serious about getting your permit and license, imma get you right, too!"

"Oh, shit!" Kai yelled as he ran towards the car and hopped into the front passenger seat. Noticing Zahir still standing in the same spot, Kai yelled, "Get in nigga! We ain't got all night!"

Nodding, Zahir strolled towards the car, tossed his belongings in the trunk, climbed in the driver's seat, and pulled off.

"How far is the new spot? Are we in the burbs, Evergreen Park? Lincoln Park?"

"Nah, we on the lakefront right off of Michigan."

"DAAAAAAMN! That rent must be higher than a muhfucka!"

"We can afford it?" Zahir responded confidently.

"How, though?! Most landlords wouldn't rent to a seventeen-year-old, and those muhfuckas up north would never."

"Cain hooked it up."

"Kai's excitement immediately subsided, disgusted by hearing Cain's name and his new home mentioned in the same sentence. Noticing his brother's reaction, Zahir looked at his brother and said, "I need you to calm that hostility down, bruh. I know you don't care for Cain–"

"Care? Nah, I hate that nigga!" Kai interjected.

"Fine, whatever, you hate him. But at the moment, you gone have to lay that hate to rest cause we need him, his money, and his connections. I don't want any shit between you and Cain. He is not the type of man that will continue to let you try him. I need you to see all this for what it is. Let me handle Cain."

"Yeah, whatever."

"I'm serious, Kai."

"Fine, I'll dead my beef with that nigga Cain. Now can we go to the pent?"

"Slow your roll, bro. I need to make a stop before we head to our new spot."

"You going to pick up Zaya, ain't you?"

"No, but I need to see her before we ride out."

Remembering where the money came from that gave them a decent place to stay, Kai calmed down.

Twenty minutes later, Zahir parked the Audi a few houses down from King David's house. Before stepping out, he instructed Kai to stay in the car and wait for him. Once he was sure his brother would follow his instructions, Zahir climbed out of the car and walked towards his destination. He made sure he held his cellphone in his hand as he walked down the block. When he got to the front of the house, the last thing he wanted was to startle the guards by reaching in his leather jacket. The evening air was much warmer than the last time he made the journey, and the pleasant breeze that blew across his face felt welcoming, unlike the crew of men waiting in front of King David's Greystone.

"Nigga, what the fuck are you doing here? Malik ain't here nigga, so I suggest you take yo black ass back in that direction!" One of them threatened.

Ignoring him, Zahir dialed Zaya's number and placed the phone to his ear. After a single ring, Zaya's excited voice filled his ears.

"Hey, babe, I missed you so much. When am I gonna see you again?"

"Right now! I'm downstairs."

Zaya nearly dropped her phone as she ran downstairs as fast as she could.

Oh my God, please don't let these niggas start nothing in front of my daddy's house. Shadow is crazy as fuck for coming here.

The front door opened, and Zaya sprinted out the house, leaping down the steps and standing between her father's goons and Zahir.

"Hey, it's cool. Back the fuck up!"

"Hey, your dad told us to regulate this nigga if we see him on the block!"

"And *I'm* telling you to stand the fuck down!"

"Zaya, no disrespect, but I answer to your father. So, I gotta do what I gotta do. I don't want him beating my ass to death with those fucking chains!"

Shadow looked at the big-mouth gangster and replied, "Nigga, it's all good. Imma bounce, I got what I came for."

"Nigga you ain't going nowhere with Zaya!"

Suddenly all of them pulled out their guns and pointed them in Shadow's direction. Zaya screamed and jumped in front of Zahir, shielding him from any potential gunfire. The men quickly lowered their weapons and yelled for Zaya to move out of the way.

"No! Like Shadow said, he's leaving, so let it ride."

"Ah-ight! Another time bitch nigga. You let your woman protect you instead of taking this shit like a man? We gone see you again, and she won't be around to protect your punk ass."

Without warning, Zahir pushed Zaya out of the way, pulled out his gun, and aimed it at the head of the group leader. Fear erupted through his body as he stared down the barrel of Zahir's Glock.

"Don't ever threaten me again! Now, I'm ready to die. Are you ready to die, muthafucka?"

Swallowing hard, the man immediately dropped his gun and raised his hands in the air. Looking around, Shadow motioned for the rest of them to follow his example, and the sound of metal colliding with concrete followed.

"Now, back the fuck up on the stairs."

The men followed his instructions, and once he was confident they were at a safe distance, Shadow collected all of their guns, removed the clips and the bullets in the chamber. He then tossed them all in the bushes on the side of the Greystone and backed away towards his car. While watching the entire exchange from the car, Kai secretly made his way directly across the street from King David's house and aimed his gun at the men threatening his brother. Once he noticed Shadow had the upper hand, he hurried back to the car and climbed in the back seat so Zaya could sit up front.

Zahir and Zaya quickly climbed into the car, and Shadow put the Audi in reverse and sped back down the block. He knew the men were searching through the bushes for their guns, and he didn't want to add insult to injury by speeding past them in his new car. He wanted to send a message, but not one that was disrespectful and reckless. He wanted King David to know he wasn't afraid of him or his crew, and no matter how much he hated him, he would never leave Zaya alone.

Trembling in the passenger seat, Zaya looked over at Shadow and mumbled, "bae, that was crazy! Why did you come over here?"

"Because I wanted to see you, and I'm tired of tip-toeing about us. I'm not afraid of your daddy!"

"And he ain't afraid of you, so what? Two unafraid niggas that love me gone be gunning for each other in these streets. I don't want my daddy trying to kill you, and I don't want you trying to kill my daddy. Shit, my daddy gone kick my ass out his house behind this shit, watch!"

"No, he won't. Listen, I don't want to hurt your father, either. We both know what's up, so me wanting to merc him would be crazy. But what I won't do is be intimidated by him either."

"You think you know my daddy?"

Shadow simply shrugged and continued to concentrate on driving. Zaya suddenly noticed the strange luxury vehicle she was sitting in and asked, "Who's car is this, babe?"

Grinning, Zahir nodded and glanced over at Zaya.

"This you?! Holy shit, bae, is this an A8?"

"Brand new!"

"Oh, baby, congratulations! This joint is off the chain!"

"Open the glove compartment!"

Zaya quickly opened the glove compartment, and four stacks of bills slid out.

"Baby, is this forty grand?"

"Yep, that's repayment of your loan, interest, and something extra on top of it because a nigga got love for you!"

Zaya grabbed the bricks of cash and held them close to her. She then leaned over, held his chin in her hand, and kissed him passionately while he continued to drive.

"Ummm, can that shit wait until we get to a red light or something!" Kai pleaded from the back seat when he noticed Zahir was driving while kissing her with his eyes closed.

Laughing, Zahir opened his eyes and kept his eyes on the road. Zaya stared at Zahir as he continued to drive as her mind began to drift away into her thoughts.

I love him so much, and the more I fall for him, the more things will get complicated with my daddy. God knows I shouldn't be dealing with Shadow, but the way he makes me feel. The way he looks at me and kisses me. Ain't no way imma be able to turn away from him. I just have to find a way to get my dad to stand down, but how?

The private elevator ride was deathly quiet as Kai and Zaya eagerly anticipated arriving at the luxurious penthouse. The soft ping proceeded the elevator door's opening directly into the large foyer that led into the penthouse. The white tiled floors sparkled like an ocean of marble, reflecting the large modern artwork on the walls.

Kai and Zaya's eyes widened as they stepped out of the elevator and reveled in the surroundings. Zahir stood behind them with his arms folded, a feeling of pride coming over him as he watched their awe at his new residence. As Zaya and Kai moved further inside the penthouse, Zahir followed them, smiling brightly as they ran from room to room, shouting with excitement.

Zaya didn't notice her phone vibrations as her father called her over thirty times. On the final call, he swore loudly and threw his burner across the living room. Gritting his teeth, he turned to his new head of security and roared, "How did you let a seventeen-year-old punk you with over nine niggas by your side?!"

"King David, listen…he had a gun pointed at my head!"

"And you think that lil nigga had the balls to pull the trigger?"

All the men responsible for guarding the front of his house answered in unison, "Yeah."

Taken aback by their response, King David ran his hand over his face, wiping the sweat of rage from his caramel-colored skin.

I wanna kill all these weak ass niggas, but I got to respect their unity trying to keep this nigga from meeting his ancestors. I wonder if that lil nigga did have it in him? That would really put Zaya's life in danger because that deviant nigga will do anything to stay alive, even put my baby in harm's way. I gotta get her from that nigga asap, and clearly, none of these soft Campbell soup ass niggas in my living room are up to the task. Imma have to call on Malik to handle this shit once and for all.

Glaring at his security team, King David pointed towards his front door and barked, "Get da fuck out of my house and stand watch. And for that weak shit y'all pulled, not a single one of you niggas will get paid tonight. I only pay hitters, so maybe tomorrow you niggas can try again. Now get the fuck on!

Without hesitation, the security team rushed out his front door, trying to push past each other in an attempt at being the first out the door. Looking at their disorganized exit, King David shook his head and aimed his gun in their direction, pretending he was shooting at fish in a barrel.

Reaching for another burner phone, King David called the only reliable hitter besides Da Rock on his team.

SHADOW OF THE JACKAL

"Malik, I need you to find Zaya, bring her back home and dead that nigga she with."

Before Malik could protest, King David ended the call and tossed the phone back on the table.

This ends tonight.

126

CHAPTER TWELVE

ZAYA RUSHED OUT ON the penthouse's terrace, calling out for Zahir.

"Hey, where's the fire?" Zahir teased as he wrapped his arms around her and kissed her on the cheek.

Swallowing hard with the frigid look of terror in her eyes, Zaya pointed at her phone and whispered, "My dad just told Malik to find me and kill you."

"Shit! Does he know where we live?"

"No, not yet, but you know that nigga Malik, he can find a hoe in a nunnery. So it's only a matter of time."

"I need to get back home and talk my daddy down!"

"I'm coming with you!"

"Shadow! No! You've definitely worn out your welcome over there. If you show up there again, I am sure he will shoot you himself!"

Shadow began to calculate every scenario and outcome of every course of action that came across his mind. He didn't have much time, and the craziest course of action seemed the only way to neutralize the threat of facing Malik as an enemy.

"I got an idea, but you ain't gone like it, and your daddy definitely not gone like it, but it's our only play!"

"As long as you don't hurt my daddy, Shadow!"

"You have my word."

"Ok, let me hear it as we get the fuck away from your spot, so Malik doesn't know where y'all live."

"Good idea, let's roll."

A few hours later, King David received a call from Malik informing him that he was still looking for Zahir and it would take longer than he anticipated because he was no longer living at the hotel. Growling into the phone, King David hissed through gritted teeth, "Nigga, I want him found tonight! I don't care who you have to pay, kill or threaten. Get it done!"

"Muthafucka!" King David yelled while throwing his phone across the room.

King David heard the men outside his house whispering to each other, clearly discussing him becoming unhinged over the actions of a teenager, so he decided to move his anger downstairs to his basement retreat. Opening the basement door, he turned on the lights and nearly fell backward when he discovered he was not alone.

"I don't want to hurt you, so don't make me, but we need to talk."

Swallowing the fear down his throat, King David nodded while holding both his hands in the air as he peered down the barrel of Shadow's Glock. Slowly backing down the stairs, Shadow kept his weapon pointed at King David until his feet met the floor, and he stepped to the side to let his nemesis walk past him.

"Have a seat," Shadow ordered, watching attentively as King David slowly sat down on his black leather sectional.

Attempting to regain some of his nerves, King David snapped, "How the fuck you get in my house!"

Looking around as if he was reminiscing, Shadow responded, "I've been in every inch of this house. It's been a long time since I was welcomed here without a gun being pointed at me. Now, things are different, but what I've never forgotten was how to get around this place without being seen."

"So, I guess you've won, huh? You're gonna be the one to take out the king! Did Cain send you to do this shit?"

Twisting his lips to the side of his face, Shadow responded, "No, sir. *You* sent me. The moment you sent Malik to kill me was the moment you left me no choice but to come see you."

"When those weak ass niggas told me they thought you had it in you to pull that trigger, I thought they were bullshitting, but now...."

"Yeah...life has a way of changing you."

"So, do it nigga! Take the throne!"

"I don't want this shit! It ain't enough! You know what I want, and if we keep at each other's throats like this, the only person that's gonna suffer is Zaya."

"Don't you fucking say her name around me nigga....you fucking freak bitch ass nigga! Don't you dare let her name come out of your mouth."

"With all due respect, fuck you, sir! Imma say Zaya all day, every day, and no matter what you think of me, she doesn't, and the only thing you'll be doing is pushing her further from you and closer to this freak bitch ass nigga! Now, what do you think will happen if she stops trusting and depending on you? Or better yet, to be with me, she decides to move in with this freak nigga?"

King David's face erupted in horror at the idea of his baby girl living with Zahir.

"Yeah, exactly. I care about Zaya. More than you can ever know. I can't change the past, but I can change the future, and I'm simply here saying let this run its course. If you know the type of woman you raised, you know she wouldn't mess with the type of nigga *you* think I am. Unless you didn't do as good of a job, you pride yourself in doing. If not, she ain't ready to run this shit when you step away in the next few years."

"You know about that?"

"I know a lot more than you think. I'm not asking you to like what we have or trust me. I'm asking you to trust her."

"You're asking a father to leave his most prized possession in the hands of a fucking monster."

"Nope, I'm asking you to allow your most prized possession to get closer to your enemy while maintaining a connection with you. Who knows what you can influence her to do."

"You expect me to believe she is capable of mercing your ass?" he scoffed.

"If it comes to that, I have no doubt she will not hesitate. She is, in fact, *your* daughter, and when you think about it, the one taking the risk is me, not you."

"Lil nigga, fuck you! I ain't one of these dumb ass niggas you be using your Jedi mind tricks on! I heard about you and how you manipulate these remedial niggas. I ain't no easy Op. I tell you what though, sooner or later, me and you will square up, and when that happens, only one of us will still be breathing when the smoke clears. But...I love my daughter more than life itself, and to have her turn her back on me for a fuck nigga like you is worse than a coward's death. So, imma fall back and give you and her your time. Let you enjoy loving her and her loving you in return. Let you invest in her, depend on her presence in your life, let her be the wind beneath your wings, nigga. Make plans for the future, even start a family, and just when you think you've made it...BOOOM! A red beam in the middle of your dome!

But as a man of my word, I won't send another nigga to do the job that I should do. So, I'll call off Malik and leave you two alone...for now. But nigga, if I find out you hurt my baby again, in any way, I don't care how many people have to die, I will set this fucking city on fire, just to make sure you burn in Hell!"

"I can respect that. I've always feared one day you and I would have to come to terms with each other, and as much as I know when that day comes, it's going to destroy Zaya, it's inevitable. So, until that day, let's agree to keep this between us."

"Now, why would I keep this to myself? Are you worried about how Zaya would feel about you holding her father at gunpoint in his home?"

"Probably the same way yo niggas running the streets would feel about you allowing a seventeen-year-old to catch you slipping in your own home."

Sucking his teeth, King David looked away and swore under his breath.

"Good point. Ok, agreed. Now, get the fuck out of my crib!"

Nodding, Shadow quickly backed away and ran up the stairs leading to the first floor. King David listened carefully for any movement on the floors above him, trying to determine the direction Shadow came from when he broke into his home. But after several minutes of deep concentration, the only reward his attentive ears received was silence.

Fuck! How did that lil nigga get in my crib?

7:00 am the following day, Zahir's phone rang. Rolling over, he reached for his phone, glanced at the number, and answered.

"Sup."

"Shadow, what did you do to my daddy?"

"Huh, I ain't do shit to yo daddy!"

"Nah nigga, I got home last night, and this nigga gone hug me and tell me you and him have a mutual understanding, and he won't interfere with our relationship anymore. Now, I know my daddy and he ain't never conceded to no nigga, especially you, Shadow!"

"Zee, you tripping. Did you see any wounds or marks on your daddy? Any bullet holes? No, so I didn't do anything to yo daddy."

"Shadow, I know you did something; I'm not stupid. You sent me home in an Uber, and that nigga conveniently got lost taking me home. A whole hour driving around the southside until he found the house. With all the apps on niggas phones nowadays, from Google Maps to Waze, no Uber driver is getting lost in Englewood. So, I know you moved on my daddy!"

"Listen, we had a conversation, that's it. We both decided it was a waste of time trying to keep us away from each other cause at the end of the day, you gone choose me."

"Ha! Nigga you burnt if you think I would choose you over my daddy!"

"You already have. Now stop jaw jacking and bring yo ass over here."

"Nigga, for what? You never have time for me since you started your *new* job."

"Well, I took the day off."

"You did?"

Zahir could hear the excitement in Zaya's voice, and he smiled to himself.

"Yep, so bring your ass over here. I got twenty-four hours and each second you waste fussing at me is a second wasted that we could be doing something that feels better than arguing."

"Like what?" Zaya responded seductively.

"Pull up and find out."

"Say less."

Zaya immediately disconnected the call and rushed around her bedroom to get ready to spend the day with Zahir.

"Hello, hello? Did this girl just hang up in my face?"

Chuckling while shaking his head, Zahir climbed out of bed to get ready for a much-needed day alone with Zaya.

A couple of hours later, Zaya walked into Zahir's building and started making her way towards his private elevator's entrance but was stopped in her tracks by the doorman.

"Excuse me, miss!"

Rolling her eyes and preparing herself to snap if the doorman tried to stop her, Zaya turned around and responded, "Yes, can I help you?"

"I'm sorry, ma'am, but Mr. Jones told me to inform you to meet him at the south entrance."

"Ok, thank you."

Zaya turned around and walked towards the south entrance. When she stepped outside, the sight of Zahir standing in front of a limousine with a dozen roses in his hand put a smile on her face.

"Boy, what is you doing? I thought we were gonna spend the day inside the pent." She protested as she climbed in the back of the limousine.

"Nah, I got other plans for you today," Zahir responded as he climbed inside the limousine and sat next to her.

"What plans?"

"It's a surprise."

"It better be a great surprise cause…I had plans of my own." She moaned before leaning over and gently running her tongue on the side of his neck.

Zahir eye's closed as her tongue sent erotic charges down his spine. Inhaling deeply, Zahir kissed her and said, oh, we gone do that too."

Shit, we better, or I'm taking what's mines.

Within an hour, the limousine pulled in front of Nieman Marcus, and Zahir stepped out of the limo and reached inside, giving her his hand to help her out of the back of the limousine. Stepping out, she looked up to the large high-end department store's name glowing above her head.

"What are we doing here?"

"You, that's what we are doing here. Shopping spree for my baby! Whatever you want, it's yours. Are you ready to be spoiled?"

"Alright, Zahir! Don't create a monster with all this lacing me up and shit! You know a boss loves to be wrapped in the finest."

"And that's why we are here!"

Taking her hand, Zahir told the driver they would be a few hours, and the young lovers strolled inside the department store. For the next three hours, Zahir escorted Zaya through the store, allowing her to engulf herself in the best shopping experience of her life. He made sure he was attentive to her every need and never made her feel like he was bored or wishing he was elsewhere. He had her undivided attention; something Zaya wasn't used to from any man in her life, including her father. With his hands filled with bags of expensive treasures, Zahir followed her to the lingerie section and took a seat in a private dressing room with eager anticipation of experiencing his own private show. Within minutes, Zaya stepped out of the dressing stall wearing a white lingerie two-piece set. Her mocha skin against cocaine white made her body shine like a black diamond. When she turned around, Zahir gasped as she gave him a glimpse of her amazing ass.

Noticing his reaction, she bent over slightly and seductively glanced back at him and moan, "You like that baby?"

Gulping down a mouthful of liquid lust to stop himself from drooling, Zahir slowly nodded.

"Hmm, I bet you do."

"I think I'll take this one. But let me try on the yellow and red one, too."

Zahir nearly fainted from the thought of her wearing the other lingerie with designs that covered much less than the white one.

Shit, she keeps this up; we gone be fucking right in this dressing room. She knows what she is doing.

After torturing him with a few more seductive modeling sessions, Zahir decided he needed to go to the men's room to relieve himself and come up for air. Handing her his credit card, he advised her to pay for whatever she decided to buy and wait for him at the register until he returned. She leaned in and kissed him passionately, and Shadow decided to help himself to a handful of ass and pull her closer to him. He then turned her around and smacked her on the ass before leaving the dressing room. As he turned down the corridor leading to the bathrooms, something caught his eye, and he slightly turned his head and smiled.

Zahir rushed inside the men's room and made his way to one of the urinals. As he began to pull down his zipper, he felt the cold steel of a gun's nozzle pressed against the back of his head.

"It ain't no fun when the bigga nigga got the gun, is it, Shadow?" Malik teased. "How does it feel to be standing there with your dick in your hand and a gun pointed at the back of your head, nigga?"

Shrugging, Shadow replied, "You tell me."

Suddenly, Malik felt the nozzle of Midas's Glock pressed up against the back of his head.

"I'll take that off you, Leek!" Midas said while quickly taking Malik's gun from his hand as he lifted his hands in the air to surrender.

"How the fuck did you know I was following you?"

Shadow continued to relieve himself at the urinal as he responded, "Is that really your concern right now, bruh? I can't believe you brought your ass downtown to pull this shit. Especially after King David gave me his word that he would call off the hit. It seems like his word is as worthless as his new security."

"KD didn't send me."

"Nigga don't start lying for him! You already caught the fuck up! That nigga sent you to your death, and you still covering for that nigga?" Midas snapped.

Zipping up his pants, Shadow moved towards the bathroom sinks and calmly started washing his hands. Looking in the mirror, he peered at Malik's reflection and shook his head.

"Leek, if KD didn't send you, why are you here?"

"KD called me and told me to leave it alone, but I needed to know where you lived and how you moved and where just in case he changes his mind."

"Oh, you wanted to be proactive when it's time for you to kill me?"

"No, so I didn't have to look all over this city to warn you to go underground."

"Oh, so you looking out for me?"

"I can't explain why right now, but Shadow, you know I've had so many chances to fucked you over, but I've always had your back. Even that shit you pulled at the club, I kept that shit under wraps."

"You didn't want to be embarrassed by the news getting out that the great Malik got caught slipping by lil ole Zahir."

"I don't give a fuck bout none of that shit! Even if that got out, not a single nigga in this city would try me, and you know it!"

"Facts," Midas mumbled.

Drying his hands, Zahir nodded towards Midas. Midas's eyes bulged in his head as he silently protested. Shadow nodded again but slower, letting Midas know he wasn't going to give the order again. Swearing under his breath, Midas backed away and handed Malik his weapon but kept his gun aimed at the muscular giant just in case Zahir's request was the wrong move.

Placing his gun back in his jacket holster, Malik turned to Shadow and said, "Thank you, I owe you."

"Yeah, you do, cause you should be dead. Don't try this shit again, Malik. If you want to warn me, you know how to contact me. I'm not that lil nigga on the block anymore, and coming at me like this will get you killed."

"I see. I never thought I'd see the day Midas would be the nigga that had your back."

"Never thought you'd put a gun to the back of my head, so I guess we are both in shock today."

Chuckling, Malik slowly backed away, quickly left the bathroom, and made his way out of the store.

"Shadow! Why the fuck didn't you let me merc that nigga?"

"Cause having Malik alive is more valuable to me than having him removed off the board. Plus, I believe he wasn't here to kill me. Have you ever known that nigga to hesitate putting a bullet in a nigga?"

"Nah."

"Exactly, as soon as he put that gun to my head, he would've splattered my shit all over the tiles. He didn't, so for me, there has to be something more to why he came here."

"Aw-ight, but you know I got your back."

"Good looking out, Midas."

"It's what I do. Now get back to Zaya before she suspects something is up, and it ruins yalls day together."

"Yeah, you right and we were just over in the lingerie section, so I don't want to fuck up what's going down later."

"Hell nawl nigga! You better run then. Shit!"

As Shadow quickly made his way back to Zaya, a mischievous grin grew on his face when he considered how he could manipulate Midas to willingly want to save his life while out with the girl he stole from him.

Diabolical as fuck. He thought with pride.

Within a minute, he rejoined Zaya at the register and placed a gentle kiss on her cheek. Zaya turned and searched Zahir's eyes as she handed him his credit card, wrapped in an awkwardly long receipt. Expecting him to unravel the receipt,

Zaya waited for his reaction to the over eight thousand dollar total, but to her surprise, he smiled at her and, without glancing at the card or receipt, casually slide the card into his jeans pocket. He then thanked the cashier and quickly led her out of the store and into the waiting limo.

As the limousine maneuvered down The Mag Mile, Zaya glanced over at Zahir staring at her, his eyes devouring every inch of her body. Her skin began to warm as she felt the rush of the flames travel to her center, causing her to cross her legs instinctively. The two of them continued their silent and sensual standoff. Each time Shadow licked his full lips, she pressed the muscles inside of her tighter, attempting to silence the building lust that was threatening to break away her self-control.

Fuck it!

Without warning, Zaya leaped into Shadow's lap and began gyrating forcefully while gripping the side of his face and kissing him wildly, her tongue exploring his mouth and biting his bottom lip. Shadow welcomed her into his lap, and as she gyrated against him, he helped himself to two handfuls of her ass, attempting to fit the firm yet soft flesh into his hands. She could feel his excitement press against her center, positioned perfectly so she could feel his curved length and girth up against her. He was impressive, much more than she considered he could be packing, and as she desperately tried to rip his shirt from his back, a silent moan escaped her lips as she imagined experiencing him inside of her.

"Fuck me, Shadow, fuck the shit out of me," Zaya grunted in his ear as she fought to unbutton his jeans.

"We're here, sir!"

The driver's voice echoed throughout the limousine, violently snatching the lovers from their sexual feast.

Zahir exhaled forcefully as he dropped his head, looking down at his undone jean button and Zaya's hand that was stuck inside them, attempting to rope him out.

"Nah nigga, roll around the block or something! We not ready to be wherever we at," Zaya yelled at the driver while glancing out of the limo's windows. Removing his hands from her ass, Zahir held them up in surrender and sighed, "He can't do that because I reserved the entire Signature Room for us."

"Wait!? You did what?!" Zaya screamed, her insatiable desire to fuck immediately dissipating as she leaned further towards the window, attempting to look up towards the top of the John Hancock building, which housed the upscale restaurant on the top floor. It was a dream of hers to dine at the Signature Room, but her father was banned from stepping foot at the restaurant due to a violent incident between him and a rival a few years ago during the Fourth of July weekend. She was too young to get a reservation herself, and her exes were too hood to consider venturing downtown.

"Baby! How did you know?!"

Zahir simply shrugged and smiled, filled with pride that he was able to impress Zaya twice...when he reconsidered her response to him a few moments ago...

Actually, that's three times.

"So, you ready, or you want to roll around the block again?"

"Shit, I'm ready, we can roll around the block any day of the week, but this is...OH MY GOD, Baby!"

Returning his jeans and shirt to their normal position, Zahir gestured for the driver, who was waiting patiently outside to open the door. As he and Zaya stepped out of the limousine, jealous and curious pedestrians looked on in awe at the young couple exiting the expensive luxury vehicle. After being greeted as "Mr. Jones," they were escorted by the restaurant's concierge in the lobby towards the high-speed elevators that led directly to the restaurant on the ninety-fifth floor. The speed of the elevator caught Zaya off guard, and she inhaled deeply as she held onto Zahir's hand tightly, trying to brace the queezy feeling of her stomach as the elevator lifted the couple at speeds of twenty miles per hour. When the elevators opened, Zaya was still holding her breath, but the stunning twilight view of the Chicago urban landscape made her exhale with a squeal of amazement.

Stepping out of the elevator, Zahir led her towards the restaurant's greeter, who welcomed them with a warm smile as he ushered them towards their table situated by the window with a million-dollar view of Lake Michigan and the world-renown Chicago Skyline. The usher attempted to pull out Zaya's chair, but Zahir held up his hand and pulled the chair out for her himself. Nodding as if he was impressed, the usher took a step back and waited patiently for Zahir to seat himself.

"We have prepared a wonderful evening for you. Can I get you two something to drink?"

"What is available to us?" Zaya asked with growing curiosity.

"The entire drink menu, ma'am. Might I recommend the Chateau Canon 2010? It has a velvet, silky style that's subtle and elegant."

Zaya's eyes widened as she glanced at a smiling Zahir. Shrugging, she replied, "Yes, I would like to try that."

"Excellent, and what can I get you, Mr. Jones?"

"Just bring us an entire bottle of the Chateau; we'll share it."

"Very well, sir. I will get that for you right away!"

The waiter then turned and went about fulfilling their drink order.

Leaning over the table so she could speak with Zahir in a whispered voice, Zaya asked, "Zahir, what the fuck is going on? I know they can tell neither one of us is old enough to be drinking in this muhfucka. Hell, they could at least card us."

"These are work perks."

"Work perks?"

"Yep, that nigga Cain run this muthafucking city. From that penthouse condo that my ass isn't old enough to own to getting the Signature Room to agree to shut down on their busiest night to let two teenagers slide in here and take over. There is nothing off-limits with this nigga."

Impressed, Zaya sat back, nodding her head.

"I heard rumors about how that nigga Cain rolls, but this is beyond what I could ever imagine. Shit, I might need to apply for a job with this nigga if I could roll like you rolling."

She suddenly considered how her father would react and immediately scoffed, "Hell nawl, my dad would burn this muthafucka down if I tried him like that."

Rolling his eyes while looking away from her, Zahir drew her attention to the far side of the restaurant as a helicopter flew past within eye view of the building.

"I want to ride in one of those," He said while staring off in the distance as if in a trance.

"What's stopping you? To ride in one of those helicopters that fly around the city ain't that expensive."

"Nah, not on no tourist shit. I want to own one and one day use it to slide down on my enemies and light they ass up from above."

Zaya's head jerked back as she side-eyed Shadow, watching him in a trance as he imagined himself reigning down death on "his enemies," which included her father.

"Shadow, you tripping."

Sighing, Zahir returned to the present and responded, "Yeah, you're probably right. But a nigga can dream, right?"

"I guess," she responded with an uncomfortable chuckle.

The waiter suddenly returned with their bottle of wine, and as he poured each of them a glass, the two teenagers watched him in silence. Once done, he gave them a few moments to sample the wine, watching their reaction as they relished in the exquisite experience of drinking the expensive wine. Satisfied with their response, he proceeded to take their orders for dinner, advising them that the entire menu was at their disposal as well.

CHAPTER THIRTEEN

ZAYA CLUNG ONTO ZAHIR'S arm as they rode the
elevator up to his penthouse. She was covered in bliss
and desire, having experienced one of the best days of
her life. Zahir pulled out all the stops for her, and the only
thing left was to get him upstairs and fuck his brains out. A
much-deserved reward for giving her such an amazing day. As
soon as the elevator doors opened, the two of them rushed into
Zahir's master suite. Slamming the door behind them, Shadow
grabbed a handful of Zaya's dress and pulled her towards him.
She instinctively jumped into his arms, wrapping her legs
around his waist.

Kissing so wildly, it seemed the two of them would devour
the other's face; Shadow held Zaya up by her ass as he moved
closer to the bed. Without warning, he tossed her on the bed,
lifted her sundress, and while gripping the top of her panties,
tore them from the waistband and snatched them off of her. A
subdued scream escaped Zaya's lips as she felt her panties
ripped from her heated skin. He then gripped her by her hips,
aggressively pulled her closer to the edge of the bed, and got
down on his knees. He quickly placed her legs on his shoulders
and started kissing her ankles and calves. Zaya watched Zahir's

head lower between her legs, anticipating the warm feeling of his tongue and lips explore her. She was already dripping on his bed, so she hoped he was thirsty and knew what he was doing because if not, he would surely drown. She could feel his warm breath as he bit down hard on her inner thighs, tasting her skin, something he dreamed of for so long, and he was getting closer.

As he moved in closer, she arched her back in anticipation…

Oh Shadow…

Without warning, the bedroom door swung open with a loud click as the darkness retreated, giving way to the light of someone flicking on the bedroom's light switch.

"Zahir! Up and at it nigga! You got a special delivery, and you were requested by name."

Cain's voice roared and tainted the room, the electric current of lust immediately fizzling out of existence.

Shadow spun around, his eyes burning with rage, and roared, "What the fuck are you doing in my house, nigga!?"

Cain's eyes became the size of silver dollars as he looked around the room and then responded, "Who the fuck you talking to, lil nigga? My name is on all this shit! So I can walk into any of the hundreds of properties I own in this city, in any room at any time I want. Now tighten up and get ready to move. Midas is downstairs waiting."

Undeterred by Cain's proclamation, Zahir wiped his mouth and began to move closer to Cain. Seeing his violent intentions, Cain took a step towards Shadow, and when the two of them was face to face, Cain leaned down towards Shadow's ear and grunted, "I will kill you right in front of her and then send her back to her daddy filled with my nut."

Zahir suddenly felt the cold of steel pressed against his chest, and as suddenly as he felt Cain's gun nozzle, Cain felt Shadow's gun nozzle pressed against his genitals.

"How you gone fuck her if I blow your dick off? If you ever decide to lose your fucking mind and touch her, even look at her like you on some freak shit, I will show you better than I can tell you, what I am capable of." Shadow responded in a low growl that matched the ferocity of his mentor.

Cain glanced down at the gun pressed against his dick and chuckled. He quickly moved his gun from Shadow's chest and returned it to its holster.

"You got heart, lil nigga. I give you that. Now, you have a job to do, and the longer it takes you to get to it, the more money I'm losing. Midas has all the information, and your content is sitting at the elevator door."

Shadow's jawline tensed as he slowly shook his head and closed his eyes, trying to calm the murderous rage that tore through him like a rabid beast. Suddenly, Shadow felt the soft hand of Zaya run across his neck, her sensual touch calming the ravenous monster inside him, causing him to exhale.

"It's cool, Shadow; I'll just leave. No need for either of you to do something stupid. But Cain, you mad disrespectful and petty for this shit."

"I'll take you home," Shadow said as he returned his gun to its holster.

"Nah, while you two were up here measuring dicks, I called an Uber. They are about three minutes away. I can find my own way home, and I don't want you having any issues with fulfilling your obligations. Just be careful, bae. You know how disloyal these streets can be. We'll have our time without fuck shit interrupting us."

Zaya then kissed Shadow and began walking out of his room. As she walked past Cain, he stared at her with eyes of resentment so cold, a frigid chill ran up her spine, and she quickened her pace to get as far away from Cain as possible. Stepping to the side to let Zahir past him, Cain gestured towards the elevator doors where two large duffle bags sat. Looking back at Cain, Zahir gasped, "You gotta be joking! That has to be about three-quarters of a million dollars worth of shit out there!"

"That's exactly seven hundred and fifty thousand worth of entertainment! You figured that out just by looking at the bags?! Damn, yo ass was made for this life!"

Still sour from Cain's intrusion, Shadow rolled his eyes in disgust at hearing Cain's voice. A reminder that the same voice stopped him from getting some pussy.

"I know you spent a grip today on that lil girl, so imma do you a solid because this is one of my more esteem clients, I'll break you off a percentage of five percent."

"Make it eight, and I'll let this fuck shit you pulled slide tonight."

"Don't fucking play with me, lil nigga. This ain't a negotiation."

"If they asked for me by name and I don't show, what you think you gone make from seven hundred and fifty thousand worth of drugs just sitting?"

"So, what is this, you on strike?"

"Nah, me and you need to get right because what you pulled tonight was some hoe shit. I'm not sure what the fuck is going on with you, but that was uncalled for. I've been loyal, and this is my first day off in almost a year. I earned enough respect from you to knock on that fucking door! At least a knock, nigga!"

Looking down at the floor, Cain nodded slowly and grinned.

This lil nigga got me feeling some kind of way. Got damn he cold with it.

"You know what, you make a good point, so how about this, five percent, but that's five percent on all your future drops instead of the flat rate I pay you now. That means you will be tripling and sometimes quadrupling your take going forward. My version of an apology to you. Deal?"

Cain then extended his hand in a gesture of peace. Shadow looked down at his hand and slapped it out of the way, and said, "Deal, but I'm not about to shake that muthafucka so you can snatch me up and say some fuck shit like, don't you ever pull a gun on me again. I know how that shit works, and I'm not about to play the intimidation game with you, Cain. I respect you, but I'm not afraid of you."

Fuck, how this nigga know that is precisely what I was gonna do.

"I'm out,"

Shadow then moved quickly towards the elevator, grabbed the two bags, and stepped into the waiting elevator. Cain observed him and, once the elevator doors closed, began to make his way towards the elevators to leave. As he got closer to the elevator, he heard movement behind him, and when he spun around with his gun drawn, he was staring down Kai, who had his gun with the red bean aimed squarely in the middle of Cain's forehead.

Holding his hands in the air and letting his gun dangle on his pointing finger by the trigger, Cain took two steps back and said, "Damn, I forgot your ass lived here, too. What's up, Kai?"

"This full clip, bitch nigga! I don't know what my brother sees's in you, and I know if I split your dome, he would be mad as fuck with me. But if you walk in this house again unannounced and pull that shit you just pulled, I will splatter your ass all over *your* condo. Now, get the fuck out."

The sharp sound of the elevator returning to the floor echoed throughout the hallway, and Cain slowly backed out of the penthouse into the elevator. He kept his eyes on Kai until the elevator doors closed. As the elevator started making its way down, Cain exhaled with relief and leaned his weight on the wall next to him, possessed with the exhaustion of deep regret.

Shit, that lil nigga really wanted to kill me.

Downstairs, a light tap on the back window made Midas spin around in the driver seat. His face lit up when he noticed it was Shadow.

He quickly unlocked the door and popped the trunk. Shadow unloaded the bags and climbed into the front passenger seat. Midas watched Shadow sit in the seat next to him and stared without making a sound. Noticing the look of surprise on his face, Shadow snapped, "Nigga, what?!"

"Nothing, you just never sat up here with me before. You always sat in the back on some driving Ms. Daisy type shit. I'm just curious as to what's different?"

"You could've let Malik take me off the board, but you didn't even though I was out with Zaya. That lets me know I can trust you. So, you gained my respect, and as long as we have respect and you remain loyal, you will never have to worry about me overstepping my boundaries or doing some off the wall fuck shit!"

"Damn, nigga! What's fucking witcho head right now?"

"Nothing," Shadow scoffed while looking out the passenger side window.

Noticing that Shadow wasn't going to share what was bothering him, Midas decided to leave it alone and drive towards their drop. After about twenty minutes of silence, Zahir cleared his throat and said, "Tell me about this drop. Who are we delivering to?"

"Oh shit! We are delivering to "That Nigga" NBA Finals MVP and four-time NBA Champion, Trey "The Chosen One" Wilson!"

"Stop bullshitting!"

"Nope, real shit, my nigga! This nigga came into town to party with these Chicago niggas and bitches. I heard about how this nigga get down and judging by those two big ass bags in the trunk, the rumors are true."

Man, I wish I could just go in there for five minutes. Midas thought as he took the next exit.

Twenty minutes later, Midas pulled into the circular driveway of a massive six thousand square foot mansion. Hip hop music could be heard rising above the trees into the night around the well-kept estate.

Fuck, it's a pool party! These niggas got naked bitches in the back, and I'm gone be stuck in the fucking car? I need a promotion!

Inhaling deeply, Zahir got out of the car and walked to the vehicle's back to retrieve the bags. Suddenly, a familiar voice bellowed Zahir's name out of the darkness, and when Midas looked in the direction of where the voice was coming from, his eyes nearly popped out of his head.

Oh shit! It's Trey and this nigga butt ass naked! This nigga higher than a giraffe's ass!

Rushing to Zahir's side, Trey Wilson gave Shadow a pound and looked down at the two bags he was carrying. Jumping up and down, causing his dick and balls to swing up and down, Trey squealed, "Is that my shit?! Is that my shit?! Nigga! Good looking out! I was told today was your day off, and much respect to you for taking the time to deliver it to me.

I heard mad shit bout, you son. Your professionalism and shit. That shit will go a long way in this business! Trey saw movement in the car's front seat from the corner of his eye and noticed the wide-eyed Midas staring back at him.

"Who is that?"

"Oh, that Midas!"

"That's your mans?"

"Yeah."

"Sweet! Tell that nigga to get out of the car and get turnt with us. We all in the back, man; it's like…maybe ten niggas and about fifty bitches…or is it seventy? Shit, I don't know. All I know is that it's too many of them and we need some help. Midas! Nigga! Come fuck with me!"

Before Trey could finish his official invitation, Midas was out of the car and standing next to Shadow with a bright childish grin on his face.

"So, y'all ready to kick it with the MVP?"

"Say less, my nigga, lead the way," Midas responded.

Shaking his head and clearly not in the mood to party, Zahir looked over at Midas and decided to reward him for his loyalty. So he inhaled deeply, forced a smile, and said, "Lead the way!"

"Fuck yeah!" Trey yelled as he turned and walked in front of them, bare ass and dancing. As they got closer to the back of the house where the pool party was raging, Zahir turned towards Midas and said, "My gift to you, bruh. Enjoy yourself"

"Good looking out, Shadow!" Midas yelled as he followed Trey into the pool area, snatching off every piece of clothing he had on. Within seconds, Midas was completely naked and running alongside Trey towards the pool. Shaking his head and laughing at Midas and Trey cannonballing into the pool, Shadow shrugged and began to disrobe.

When in Rome.

As they enjoyed themselves at the wet and wild orgy, Midas quickly became the most famous person at the party, and before long, he and Trey were laughing and hanging as if they were partners since grade school. Shadow watched Midas speaking into Trey's ear from across the other side of the pool as he listened attentively. Shadow received a much-needed release as two women sucked his dick, taking turns and kissing each other as they both tried to see who could take him entirely down their throats and make him cum first. Although they were good at what they were doing, Shadow's attention was on Midas and Trey. He felt Midas was up to something, but he also knew whatever it was, it would be something to help grow Cain's empire.

Midas was a great salesman, manager, and an even greater wingman, but a king, he was not. So, Shadow knew that whatever he was doing, it was for the best benefit of his employer. Eventually, Shadow could see Trey becoming increasingly interested in what Midas was saying, so he reached down and held onto one of the women's heads and started to force-feed his dick down her throat. The other woman, aroused by his sudden aggressiveness, slid down between her partner's legs and began to devour her. Shadow sped up his feeding frenzy as he felt himself reaching his climax, something that Cain deprived him of earlier that evening, and he was determined to get one-off, and he didn't care if it wasn't Zaya's mouth giving it to him. His eyelids began to flutter as she paused, keeping him down her throat without moving her head, closing her throat and jaws around him. It was more than enough and within a few seconds…

"Oh shit!" he roared as he unloaded down her throat. Once he was sure he was done, he pulled his dick out of her mouth while carefully making sure her lips cleaned every ounce of his excretions from it. He then grabbed a towel and his drink and made his way towards Trey and Midas. Noticing Shadow walking towards him with a towel wrapped around his waist, Trey reached for his own towel and gestured for Midas to grab his.

Once Shadow was in range, Trey pulled his arm back as far as he could, and the both of them slapped fives multiple times."My nigga! I saw you over there getting served up by the Doublemint Twins."

"Wait, those are twins?! Midas asked while looking in their direction.

"No, nigga! But I have an idea why they earned that name." Shadow responded while nodding his head in Trey's direction.

"Hey, your boy here was telling me that you guys have the product and set up to supply some of my more…discrete…associates. Is that true?"

"You damn right! Let them know that we will provide without fear of their extracurricular activities getting out in public if they mess with us. With all these camera phones and social media, no one is safe unless you fuck with us!"

Nodding while taking two pills and following them with a heavy gulp of Hennessy, Trey appeared to be in deep thought. After about thirty seconds, Trey had made up his mind.

"Listen, man. This muhfuckas I'm talking about be on Forbes every year, billionaires and world leaders. If I make the introduction, I have to be assured y'all won't fuck me! I don't even want a cut because if I can get these muhfuckas connected to you and your product, which is top fucking notch, by the way, it would open some major doors for me. Like financing to be the sole owner of a team and the access to be voted in as a team owner without the racist red tape. You feel me?!"

"Shit, you know I do, MVP!"

Smiling, Trey pointed at Shadow and said, "You know how to get a nigga's attention and make them comfortable. I like that shit! That's gonna go a long way with these people. Ok, let me get my contacts together, and I'll have them reach out to your employer, and then they can iron out all the particulars. Shit, if we pull this off, soon you two niggas might be running this shit!"

You damn right, Shadow thought as he smiled at Trey and lifted his glass of Hennessy before taking a sip.

The chill of the early morning breeze jolted Zahir out of his drunken slumber, and he sat up holding the side of his pounding head, trying to keep at bay the earthquake of a headache that kept rocking his head. Yawning, he glanced around the pool area and shook his head at the damage caused by the party the night before.

Shit, I need to call Zaya.

Looking around, Zahir searched the pool chairs and towels for his phone and eventually found it resting next to three sleeping blonds. He reached down to grab his phone, careful not to wake the women. Turning on the screen, Zahir noticed he didn't have a single missed call.

She didn't even call a nigga to see if I was cool? Shit, she a savage.

"Hello."

"What's up, Shadow? You good?"

"Yeah, I'm good."

"You made your appointment?"

"Yeah."

"So, why you calling me so early?"

Rendered speechless by her uncaring demeanor, Zahir shook his head and smiled.

"I just wanted to hear your voice."

"Well, now you've heard it, it's too early for this romantic shit, Shadow. You know, on the weekend, I don't wake up till after twelve, and here you are calling me at fucking six. Hit me up after twelve, ok?"

Zaya quickly ended the call before he could respond. Shadow stared down at his phone as the screen went dark after a few seconds. He was initially concerned that after speaking to Zaya, he would be burdened with guilt, but he discovered he didn't feel an ounce of guilt after a few moments of clarity. It was as if his moral compass had gone awry, pointing in any direction that leads to his goal of money and power...and he loved it. Last night was about connecting with an important client. Had he stood on the sidelines and not participate, Trey would have found it hard to trust them, and a great opportunity would've been missed. It just so happen that what he had to do to earn Trey's trust was fun...a *lot* of fun.

Smiling to himself as he reminisced about the night before, Shadow began searching the pool grounds for his clothing and Midas so the two of them could leave before everyone woke up and started to party again.

CHAPTER FOURTEEN

Two weeks later

ZAHIR JOGGED ACROSS THE street and hopped in the waiting Black Mercedes Benz. As soon as the door closed, the car sped off, joining the heavy traffic.

"So, you know why I called you, right?" Cain asked while he slightly turned his head to check the side-view mirror before switching lanes.

"Yeah, you heard from Trey's people?"

Nodding, Cain responded, "Your job was to drop off the product, not broker another deal with someone you just met."

"I didn't have to know him since he's your customer. If he's good with you, he's good with me."

"Oh, like Zaya?! Yo ass was about to stick your whole head up that girl's pussy and probably raw dog it…am I right? You don't know how many niggas she done had up in her, and you were ready to taste the entire rainbow coalition. But my biggest concern is who her daddy is! King David!? Out of all the fathers in this city, you chose that one to try and fuck his daughter?! Imagine getting her pregnant! What that baby shower looking like, lil nigga, a fucking bloodbath. Shit, yo ass so smart, you dumb as fuck! Gad damn, Zahir!"

Confused by Cain's outburst and his investment in who he sleeps with, Zahir gave him the side-eye before responding,

"I've known Zaya all my life; you don't know her like I do. She ain't like that. And I had a condom."

"Yeah, I'm sure you had a condom on your tongue, too. It's not about who I know and how long you've known them; it's about you knowing how shit plays out. You can't play leapfrog in the game or cut corners, Zahir! There's an order to this game called life, and what you do can throw shit out of balance and cause a lot of heat to come down on people more dangerous than me."

Turning and looking at Cain, Shadow asked, "Who could be more dangerous than you?"

Swallowing hard, Cain grunted, "The Jackal."

"Who?"

"Mateo "The Jackal" Ayala, head of the Cazadores Nocturnos cartel and the one that supplies the entire Midwest and East Coast. Every ounce of product, including synthetic, comes from the Cazadores Nocturnos. The plug buys from him, we buy from the plug, and we sell to the customers. That's how it's been for over twenty years. No one oversteps or tries to leapfrog over the other. That's what keeps the engine working without any hiccups. When you do shit like what you did, you create chaos, something that The Jackal does not tolerate. Many a nigga found themselves swallowing their balls and being tossed in the lake because they didn't respect the game's rules. You and Midas came this close to being another cautionary tale.

"Why do they call him The Jackal?"

Adjusting himself in the driver's seat, Cain continued.

"Mateo was the most skilled and feared Sicario in Central and South America. Hell, that muthafucka had the feds shook here in the U.S. He had a one hundred percent success rate. If they sent The Jackal for dat ass, dat ass is got! Well, when you're that good, you become a threat, even to the people you may be working for. His boss, Arturo Fuentes, felt like he was gaining too much respect in the game, especially with his own crew, so he tried to take him out. Arturo sent twenty hitters after Mateo, and when the smoke cleared, the hitters, his wife, and his baby boy, Antonio was dead. Arturo thought that he would go into hiding, but he was wrong. Mateo came straight at him and killed Arturo and his entire family. And when I say his *entire* family, I mean this muhfucka even killed the pets. There are no more Fuentes alive today. He wiped the entire bloodline out. After what he did to the Fuentes, no one dared fucked with Mateo on any level, and that's why he's been able to run the Cazadores Nocturnos Cartel for over twenty years without a single attempt on his life."

So, if you want to become the master of the game, you have to know the rules. Once you know the rules, you'll understand which rules can be bent a bit and which ones can be broken. And crossing Mateo is one rule that you don't bend or break. So, don't ever try that shit again."

"I saw an opp and decided to take it."

"I get that, but that wasn't your opp to take. Now we have to up our intake to accommodate the added customer roster. Now don't get me wrong, that little stunt you pulled increased our profits by over seventy-five percent, but this new customer base will take careful handling. That is why you and Midas will be handling those drops. You two seem to be a fan favorite with them, muhfuckas, so if those billionaires and politicians feel comfortable with you two, I'll let them have it their way."

"If that's the case, I want Midas out of the car and next to me on these drops."

"Yeah, I like that lil ambitious nigga, too! Cain chuckled, nodding his head in agreement. "Done, I'll get another nigga to drive you two to your drops."

"Cool."

"Smile, nigga, with the amount of shit you two will be delivering, you're not gonna know what to do with all that paper you about to make."

Shadow nodded and turned his attention to the world outside the car, quickly passing before his eyes. He knew there was something else Cain wanted to discuss, and he was anticipating the next topic to spring out of his mouth in a few moments.

"So..."

Rolling his eyes, Shadow thought, *Here we go*.

"I heard about what you did to King David a few weeks ago. You actually snuck in that nigga's house and held him at gunpoint?"

Shadow simply nodded and continued to look outside the window.

"Where did you learn how to move like that? Was it from that cat burglar your momma was fucking...what's his name...Jose or Julio, right?"

Cat burglar? Who says that anymore. How old is this nigga?

"It was Daniel."

"Yeah, that muthafucka. So, you learned all that sneaky hitman shit from him?"

Shaking his head, Shadow responded, "He taught me a few things and got me interested in boxing and MMA fighting."

"Shit, he taught you more than a few things. Your ass be moving like a Sicario, too. Shit, Mateo would love you. Anyway, whatever happened to him?"

Shrugging his shoulders while still staring out the window, Zahir responded, "He left one day and never came back."

Cain could feel the tension in Zahir's voice. The sting of abandonment still prominent despite the years passed since Daniel left him behind.

Wanting to dig deeper, but knowing he needed Zahir focused on what he had planned, he decided to leave the topic of Zahir's relationship with Daniel for another day.

"Imma cut through the chase because we don't have a lot of time before we get to where we're going. Because of the type of people you'll deliver to going forward, I need you to meet the plug in person because you and Midas will be the only ones allowed to pick up the product for the clients you'll be serving. That way, we don't mix this shit up because what we will be providing them will be a step above what we supply everyone else.

Fixing his slouched posture, Shadow turned to Cain and asked, "The Russians?"

"Yeah," Cain responded, the stress in his voice making it clear to Shadow that dealing with the European middlemen was not a pleasant experience.

"Them commie bastards are a pain in the ass, but a necessity. No matter what they say, do not retaliate or insult them. If we cross the Russians, we cross the feds, cause that's who they work for."

Inhaling deeply, Shadow gasped, "Wait, what the fuck?"

"What? You think that amount of weight can move through the borders, and some badge-wearing asshole ain't behind the scene giving orders and turning a profit?

"I never considered it."

"Of course you didn't, why would you? The game is a federally funded fuck fest, and at any given moment, if they think you can't handle the job they give you, you'll get your walking papers and a toe tag to match. That's why I need you to get your mind right. I'm trusting you to handle this meet and greet with professionalism. You need to leave a great impression on these muhfuckas, so the next time I send you to make a pickup, you can do it without me babysitting. Now, can you handle that?"

"Yeah, I can handle it."

"My nigga." Cain responded while lightly tapping Shadow on the chest.

An hour later, Cain pulled his Mercedes Benz into the parking lot of a police station. Shadow's body jumped up as he looked around, his head bolting back and forth as if he had just heard a gunshot. Chuckling at his response, Cain tapped him on the shoulder and said, "Calm down, we in the right place. This is where we re-up."

As they both got out of the luxury vehicle, Shadow looked around him and carefully took inventory of the surroundings and the players. There was a police captain and two on-duty officers waiting for them at the entrance into the police station. A few cars down from them were two men in suits sitting in a dark foreign luxury car, looking at the car's hood; Shadow could make out the unmistakeable Bently emblem. Judging by the type of vehicle they were sitting in, Shadow knew they were not law enforcement and, more than likely Russian Mafia. At first glance, they appeared to be the backup just in case things went south, but judging by their relaxed silhouettes, they were here to supervise, which means whoever was inside the building answered to them. One thing that piqued Shadow's curiosity was that he and Cain were the only people of color involved in this transaction. Something he promised himself to pay close attention to for the foreseeable future.

I don't like how this is set up. Cain is always at a disadvantage.

Watching Cain stroll towards the police and slapping fives with them, Shadow concluded that these transactions were a regular occurrence at this station. Everyone had a less than professional reaction to each other. But that all changed once Shadow made his way out of the darkness on the other side of the Mercedes and stepped into the light.

"Wait, Cain, who the fuck is this?" The captain asked, quickly reaching for his sidearm.

Shadow didn't hesitate or flinch as he watched the captain nervously reach for his gun.

I wish I would let this corrupt bacon, cracker, and cheese-looking muthafucka intimidate me.

Shadow didn't lose the rhythm of his stride as he continued to close the distance between him and the captain, staring directly in his eyes, daring him to pull his weapon. Noticing Shadow wasn't intimidated by his reaction, the captain started laughing while pointing at Shadow and said, "Damn Cain, you were right; this one has it in his blood!"

Turning and looking back at Shadow, Cain flashed a look of pride while nodding his head in agreement.

Yeah, that boy is special.

Joining the four men at the door, Shadow looked the captain up and down before turning to Cain and shaking his head.

"Let's get this shit out the way. My wife is making her famous tuna fish casserole," the captain joked while attempting to pat Shadow on the shoulder. Instinctively, Shadow pulled his shoulder out of reach; the idea of having a police officer pretend they were cool didn't sit right with him. The captain's hand came down and completely missed Shadow's shoulder, and he momentarily lost his balance. Catching himself before he stumbled to the ground, the captain's face turned red and crumbled in disgust as he scoffed at Shadow's reaction to his friendly gesture.

"Oh, it's like that, huh?"

Shadow refused to address him and turned his attention to the inside of the police station.

"Fine…fine, let's get this shit over with then."

"Nigga, you ain't in a rush to get to your wife's disgusting ass casserole. That shit smells like defeated pussy at the Shamrock. Fuck you talking bout, get this shit over with!" Cain blurted out while laughing hysterically at the captain's reaction to his jab at his wife's cooking.

"That's fucked up; you can call me the "N" word, but I can't, and I'm not even…."

Suddenly, a voice in the captain's head warned him against finishing his statement, and he decided to inhale and lead Cain and Shadow inside the police station.

"Fuck it!" The captain continued while leading Cain and Shadow inside the building. The captain led them deep inside the police station until they came to the lock-up area. After walking past several cells filled with prisoners, mostly young black men, Shadow made sure not to look at them and pretend they didn't exist. The last thing he needed was for one of them to be from around the way and notice him.

After being led through another series of hallways and entrances, they arrived at a large storage room filled with pallets of cash and drugs. Shadow's mouth almost hit the floor as he walked past millions of dollars in cash and drugs in a police station on the northside of Chicago.

Man, if people knew how fucking corrupt this city is. They would burn this muthafucka down. Shadow thought as he continued to follow Cain to the back of the storage room.

"Cain, Privet moy drug, (hello, my friend)," a large man wearing a black suit greeted Cain in a heavy Russian accent flanked by two equally large Russians. *"Kak biznes? Sudya po rostu vashikh pokupok, biznes, dolzhno byt', idet khorosho. YA byl shokirovan, kogda mne pozvonil Mateo s pros'boy uvelichit' vashu kreditnuyu liniyu."* (**How's business? Well business must be doing great judging by the increase in your purchases. I was shocked when I got the call from Mateo to increase your credit line.**)

Shaking the man's hand, Cain responded, *"khoroshiy biznes rastet, tak chto eto ne dolzhno byt' syruprizom, Yuri."* (**Good business grows, so it shouldn't be a surprise, Yuri.**)

Shaking Cain's hand while pointing at him, Yuri smiled before saying, "It's always entertaining to hear you speak Russian in such perfect tone and pronunciation, Cain. Especially coming from a face as dark as that. Always entertaining."

Shadow stood next to Cain and folded his hands in front of him, refusing to show any reaction to Yuri's overtly racist remarks. Looking in Shadow's direction, Yuri's eyelids lowered halfway over his eyes as he strained to study Shadow's face.

"This one, he looks familiar, Cain. Like I've done business with him before. I know they say you all look alike, but this is a face I wouldn't easily forget."

"Nah, you've never done business with this one, trust me on that."

"How can you be so sure? I've been in this business for almost thirty years, and I've seen men come and go, but there are some faces I never forget, and that face…it looks like I've seen it before. Or could it be, you all do look alike, and I've seen so many of your black faces that they are all running together, like black paint pouring over a perfectly painted white wall and ruining the purity of its perfection."

The two men stared at each other without saying a word until Yuri couldn't hold in his laughter and pointed at Cain and yelled, "Ahhh, my friend, I can never get you! Fuck! You are a bear! Come, let's get your order filled and send you on your way. We don't want to keep your customers waiting, no?"

"Yeah, let's get down to business."

An hour later, Yuri and his men watched Cain and Shadow leave the police parking lot with curious anticipation. Once they felt Cain was out of sight, the two men waiting in the Bently exited their vehicle and walked towards Yuri, and they greeted each other warmly. One of the men looked Yuri in his eyes and said, *"Eto mozhet stat' problemoy dlya nas, Yuriy. My dolzhny chto-to delat' s etim novym razvitiyem. Komandir yasno dal ponyat', naskol'ko vazhno dlya nas privlech' nekotorykh grazhdan SSHA k nashemu delu. Kogda oni budut snabzhat' etikh grazhdan, ikh budet ochen' trudno ubedit', potomu chto oni ne zakhotyat narushat' tekushcheye soglasheniye s Shakalom"*

(This can pose a problem for us, Yuri. We have to do something about this new development. Komandir made it perfectly clear how important it is to get certain US citizens to join our cause. With them supplying those citizens, it will be challenging to convince them because they wouldn't want to upset the current agreement with The Jackal.)

"Ne volnuysya, Sasha. Skazhite komandiru, chto vse pod kontrolem. My vsegda mozhem rasschityvat' na amerikantsev i ikh lyubov' k nenavisti drug k drugu, osobenno k chernym. Mateo ispol'zoval ikh degenerativnoye povedeniye protiv nikh, i u nego yest' negr v kachestve yego predstavitelya. Vse, chto nam nuzhno

sdelat', eto zaverit' ikh, chto, yesli oni vstanut na nashu storonu, my ne tol'ko predostavim im tot zhe produkt po gorazdo boleye nizkoy tsene, no i sokhranim ikh sekrety v belykh rukakh, a ne v rukakh obez'yan. Oni ukhvatyatsya za shans izbavit'sya ot nikh."

(Don't worry, Sacha. Tell the Komandir that we have it under control. We can always count on Americans and their love for hating each other, especially the blacks. Mateo has used their degenerate behavior against them to keep them compliant, and he has a nigger as his representative in this city. Two things these Americans don't care much for. We need to assure them that if they side with us, we will provide them with the same product at a much lower price and keep their secrets in white hands instead of the hands of the monkeys. They will jump at the chance to be rid of them.)

"What about Cain?" Sacha asked while pointing in the direction where Cain's car turned the corner.

"It's already being taken care of," Yuri responded, staring off into the night. After a few moments of reflection, Yuri walked back inside the police station with his two bodyguards at his side.

CHAPTER FIFTEEN

Two months later...

ZAHIR'S SKIN PROTESTED FROM the summer's heat as rivers of sweat poured all over his body, reflecting the glaring sunlight pouring down on him as he jogged down the outdoor basketball court flanked by Midas and three other young black men that he'd recruited over the past few weeks. They formed an airtight crew that soon garnered the name "The Franchise" due to how they could expand Cain's empire with each drop they made to their new roster of high-end clientele. In eight weeks, The Franchise helped increase Cain's revenue by sixty percent, quickly making Shadow a millionaire before his eighteenth birthday.

The court was surrounded by onlookers, watching the five members of The Franchise take apart the opposing team with precision, passing the ball and confusing the defense. Suddenly, Shadow increased his speed and then came to a complete stop while crossing over the ball behind his back to his non-dominant hand and back again. The man guarding him tried to come to a full stop but lost his footing and stumbled backward, and Zahir reacted immediately by driving to the basket. Midas lifted his hand in the air and ran towards the paint. Seeing Midas from the corner of his eye, Shadow lifted his eyes towards the basket while he continued to drive towards the paint. Midas then took off into the air after Shadow tossed the ball in the air above the basket.

The loud boom of Midas forcefully slamming the ball into the hoop was overshadowed by the crowds howling and cheers. Onlookers began running onto the court, celebrating and teasing the losing team, gesturing for them to leave the court.

"Game, niggas!" Midas yelled as he landed back on the ground. "Fuck off our court. Rainbow beach belongs to The Franchise now, niggas. Look at me, look at me, Shadows' the captain now."

Laughing, Shadow jogged over to Midas, and the two friends gave each other a pound before heading off the court.

"Bro, are you ready for tonight!? It's gonna be wild as fuck! You gone be a grown-ass man at midnight."

"Nigga, I've been a grown-ass man for a while now."

"Facts, but tonight the shit will be official. No more dealing with Cain and his shit. Whatever you want, you can get that shit in your name."

"That's definitely the plan, cause Zaya won't even take her fucking shoes off at the pent after that fuck shit Cain pulled."

Midas began laughing so hard he started to stumble forward and lean on Shadow's shoulders.

"Niiiiiiiiiiiiiiiggggggggah!!! When you told me what Cain did, it took all of my strength to not laugh in your face cause that shit was funny as fuck!"

"Fuck off me!" Shadow growled while playfully pushing Midas off his shoulder.

"I knew yo ass wanted to laugh. Fuck, sometimes I laugh when I think of the way I jumped when that door opened. I swear it felt like my mom busted us."

"What a way to get caught by a parent with only yo neck showing cause you got your whole head in a girl's pussy."

"Fuck you, Midas! My whole head wasn't in her pussy. Fuck, I hadn't even started before that nigga busted in!"

"That's even worse! I would've had to see that nigga Cain for that shit!"

"Nigga, shut yo goofy ass up. You know damn well you weren't gone do shit if that were you. This is Cain we are talking about."

"Whatever, you don't know what I'm capable of...."

Noticing Shadow twisting his mouth to the right side of his face while looking at him from the side, Midas decided not to finish his statement.

"Yeah, that's what I thought. Talking bout you was gone do something. You weren't gone do shit, but do the same shit I did. Got dressed and went to work."

"Whatever, just don't be late and don't bring no sand to the beach!"

"Nigga, you know damn well Zaya is coming. I don't even know why you talking like she ain't coming with me."

"Yeah, I figured. Well, don't let her make you late. We got a full night laid out for you. We got the whole VIP locked."

"How the fuck you pull that off."

"You know how!" Midas responded and then reached into his backpack and pulled out a single brick of cash.

"Nigga! Put that shit away! You know the rules!"

"Aww, man, these niggas need to know how The Franchise really gets down. Knowing us as a basketball squad ain't enough. These muhfuckas need to know there be rich niggas in the mist!":

Looking around, Shadow forced Midas's hand back in his backpack and roared in his ear, "Nigga, I don't care if these niggas think I'm homeless. You fucking with our lives pulling this shit. Nigga, don't make me regret letting you live. I'm not trying to die so you can shine for these remedial niggas. You know the mission and the risks, so don't act like you don't know the consequences to all of us if the wrong person sees you flashing large amounts of cash. There are too many eyes and ears around this muthafucka that ain't one of "us". The whole hood infiltrated."

Noticing the seriousness in Shadow's voice, Midas's arrogance dissipated immediately, and he apologized repeatedly.

"Apology accepted, but this is your last pass from me, nigga. Don't do this shit again. I'm out!"

Shadow quickly turned and walked away, heading for the bus stop. As Midas watched him walk off the court, he noticed as he reached down to pick up the rest of his belongings that his hands were trembling, a direct connection to the threat Shadow just made on his life. Being five years younger than Midas didn't make Shadow less terrifying when he was angry. Shadow's rage was only rivaled by Cain but no less potent because one could feel the malice of the threat and left no doubt that they would carry it out without hesitation.

Within a few minutes, the bus pulled up, and Shadow joined the crowd of people trying to get on the bus. Moving towards the back, a passenger stepped out of Shadow's way and allowed him to stand in their space. Thanking him, Shadow held onto the overhead bar and placed his backpack on the floor between his feet.

"Ahhh shit! I know that ain't who I think it is!" A loud voice exclaimed from behind Shadow, and when he turned around, he rolled his eyes and gritted his teeth.

I don't need this shit right now.

Three men stood up and began making their way towards Shadow, shoving passengers out of their way.

"I know you thought you was gone get away with that shit you pulled in front of King David's house, didn't you?"

Shadow slowly turned around, keeping his back towards the window so none could attack him from behind.

"Looking down at his feet, one of the men pointed at his backpack and said, "What's in the bag, op?"

Shadow refused to respond while keeping his attention on the three men that had now flanked him.

"Fuck it, we gone find out on our own." And he began to lean down, attempting to open his bag. As the man got lower, the entire back of the bus stood to their feet, and before he could reach down to touch the bag, the passengers had guns drawn, aimed at the three men. One of the men began to frantically tap the shoulder of the man reaching for Shadow's bag.

"Nigga, what?!" He yelled while turning around to face his partner, and after glancing around the bus, he immediately recognized the volatile situation they were in. He quickly threw both hands up and took a step back away from Shadow and his bag. An evil grin grew on Shadow's face as he looked at his crew and then back at the three men. He then pointed at each of them and said,

"7614 South Essex, 8219 South Green, and 6826 South Racine. Ain't that where y'all mommas' stay?"

"Nigga, the fuq you say?!" The largest of the three men growled. Smiling, Shadow responded, "You heard me, now, I would suggest you get off at the next stop or…well…you know how wild the jungle can get in the summer. You never know what might happen, but if you get off at the next stop, the chances of you getting to see your mothers alive again goes up, drastically."

The loud hissing sound of air brakes stopping the bus filled the men's ears, and they quickly turned to rush out the back of the bus. But the passengers refused to step aside, and the men began to panic and started to yell at the bus driver to open the back door. Their pleas went on deaf ears as the bus driver continued to welcome new passengers on his bus. Looking back at Shadow with eyes filled with terror, the three men started to protest, and Shadow nodded, and immediately the passengers made a path for them to leave.

"Driver, open the back door, please!"

The back door opened as if on cue after his request. A puzzled look erupted on the men's faces as they backed out of the bus. Walking towards the back door, Shadow leaned out the door and said, "Y'all be careful out in these streets. It's been a wild summer, my niggas!"

Running away from the bus as it began to move, just in case Shadow and his crew decided to fire out of the windows, one of the men yelled back, "Fuck you, bitch ass nigga! We'll catch you another time when you don't have your niggas with you!"

Shaking his head, Shadow leaned back into the bus and watched the back doors close in front of him. Looking through the door's narrow windows, he watched the three men run around a corner and out of sight. Walking back towards his place on the bus, one of his crew members handed him his bag and said, "Here you go, Shadow."

"Good looking, Tre'. I appreciate it."

"Ah, nigga you know The Franchise got you, by the way, happy birthday!"

Smiling, Shadow held onto the upper bar and watched the city roll past the windows of the bus, dreading when he'll have to face King David's foot soldiers again.

Shit, I already have beef with King David, now I got to deal with his unorganized crew too. Fuck!

A few hours later, a black limo pulled in front of King David's Greystone mansion and parked across the street. Zaya's phone came to life as it vibrated and started to dance on her nightstand. Seeing who was calling her, she quickly picked it up.

"I'm outside." Zahir's voice seemed stressed, and Zaya felt like although he was becoming a force in Cain's organization, the rise and speed were getting too much for him, and he needed a moment of peace, and she decided to make sure he had the time of his life tonight.

"On my way now, baby." She quickly ended the call and made her way downstairs as quickly as her six-inch Red Bottoms would allow her on the smooth black and white marble tiled floors. As usual, her father was sitting in the living room, looking at his laptop screen. Hearing the sharp collision of her shoe heels on the floor, King David looked up and momentarily smiled as he admired how stunning his daughter looked. Her black designer dress elegantly hugged her frame like an entranced lover, and as quickly as his admiration appeared, it vanished when he reminded himself who she was going out with in that dress.

"Zee, let me holla at you."

"Daddy, I gotta go. You already know those niggas outside ain't gone be able to control themselves, and Zahir is out front."

175

King David's cold stare back at her let her know that he wasn't processing anything she was saying, so she exhaled forcefully and stormed over to the living room.

"You look beautiful, baby."

Rolling her eyes and placing her hands on her hips, Zaya responded, "Thank you, Daddy."

"I'm not trying to ruin your night; just please be careful and keep an eye on your surroundings."

"Why, daddy? What did you do?"

"Nothing, it's a hot Friday night in Chicago. You already know how this city gets down at night. So, watch your back. You got your heater?"

"You know I do."

"That's my girl. Hopefully, your *man* does something that forces you to use it on him."

Shaking her head, Zaya leaned down and kissed her father on the cheek and whispered, "I will see you later, daddy. I love you."

"I love you, too. Have fun."

The encouraging words to wish his daughter to have a good time while out with Zahir almost made him puke in his own mouth, but he made a pact with Zahir, and there were a lot of things he has broken in his life, but his word was never one of them. So, he had to pray everything he's taught his daughter would protect her if anything were to happen while she was out on the town with Zahir. As Zaya walked out the front door, King David stood up and looked out the window as she strolled across the street and climbed into the back of the waiting limousine. He stood there, heart pounding and his stomach in knots as the limo pulled away. An artic chill suddenly ran up his spine, chilling his blood, and he cursed

himself as he rushed outside to call a few of his guards to join
him inside the house.

Standing in his foyer, King David pointed at the same
three men that had the run-in with Zahir earlier and gave them
specific instructions for the evening. Once he was done, they
rushed out the front door and hopped inside one of the black
SUVs parked out front, and drove off.

Lincoln Park, Chicago IL

Patrick leaned back in his easy chair and reached for the
remote, but the gentle hand of his wife stopped him.

"Baby, before you relax, can you help me put the girls to
bed. I need to clean the kitchen."

Sighing, Patrick returned the chair upright and nodded.
Climbing out of his chair, he stretched before heading upstairs
towards the twin's room. The closer he got to the girl's room,
he could hear them screaming and laughing. Walking down
the long hallway, Patrick momentarily paused at the portrait of
his parents and placed two fingers on his lips and then on the
picture.

I miss you guys so much. He thought as he took a few more
paces and turned to open the girl's bedroom door.

"Ok, girls, time for bed."

"Why, we are just getting started."

A deep European accent filled Patrick's ear, and he quickly
pushed open the door. The three men in black suits paired with
the hot pink walls of the girls' room created a contrast of panic
inside of Patrick, and he rushed across the room towards the
man who had his daughters sitting on his lap, bouncing them
both on either knee. Pretending they were riding a horse. As he
ran past the threshold of the girl's room, he felt a sharp pain as
the man hiding behind the door struck him in the back of the
head with his gun. Patrick collapsed to the floor, losing

consciousness with each passing second. But he continued to move towards his daughters, crawling, as their screams of terror became muffled until....darkness.

Patrick's face felt like it was on fire as the heat caused by a slap across his face brought him back from his slumber.

"Wake up, Detective!" Yuri said while wiping blood from his hands with a white towel. Patrick's vision became clearer as his head swayed from side to side. He immediately noticed Yuri's blood-soaked hands and began to struggle violently to free himself from the chair he was tied to.

"Who's blood is that?! What did you do!?"

Turning and looking at Patrick while cleaning the blood from underneath his fingernails, he responded calmly, "Oh, it's your wife's blood. We could've tortured and raped her and made you watch, but we really don't have time for that. Plus, your wife was pretty fucking ugly. None of us could get it up to even let her suck us off. So, I slit her throat. Don't worry; we didn't let your twins watch her bleed out—something we usually do, but not this time. You can thank me later. Instead of the usual merry going around in these situations, I decided to show you just how serious we are to understand how far we are willing to go to get what we want. Patrick's chest began to expand and contract as his breathing became labored with rage and grief. Noticing his reaction, Yuri pointed to one of his men, and they quickly landed a right hook to his face and left to his midsection. The first strike nearly sent Patrick and the chair reeling to the floor, while the punch to his mid-section caused him to almost blackout as the air was forced out of his body.

"I would advise you to remain calm, detective. I wouldn't want your beautiful daughters to watch us beat you to death."

Forcing himself to speak, although he barely had enough air in his lungs, Patrick groaned, "You're gonna kill us anyway, now that we've seen your faces."

Yuri's eyebrows lifted as he walked closer to Patrick and leaned in so that their faces were mere inches from each other.

"Does it look like I care if you've seen my face, detective? If we wanted you dead, you would've awakened in the arms of your sweet baby Jesus and not tied to that fucking chair. But I can assure you that once I've spoken to you about our proposition and the rewards for doing what we ask, you won't care either. Now, please try to shut the fuck up while I explain to you how we all can help each other. And, those tears for your wife, save them. You've been cheating on her since you walked down the aisle. And with her sister, who is a beautiful woman and recently divorced. So, consider me killing your wife the first of many gifts from me," Yuri said while standing straight up and pointing to the detective and then to himself.

"Now, listen carefully because I will only go over this once...."

Downtown Chicago

As the limousine pulled into the parking lot, Zaya looked outside the window and glanced over the crowd of people waiting in line to get into the Black Tower nightclub. The Black Tower was the most exclusive nightclub in the city, a hot spot for the rich and famous coming to Chicago to enjoy the incredible nightlife. Nestled across the street from Lake Michigan, the four-story all-glass night spot gave its patrons an uninhibited view of the beautiful lakefront at night. The building was illuminated by blue neon lights that created an alluring aura that begged for anyone walking past to want to enter. But judging by the line that stretched around the block, many were called, but very few were chosen.

The limousine pulled in front of The Black Tower's front entrance, and two club security personnel rushed to open the door and help Zaya out of the car. Stepping out behind her, Zahir pulled down on his black and silver print European-style blazer and held out his arm. Zaya instinctively wrapped her arm in his, and as one of the security guards led them inside the club, the other followed, keeping a close watch on the people in the line on his left. Shadow could feel the crowd's eyes fixated on them, their covetous gaze attempting to pierce through their confidence, but mumblings only added fuel to their arrogance. The closer they got to the door leading into the nightclub, the higher they held up their chins until, by the time they were walking through the black double doors, they were almost looking directly up at the ceiling.

Laughing at themselves, Zaya and Zahir continued through the entrance and down a long corridor. The club's exterior was covered with soundproof glass, so once they were in the hall, the concussive blast of the bass from the massive speakers on the main dance floor rocked their entire bodies. Making their way through the crowded corridor, they eventually walked into the main dance floor. The room was the size of a sports arena built in a circle with bars lining each wall. Where ever a party goer turned in the vast room, a drink was just within a few steps from the dance floor. Something above his head caught his attention, and Zahir looked up and nearly gasped at the sight of scantly clad women dancing on silver poles that appeared to be levitated above the dance floor. Tapping her shoulder, Zahir pointed above his head so she could see what he was seeing, and her mouth began to lower the longer she watched the women spin up and down the levitated silver poles.

"How the fuck did they pull that off? They look like they are stripping on air, bae!"

Shrugging his shoulders without taking his eyes off the elevated erotic entertainment, Zahir whispered, "I have no idea. But I like it!"

Playfully punching him in his chest, Zaya tugged on his arm so they could continue following the security guards. The dance floor was packed with gyrated bodies, dancing to the sensual rhythm of an Afro beats mix, and without noticing, Zahir found himself bouncing his head to the beat. The security guard began leading them up a flight of stairs that led to another floor filled with couches and more bars. Turning their attention to his right, the security guard politely said, "Right this way, Mr. Jones," leading them inside a private elevator. Once inside, the security guard joined them and pressed the fourth-floor button. Within twenty seconds, the elevator doors opened up to an ultra-modern and luxurious floor filled with blush couches and a single bar. Stepping out of the elevator, Zahir looked to his left and was excited to see that they had a front-row seat to the floating strippers. Even at an advantaged distance, he couldn't figure out how the builders could pull off the optical illusion.

Looking to his right, he was greeted by his Franchise crew, lifting their bottles and glasses and yelling his name over the loudspeakers. Noticing his job was done, the security guard backed into the elevator and said, "Have fun, sir," before the elevator doors closed.

Midas walked over to Zahir and Zaya and greeted them both warmly.

"Damn, Midas, I see you rocking the Armani three-piece." Zaya complimented, smiling brightly while looking her ex-boyfriend over. "But um, you ain't as fine as my baby, though." She continued, her smile vanishing as quickly as it appeared.

"Whatever, Zee! What's up, Shadow, you ready to shine? It's your night, my nigga!"

"For sho! Let's get it!"

"Follow me, sir! Let the festivities begin." Midas responded, imitating a British accent while bowing slightly and point in the direction where everyone was waiting.

Willing to play along, Zahir responded in his own British accent, "Indeed, lead the way, fine sir."

Giggling, Zaya shook her head and said under her breath, "Y'all slow."

Time seemed to move to a crawl as Shadow and his crew partied, ordering expensive bottles of alcohol while dancing and yelling in celebration of Shadow's eighteenth birthday. From the other side of the fourth floor, the three men that King David sent on a mission observed the crew.

"Byron, how da fuck that lil nigga got up on this floor? It costs at least ten thousand to reserve this floor on a slow night, but on a Friday, the shit gets past twenty K."

"Shit, I can't call it; all I know is that lil nigga need some act right cause he thinks he some fucking boss or some shit."

Letting out an uncomfortable chuckle, Byron scoffed, "Jamal, fuck what you talking about, the way he had the whole bus on our ass, that nigga definitely moves like a boss."

"Fuck that nigga! It would be so easy to pick that nigga off," Jamal responded while pulling out his gun and pointing it in Zahir's direction. Byron reached over and pushed Jamal's hand down.

"Nigga, what the fuck are you doing? Are you trying to get us arrested or fucked up? You already know what King David said, and mercing that nigga wasn't it."

"Man, fuck dat nigga. King David is getting soft out here. Fuck, I miss the Da Rock. If he weren't down, he would be on this nigga ass for the disrespectful shit he's done. King David got us out here babysitting Zaya instead of having us putting in work on this nigga."

"Nigga, you talking reckless as fuck right now, and I don't want no parts of it."

"Me either," Terrell responded while tapping Byron on the shoulder.

"Let's go downstairs, Byron, cause this nigga Jamal on some wild shit."

"Yeah, we out nigga. We don't want no parts of whatever you trying to do right now."

"Do you see me begging for you bitch ass niggas to stay? Get the fuck on!"

After Byron and Terrell left him alone, Jamal began to imagine the many ways he could kill Shadow and his entire crew. He imagined walking over to them and putting the first bullet in the back of the Midas's head, and then he would gun them all down one by one, leaving Shadow for last. He could see him, lying on his back on one of the red couches, begging for his life right before he emptied the clip in his chest and face. He would then snatch Zaya up and take her home to her father, who would be grateful to him for getting rid of Shadow and his entire squad. The more his dark fantasy of murder and mayhem played inside his mind, the more determined he became.

How the fuck did this lil nigga get the drop on us on that bus. I know he had either some weight or a shit load of cash in that bag.

And there is only one nigga in this city that can lace a motherfucka like that, and that's Cain. And I hate that nigga Cain more than I hate this bitch made nigga. Who the fuck these niggas think they are? Popping thousand dollar bottles and having bitches running up through this muhfucka. Even the stripper bitches are partying over there with them. Nah, I can't let this shit slide. These niggas gotta die.

Without giving it another thought, Jamal rose to his feet and began reenacting his plan to murder Shadow and everyone around him. Jamal started to taking long strides as he lifted his gun, heading straight towards Midas, aiming for the back of his head. One of the strippers was handing Midas a drink when she noticed Jamal coming towards them out of the dimly lit foyer and screamed, "He got a gun!"

Midas ducked and rolled on the floor without hesitating, just before Jamal fired, his bullet tearing through the neck of the stripper and sending her body to the floor. Her body collided with the carpeted floor with a sickening thump as she wrapped her hands around her neck, trying to subside the excruciating pain that exploded through her body. A crimson river poured out of her neck and over her hands as she shook violently from her body, losing massive amounts of blood.

Noticing his missed, Jamal began firing along the floor, trying to kill Midas, but his aim was obscured by the dim light of the VIP section. The loud pop of the gunfire sent the entire club into a frenzy as a stampede of bodies rushed towards the exits. Noticing he wasn't in the proper position to hit Midas, Jamal began firing at people running towards the elevator or the stairs leading down to the lower levels. His bullets tore into the flesh of those retreating, and the more bodies that dropped, the more he became drunk in his blood lust. He continuously reloaded his gun, trying to kill as many people as he could.

Midas, Zaya, and Shadow hid behind a group of pillars on the darkest side of the floor, watching Jamal gun down their friends. With each body, the fire of Shadow's rage burned hotter as he waited for Jamal to reload again so he could make his move.

There was a brief moment of silence, and Shadow waited a few seconds to make sure it wasn't a ruse and that Jamal was going to reach for another clip to reload. He'd been timing Jamal's reload times, and he figured it would take him fifteen seconds to get another clip out of his jacket and reload. He would be able to cover the distance by the time he'd fully completed his reloading routine. Still, he wouldn't have much time after that, maybe three seconds, and as skilled as he was as a fighter, trying to take down Jamal with a gun in three seconds would only lead to him catching a bullet. But he knew he couldn't let his entire crew be wiped out while he hid in the dark like a coward.

As Jamal reached into his jacket for another clip, Shadow rushed him from behind. He noticed an intact liquor bottle on his way towards Jamal, unopened and filled with expensive mind-altering fluids. In a single motion, he scooped the bottle from the floor and threw it with all his strength at the back of Jamal's head. The bottle collided with Jamal's head, breaking in countless pieces of glass. The force of the bottle hitting his head pushed Jamal's body forward, nearly knocking him to the floor, interrupting his reloading ritual and forcing his new clip out of his left hand. This gave Shadow enough time to run and lift Jamal's body off the floor from his legs. The sudden violent upward motion caused Jamal's grip on his gun to loosen, and the weapon fell to the floor. Shadow began running with Jamal lifted above his head towards the open railing that overlooked the entire club from the top floor. Noticing what Shadow was doing, Jamal tried to free himself, but his body's position left him at a disadvantage, and before he could grab ahold of the railing, Shadow threw him over.

Jamal's high-pitched screams could be heard throughout the upper levels as he fell four stories to the bottom floor. Within seconds the screaming stopped as his body hit the concrete floor with a loud and sickening pop. Shadow looked down at Jamal's body, sprawled out on the floor. Through the darkness and chaos, he could see a dark pool of blood flow from under his body, and then he noticed one of his legs moving. Shadow's eyelids lowered as he took a second look to make sure his eyes weren't deceiving him.

This piece of shit is still alive?

Swearing loudly, Shadow stormed over to where Jamal's gun landed on the floor. Searching for a few more seconds, Shadow found the full clip and within seconds, was loading it inside the gun and storming back over to the railing. Throwing his arm over the side of the railing, he took a few seconds to measure his aim, perfected by the countless hours of target practice with Cain, and proceeded to squeeze the trigger and didn't release until the gun's ammunition was exhausted. Midas and Zaya rushed to Shadow's side and looked down at the morbid scene below. They both slowly turned and looked at Shadow with their mouths agape, and their eyes were bulging out of their heads when they noticed Shadow's barrage of bullets hit no one else but Jamal despite hundreds of screaming people running within his line of sight.

Shadow remained still, his breathing calm, his mind clear. He knew this day would come but never thought it would be on his eighteenth birthday and at such a high cost. As Jamal went on his murderous rampage, he counted at least five of his crew was either dead or dying on the club's floor, and there was nothing he could do about it. He was afraid that killing a man would make him regret the choices he made in life, but as he stared down at Jamal's body, he felt a sense of liberation, as if this was his final moment to shed the last pieces of Zahir and only Shadow would remain. As he, Midas, and Zaya made their way around the VIP section to help those who were still alive, Shadow recalled the confrontation earlier that day, and the recollection of Jamal's face enraged him further. At that moment, he knew that he and King David would have to come to terms with their beef, and only one of them would remain alive after it was all said and done.

This muthafucka gotta go. I don't care how much it's gonna hurt Zaya. This will never happen again, and if Malik wants to get in my way, he can join his boss in hell.

Surrounded by police and first responders, Shadow, Midas, Zaya, and the few unharmed survivors of The Franchise walked through the chaotic parking lot seemingly in a daze. A few minutes before they walked out of the club, the police questioned them about the state they found Jamal, and on code, all of them repeatedly said, "We didn't see nothing."

Frustrated but relieved the shooter wasn't on the lose, the investigating homicide detective let them go but warned them not to leave town for the next couple of weeks until they can close out the investigation.

Within a few minutes of them standing outside the club, Shadow's limousine pulled in front of them, and before Shadow and Zaya climbed into the back, Midas reached over and hugged Shadow.

"You saved our lives tonight, Shadow. Thank you. If you ever need me for anything. I'm ready to ride. I know tonight changes everything, so whatever you decide to do, even if Cain ain't with it, I'm on whatever you on."

Nodding, Shadow returned Midas's embrace, and the two men released, and Midas stepped back to watch Shadow and Zaya pull away in the limousine. A few blocks down the street, Zaya sat across from Shadow, refusing to look him in the eyes. Watching her closely, Shadow tried reading her body language. He didn't know if she was upset with him or if she was feeling something else. Something carnal and animalistic, as he did. He needed to be inside of her, to feel her skin against his skin, hear her call his name, and violently fuck his brains out. The longer he thought about it; the more potent his desire for her became until he was hypnotized by it. He didn't notice Zaya had been staring back at him, whispering his name until one of Chicago's infamous potholes shook him out of his waking fantasy.

"Shadow. I need you to fuck me, right here, right now."

Here command filled his ears like a cool breeze on a scorching afternoon, a momentary reprieve from the torture of desire unfulfilled. Without hesitation, the two lovers leaped into each other's arms and began tearing their clothes off. The driver hearing their passionate grunts and moans behind him, quickly closed the divider to give his passionate passengers some privacy.

Completely naked, Zaya mounted Shadow, grabbed his throbbing and rock-hard dick, and slowly guiding it inside her. As his girth and length expanded her pussy, the sweet agony forced her to brace herself as she bit down hard on his bottom lip, breaking the flesh of his full lips allowing drops of his blood to fall into her mouth. Unable to wait for her to submerge all of him inside of her, Shadow grabbed her ass and forcefully pushed her down. The sudden feeling of taking all of him inside her caused her to squeal and dig her fingernails into his chest as she sat on top of him and began to ride, only using her hips to bounce her lower body up and down on his dick. The continued friction pushed her flood gates to their limits as her nectar began to pour out of her, drenching his dick and pelvis. Her hips rocked back and forth as the force of her pussy bouncing up and down on his dick became more aggressive as she felt the heat of her eruption building in her chest and moving down towards her pussy. Shadow began clenching his fist, trying his best not to allow his eruptions to end their violent sexual encounter before Zaya reached her climax.

Feeling herself getting closer and closer, but not quite there, she leaned back so that she can experience Shadow's curve. Then tightening the muscles inside of her, she began pushing and pulling, Shadow's angle now pushing the intensity of her climax to the next level.

"Oh my Gawd, Shadow! Stay right there, don't move, oh shit! Yes, fuck me, fuck me, fuck me."

Under extreme pressure, Shadow did his best to keep the same position he was in while trying to count to twenty. But he was losing his grip on her hips, along with his self-control. Zaya's riding became wilder with each passing second she felt herself getting closer. Zaya's eyes suddenly popped open as she screamed to the top of her lungs, shaking violently and collapsing on top of Shadow out of breathe and covered in sweat.

Whew, I almost fucked that up. Shadow thought to himself while he began to forcefully move her ass up and down, wanting to have his own moment of satisfaction.

Noticing what he was doing, Zaya began running her tongue along his neck and then tightened her pussy around his dick. Within a few strokes, Shadow was digging his hands into the flesh of her ass, trying to keep the loud moan dancing on the tip of his tongue from betraying him as he exploded inside her. Allowing his arms to fall to his side, Shadow looked around the limousine, noticed the foggy windows, and chuckled.

"I think everyone in traffic knows what's going on back here."

"So, I don't care. Do you?"

"What you think?"

Smiling, Zaya laid her head on Shadow's chest and began listening to his heartbeat. The longer she laid on his chest, her breathing rhythm slowly began to match his until they were breathing in harmony, their exhausted bodies singing to one another. The sudden knock on the divider woke the two young lovers from their bliss, and Shadow sighed as he tried to sit up with Zaya still lying on top of him.

"Sup?"

"Sorry, sir. I didn't mean to interrupt, but I thought you should know we are about five minutes away from your date's house."

"Oh shit!" Zaya gasped as she jumped up and started looking around the limousine for her clothes."

Shadow joined her as the two of them laughed hysterically when he found her panties instead of his boxers. By the time the limousine pulled in front of King David's home, they were both fully clothed and had cracked the windows to ease the smell of sex out of the car. As soon as the limousine came to a complete stop, about twenty men appeared from the cover of darkness and surrounded the vehicle with their guns displayed.

Fuck! Shadow thought as he looked over at Zaya and shook his head.

Looking outside, Zaya began to panic and started screaming her father's name from the limousine window.

"Zaya! Stop, it's ok. There is nothing we can do about this. Your dad played his hand perfectly. I don't want you to get involved. Whatever happens, just know that I love you, have always loved you and whether in this life or the next, you will always be my queen."

"Zahir?" Zaya pleaded, but before she could reach out to him, he opened the door, stepped out of the limousine, and closed the door behind him.

"All right! Now what?" Shadow yelled towards King David's front door with his hands raised in the air. From behind a couple of the armed men, King David stepped out of the shadows. His victorious stroll towards him burned Shadow deep in his soul.

Smug bastard, the only reason why you got me tonight was because of your daughter.

"Well, well, well. It seems like you ain't the only nigga able to pull some ninja shit, huh?"

"No, but it seems I'm the only man out here willing to keep his word."

"You watch your fucking mouth, lil nigga! I did not order that hit!"

"Nigga, you got me! Why stand in front of me and lie?! Those were your hitters tonight!"

"Yeah, about that, I need you to come with me."

Shadow scoffed at the idea that King David would expect for him to follow him into his house.

Turning around and looking at Shadow like he'd lost his mind, King David snapped, "Nigga, you better move your feet, or I'll have a couple of these niggas move them for you! You can walk on your own power or the power of a pistol-whipping, your choice...*Shadow!*"

Accepting he had no choice in the matter, Shadow began to follow King David into his house. From behind them, Zaya began screaming from inside the limousine for her father not to hurt Shadow.

"Turning around abruptly, King David roared back at his daughter, "You keep your ass in that car, Zaya!" Looking at the remaining men standing around the limousine, King David ordered them to watch Zaya and keep her inside the car. He then turned and continued to lead them to the side of his home. On the side of the Greystone was a flight of stairs leading down to the lower level of the massive house. The walk down the stairs was slow as Shadow carefully navigated his way to the lower landing and waited for King David to open the door and lead the entourage inside.

As soon as the door opened, Shadow's nostrils were assaulted by the putrid odors of sweat, piss, and blood. Although the horrid smells burned the inside of his nostril, causing his eyes to water, he refused to cover up his face. He didn't want to display an ounce of weakness because he knew King David was watching his every move, every reaction to whatever he had planned for him. As his eyes adjusted to the sudden exposure to light of the lower basement, Shadow could hear the faint sounds of whimpering further ahead of him. His escorts walking in front of him, suddenly stepped aside to reveal Byron and Terrell on their knees, naked and chained to one of the metal foundation pillars. Their bodies were soiled with the filth of blood and their body excretions. Their eyes screamed the terror they felt, replacing the whimpers coming from their duct-taped mouths.

King David, wearing rubber gloves, reached down and violently snatched the duct tape from Terrell's mouth and roared, "Tell this nigga what was really supposed to go down tonight!"

Terrell's fear of death was palpable as he went over every minute detail of the events leading up to the mass shooting at The Black Tower. He ensured that they were only supposed to watch Zaya's back, and King David didn't give a hit order on Shadow or his crew. When he was done, Terrell looked up at King David with eyes wet with regret, silently pleading for his life. King David responded with a devastating backhand slap across his face.

"Nigga, don't be looking up at me like some begging bitch! You should have never left Jamal by himself after you knew what that nigga was on. My daughter could've been killed tonight because you two bitch ass niggas didn't have the fucking balls to check another bitch made nigga!"

Pointing down at King David's captives, Shadow interjected, "Listen, clearly you have already beat these niggas half to death, and to stay alive, they will say and do whatever you say. How am I supposed to believe these niggas now? Your man made an attempt on my life and murdered five...FIVE of my niggas, and you think this display will make that shit right?"

"Oh, you think I'm doing this to prove something to you? Look where you at nigga! I don't need to prove shit to you or anyone else! You can join these niggas on your knees, naked and begging like a bitch. All it takes is one word from me!"

"You and I both know if you do that, you'll have to answer to someone that you ain't trying to see right now!"

"Fuck that nigga and fuck you! I'm King David nigga, and I run these streets! All I have to do is point at any nigga, and it's over! Life, death, wealth, peace, and war in these streets is my domain! I'm the only reason you're still breathing, so don't let the fact you're able to use those lungs to speak fool you into thinking I can't change that with a single bullet."

"Yeah, you run the streets, but what's running the streets to a nigga that rules the city?"

Shadow's response momentarily silenced King David; noticing he didn't have an answer, King David became enraged and stormed over to the other side of the basement. The sound of metal dragging across the concrete floor echoed in the basement as King David retrieved the chains that made him infamous on the streets of Chicago. The chains were massive, weighing sixty pounds. They were discolored with the dried stains of the blood from past victims, giving them an ominous appearance. When King David returned, his entourage stepped back, not wanting to be in the path of the chains once he started swinging them.

King David started to wrap one end of the chain around his hand while staring directly into Shadow's eyes. Unwilling to be intimidated, Shadow stared back at him, seemingly unbothered by what he knew was coming next. Byron and Terrell, watching King David prepare himself to be the weapon of their demise, began wailing and begging, looking into the eyes of everyone in the basement, attempting to garner sympathy. Still, no one dared look in their eyes besides Shadow. He returned their pleas of mercy with eyes filled with malice and rejoiced anticipation. He looked forward to seeing them die, and he didn't want to miss a single swing.

Shadow began looking around the basement until he found an empty paint bucket. He then picked it up, turned it upside down, and sat it directly in front of Byron and Terrell, making sure he was away from the path of the chains when King David started his rampage. He knew getting too close would encourage an *accidental* hit from his nemesis. King

David, puzzled by Shadow's action, observed him until he was seated on top of the bucket. He then turned to Byron and said, "You first." He then pointed at Terrell and said, "I liked you better than this bitch nigga, so you can live a little longer than him."

Flexing his muscular arms while rolling his neck, King David pulled back and struck Byron on top of his head with the metal chain. Byron's head cracked open like a Halloween pumpkin, exposing the fleshy interior of his skull. His eyes rolled to the back of his head as he began to lose consciousness, but a strike across the chest with the chain caused his eyes to return forward as the strike collapsed his rib cage. Terrell watched in horror as Byron's body was assaulted by the massive chains, tearing flesh and breaking bone. On the other hand, Shadow watched the morbid scene unfold in front of him as if he was watching his favorite television series.

An hour later, Shadow calmly walked out of the basement door, up the stairs, and out into the cool morning air. The night was slowly retreating to the sunrise, clearing away the darkness of the night before. The limousine was still parked in the same spot, surrounded by King David's men looking across the street. Walking up to the limousine, Shadow opened the door, and Zaya leaped out into his arms, kissing him all over his face and holding onto him as if her life depended on it. Looking him over, she asked, "Are you ok? Did he touch you?"

Smiling, Shadow responded, "Nah, but I need to go. He's asking for you."

Looking past Shadow at her father's home, Zaya swallowed hard as the only home she's ever known cast an eerie shadow on the street. Looking back at her love, she shook her head and said, "No, I don't want to go back in there! I want to stay with you."

Removing her hands from his face and holding them firmly in his own, Shadow responded, "That can't happen. After last night, me and your father have reached a point of no return, and I don't want you caught up in the middle of that. He is your father, and you and I both know his hatred for me is fueled by a lie that neither of us can afford to expose."

"So, you're breaking up with me?" Zaya said, searching Shadow's eyes for answers.

"Hell no, but being close to me right now is too dangerous, and just like that idiot Jamal, how many of them wouldn't mind taking you out just to get to me? I'm sure he's not the only one. And I can't have you caught up in this shit."

"Shadow, I knew exactly what I was signing up for when I chose you to be my man."

"Oh, *you* chose me?"

"You better believe it. I've been in this game for much longer than you have, and although it seems like you were born for this shit, I was also made for this shit. So, I'm not going back to that house. So, either I can go with you or go elsewhere, but I won't be spending another night in that house either way. So, what you wanna do?"

Rolling his eyes, Shadow shook his head, opened the limousine door, and gestured for her to get back inside. Smiling, Zaya climbed into the back. Turning around, Shadow noticed King David staring at them from his living room window. Smiling, Shadow playfully saluted in his direction, stepped inside the limousine, and ordered the driver to take them to his penthouse.

As soon as the limousine turned the corner, Zaya's cellphone began vibrating. She sighed as her father's number flashed across the screen.

"Sup?"

"I know after what happened last night, I really don't have much I can say to convince you I didn't order a hit on Shadow. So, I'm not going to waste your time with that. All imma say is, be careful around him; there's something off about that boy. The way he wasn't bothered by me deading Byron and Terrell was disturbing."

"I'm sure not as disturbing as watching you beating them to death with sixty-pound chains, daddy. But go off!"

"That's the thing, that boy literally grabbed a seat and watched till the end. Clearly enjoying it." "Hmmm," Zaya responded while quickly glancing over at Shadow before returning her attention to her phone.

"Daddy, I'm not upset that Jamal tried to kill Shadow. Well, I am, but the attempt isn't my main concern. I'm upset that you are losing your grip on your empire. You are so preoccupied with Shadow and keeping him away from me that these niggas don't respect you anymore. How long will it take for one of them to try you now? You need to lock your shit down, daddy. Last night shouldn't have happened. These niggas are getting reckless, especially with Rock being down. I know Malik was the obvious choice to take his place because these niggas are scared of Malik, but they respect Rock. Big difference."

Remaining silent, King David began to consider his daughter's prognosis of the root of his growing problems with maintaining control of his empire.

"Seems like I may have taught you better than I was taught."

"Seems that way. I love you, daddy, but what's going on, ain't it."

"Then you shouldn't be running off with Shadow; you should be here with me, helping me solve this shit!"

"Wait a minute; weren't you the one that said, if you create the problem, you should be the one to create the solution. Wasn't that you? If you need me, I'm there. But if it's anything involved with Shadow, don't call me."

"Zaya, please. Don't do this."

"Bye, daddy, I love you."

Tossing her phone on the seat across from her, Zaya began massaging her temples, attempting to hold the coming migraine at bay. Shadow watched her silently, giving her time to process her decision and hoping she would change her mind and have him take her back to her father, but after a few minutes, she looked at him and smiled.

Damn, she ain't changing her mind.

Shadow wanted nothing more than having her with him, waking up next to her every morning and having her amazing pussy at his disposal twenty-four hours a day, but the events of the previous night led him down was a path he didn't want her to ride along. The last thing he wanted for her was to choose between loving him and accepting her father's death because the war was coming.

"You hungry?"

"Nah, I just need to soak in a hot ass tub, ride that dick again, and then go to sleep."

"Say less!"

Maybe it won't be so bad. He thought, getting excited at that thought of Zaya bouncing her phat ass on his dick in his massive soak tub back at the penthouse.

Twenty minutes later, the limo driver pulled in front of Shadow's building and opened the door for them. As Shadow got out of the car, he noticed Cain standing in his building doorway and swore under his breath. Grabbing Zaya's hand, he whispered in her ear, "Go upstairs and wait for me. I got to handle something."

"What you got to handle…."

She paused her questioning once her eyes looked in Shadow's direction and noticed Cain standing in the building's doorway.

"Oh, no! I'm coming with you; I don't trust that nigga!"

"I do, I don't why, but despite how many times the nigga oversteps, I trust him. I got this. Just go upstairs. But, if anything goes wrong, I got a stash in my room, Kai knows where it is, and the both of you get out of there. Kai knows where my other spot is. Let him take you there."

"Ok, I love you, Shadow!"

"I know, I love you too, now get yo ass upstairs cause as soon as I get back, I want dat ass naked and my pussy wet and ready to receive this dick."

Zaya kissed him passionately before turning and heading for the entrance of the building. Walking up the stairs leading to the door, Zaya looked up at Cain. The two of them exchanged looks of disgust as she walked past him and into the building. Cain turned and watched her walk past him and shook his head. Feeling Cain was watching her, she turned and looked him in his eyes and said, "If anything happens to him because of you, I *will* kill you."

Cain looked into Zaya's eyes and saw the unquestionable truth in them, which momentarily startled him. Nodding, he responded with a hint of admiration in his voice, "I have no doubt you would try."

The two of them stared at each other for a few more moments, both accepting the other's commitment to keeping Shadow safe and their resolve in regulating anyone responsible for his demise. At that moment, Cain gained a level of respect for Zaya that he could never muster up for her father. She was her father's child, but she wasn't her father. Zaya would be much better at the helm of her father's empire than he could ever be. It was a shame that because of her father, she may not ever get the chance.

Impressive. Shadow chose a real one.

Across the street in an unmarked car, Detective O'neil watched Cain and Shadow get inside a blood-red Lamborghini Urus. Once the Lamborghini pulled away, Detective O'neil waited a few moments before tailing them. He made sure he kept his distance while hiding behind several cars so that Cain couldn't tell he was being followed. O'Neil pushed his knees up to the bottom of the steering wheel while he used his free hands to sprinkle a small mound of cocaine on the side of his hand and inhale it up his nose. The salty drip caused him to clear his throat as he waited for the euphoria to take hold, and he didn't have to wait long. His eyes watered as his mouth slowly hung open, riding the wave of the high.

This shit is the best I've ever had; he thought as he returned one hand to the steering wheel and placed his small bottle of white powdered heaven in the middle console. As his high increased, his mind became sharper, and his confidence skyrocketed.

I can do this. I can do this. He kept repeating in his head as he maneuvered through traffic, keeping his distance but making sure he didn't lose Cain in the bustling rush hour.

Inside the Lamborghini, Cain kept looking over at Shadow, the concern on his face making Shadow suspicious.

"What's up, Cain? Where are we going?"

"Someplace special, I wanted to wait until you were eighteen before I did. I wanted to bring you earlier, but I wasn't sure you were ready, but after last night, I am confident you are ready."

"What place? Where the fuck are you taking me, Cain?" Shadow asked, the concern in his voice growing with each passing second that Cain remained cryptic on their destination.

"It's better if you see it for yourself because if I told you where we're going, you wouldn't believe me. But, listen, everything I've ever done, even the disrespectful shit, was to help you grow in this business. To protect you and help you develop a skin of steel when dealing with the snakeskin muthafuckas in this business. When I heard what was going down last night, shit....I didn't know what to do. I raced over there, but by the time I got there, everything was over, but I waited until I saw you walk out of the club with Zaya and Midas. I didn't know what to think...I know you lost some of your crew, and trust me, King David will pay for that fuck shit he tried to pull. Nobody moves on my...nobody moves on my niggas and get away with it!"

Cain was enraged and rambling, making Shadow nervous because he was always calm and calculating. Even when he was angry, he didn't stutter or have a hard time finding the right words to express himself. This was a side of Cain Shadow didn't know existed, and it wasn't reassuring.

"King David didn't give that order. One of his foot soldiers decided to take matters into his own hands."

"And how do you know that shit, Shadow?!"

Did he just call me Shadow? He thought as a feeling of pride came over him. But he didn't have time to revel in Cain's respect for him. He needed to tell Cain precisely what happened in King David's basement.

"I saw him dead the other two niggas that were there. They left that nigga Jamal by himself when they knew what he wanted to do."

"But why was the niggas there in the first pl.."

Zaya's face suddenly flashed across Cain's mind, and he stopped talking and nodded his head.

"Yeah, they were there to watch her back, but I ran into those same three niggas on the bus earlier yesterday, and Jamal felt a way about the crew and me embarrassing them. The other two niggas seemed to let it go, but some niggas are too weak to see past their egos, and Jamal was such a nigga. But, King David is still a problem, and I will deal with that problem myself because if he can't keep his niggas in check, then another nigga needs to be in charge."

"And you're willing to make that move knowing what it will do to Zaya?"

"She left him and decided to live with me, and she is more than capable of understanding what last night means."

"Gad damn, that girl is a fucking savage!"

"Well, I'm not going to let you go at it alone because you work for me, and one of his clowns moved on one of mines, so he got more trouble than he bargained for."

Nodding, Shadow smiled, relieved to have Cain on his side and ready to retaliate against King David. Shadow knew he didn't have the numbers, but King David's numbers didn't matter with Cain and his influence.

"So, are you going to tell me where you are taking me?"

"Not yet. It's a surprise." Cain responded while turning down an alley.

"You know I don't…"

Without warning, the flashing red and blues engulfed the interior of the SUV, followed by the loud screech of the police siren. Cain swore loudly and pulled his SUV over in front of a garage door, looking in his rearview mirror. Shadow's brow crumbled as he looked in the side-view mirror and recognized the officer walking towards the back of the car.

"Hey, that's the detective you sent to test me!"

"Patrick? Why the fuck is that idiot pulling me ov…shit get down!" Cain yelled when he noticed Patrick drawing his gun and aiming it at the back of his SUV. The back window exploded, sending shards of glass all over the interior of the Lamborghini. Patrick kept firing, trying to hit his targets, switching his angle, hoping a bullet would penetrate through the back of one of the seats and find its intended target.

"Stay down, and no matter what happens, don't you get involved in this. I will handle this and whatever happens, remember, that picture in the dining room can save your life!" Cain yelled while he reached for his gun in the side panel of the driver's side door. Readying his gun and removing the safety, he peered around his seat as he ducked down. He aimed at Patrick's chest and fired four shots, each one hitting their target and knocking Patrick to the ground. Hearing his body hit the concrete, Cain opened his door, enraged while wiping the broken glass from his clothing.

"You spineless piece of Irish shit! Who sent you!" Cain screamed as he stood over Patrick, aiming his weapon down at him. Patrick squirmed and moaned in pain as the agony of the bullets striking his bulletproof vest erupted through his body.

"I should've busted your head wide open, but I need to know who sent you?!"

"Please, I have a family!"

"I don't give a fuck! You had a family muthafucka! Once I'm done here, I'm going over there and finishing the job. Now, tell me who sent you, and I'll make their deaths quick, but if you play with me, I will make them suffer for weeks before I put them out of their misery. Including those beautiful twin girls of yours! Now talk muthafucka!"

Inside the SUV, Shadow remained tucked down, but something didn't feel right.

Patrick wasn't skilled enough to take Cain down. He was barely competent enough to be a police officer. So a hitter sent to take down a man like Cain was a suicide mission. So, whoever sent him knew he would fail, so why send him? What was the goal?

From the corner of his eye, Shadow saw a red beam of light, and before he could scream to warn Cain, The back of Cain's head erupted in bone and brain matter as the sniper's bullet penetrated his skull and traveled out the front of his face, tearing it to pieces. Cain's body swayed for a few seconds before his large, lifeless frame collapsed to the asphalt. Shadow screamed in agony as he witnessed the murder of his mentor. Patrick quickly jumped to his feet and ran towards the passenger side of the SUV, reloading his gun along the way. Shadow climbed over to the driver's side and fell out the door. A single bullet whistled past his head from the sniper, and he quickly dove behind a metal dumpster sitting in front of a garage.

Patrick began running around the front of the SUV to flank Shadow, but Shadow anticipated Patrick would pursue him, so he kept his head low, using the dumpster as cover as he ran and jumped over the fence next to the dumpster. Remaining low, Shadow ran towards the front of the house and then ran across the street through another yard. From the corner of his eye, he noticed a garbage truck moving down the alley, picking up dumpsters and loading them into the back of the truck. He gritted his teeth and jumped into the dumpster closest to him, and closed the lid.

Within a few minutes, he could hear footsteps running back and forth. They were lifting dumpsters and kicking over garbage cans looking for him. He could hear the garbage truck getting closer, but his pursuers were also getting dangerously closer as well. Suddenly he heard metal being hit against the dumpster's side and Patrick saying, "What about this one?"

He looked above his head and saw the metal lid on top of the dumpster lifting, and he readied himself to see Patrick looking down at him with his gun aimed at his head…then boom.

"Hey, what are you doing?!"

"I'm checking the garbage!"

"Do you live here?"

"Ummm…no…but I'm a police officer!"

"I don't give a fuck if you're the president; you can't be going through people's trash without a warrant, buddie. I'm going to have to call this in to dispatch!"

"No need, I'll just leave."

"Yeah, you do that."

Shadow could hear Patrick's footsteps getting further and further away from the dumpster.

"Fucking pigs always on that bullshit." The sanitation worker complained as he lifted the dumpster's lid and gasped when he looked into Shadow's terrified eyes. He looked down both ways of the alley and then gestured for Shadow to stay low.

"I got you, buddy; I'll let you know when they're gone." The blond-haired sanitation worker promised while he started to grab the garbage bags around him.

"Hey, just drag the dumpster over here so the truck can lift it, his co-worker instructed. Confused by him walking towards the back of the truck with two garbage bags in his hands.

"Nah, give it a few minutes, and then we can do that one. Grab that other one. We'll get that one last."

"Why?"

The sanitation worker gestured towards the end of the alley where Patrick's car was sitting at the end and then back at the dumpster. His partner quickly caught on and nodded his head in agreement.

"Fucking pigs."

"Exactly"

Ten minutes later, the sanitation worker lifted the lid and reassured Shadow that the coast was clear, and he slowly climbed out of the dumpster, trying to clean the filth off of his suit. Seeing how Shadow was dressed confused them as they couldn't understand why the police would be pursuing a young black man in such an expensive suit. But neither of them was prepared to find out.

"Thank you; I owe you both."

"Aye, buddy, no need. We hate CPD as much as anyone. Just get home safe."

Shadow thanked them again and then hopped over another fence as he made his way out of the area.

CHAPTER SIXTEEN

ZAYA HEARD THE PING of the elevator's arrival to the penthouse floor and rushed out to greet Shadow in a robe with nothing on under it. Shadow sprinted out of the elevator, completely ignoring her, and ran into the dining room. Cain's last words kept repeating in his head, and it tortured him on his journey back to the penthouse. Zaya got a whiff of the stench of rotten food when Shadow ran past her, and she gagged as her stomach protested.

"Oh my God, baby, you stink! What did y'all do, dumpster dive for your birthday?! Following Shadow into the dining room, she said but keeping a safe distance to prevent herself from experiencing his stench again. Watching him frantically run his hand around the edges of the massive painting that hung on the elegant dining room walls began to send chills up her spine. She was all too familiar with her father's moments of doom when the feds or CPD was about to raid their home looking for drugs or evidence.

"Baby, what happened?!"

Shadow didn't acknowledge her as he carefully lifted the picture off of the hanging hooks and let it drop the floor. On the wall in its place was a small door, the bottom of the door about three feet from the floor.

"Hand me that chair!" Shadow demanded. Zaya complied but continued to drill Shadow.

Pushing the chair against the wall, Shadow stood on it and pushed the door, but it didn't move. Because the door's edges were flush with the wall, he could not pull it open, so he started to look around the wall surrounding the secret door for another way to open it.

"Shadow! What the fuck is going on?!?"

"He's dead! They murdered him! I don't have time to go into details right now, but we have to get the fuck out of here, but I need to get to whatever is behind this door. Cain made it clear that whatever is in there is important. Now go get Kai!"

His raised voice startled Zaya into action, and she ran towards Kai's room.

How do I open this muthafucka. Come on, Shadow, think. How would this nigga protect this? Wait a minute.

Shadow got down off the chair and walked over to the picture he just took down from the wall. Turning it over, he noticed a metallic square on the back of it. Pushing it with his forefinger, the square vibrated, and from behind him, he heard a low clicking sound. Turning around, he watched as the door slid to the side, and he quickly jumped on the chair. Behind the door was a small space big enough to fit a single door refrigerator or the six large duffle bags that were filling the room. Shadow opened one of the bags and discovered brinks of cash with a note on top of them that read, ten million.

Sixty million dollars?! Why would he give me access to this cash?

"We ready!" Zaya's yelled as she and Kai stood at the elevator door's entrance.

"Help me with this, Kai!" Shadow said while tossing the six bags of money out of the hidden space. As soon as he pulled his body from inside the empty space, the secret door closed. Shadow and Kai then put the picture back, and the three of them rushed out of the penthouse into the elevator.

Shadow's car was waiting out front when they got downstairs, and the confused look on his face made Zaya giggle.

"I called the front desk to have them bring your car around front."

"Good looking out."

The three jumped into the car, and Shadow sped down Lakeshore Drive heading towards the north suburbs, trying to increase the distance between the penthouse and those he cared for the most. In the car, Shadow called Midas and began telling him what happened to Cain and warned him to leave the property where he was staying. Midas assured Shadow he was leaving immediately, and confident that Midas was a man of his word, he ended the call and began calling the remaining members of The Franchise. Upon hearing about the demise of Cain, they became infuriated and wanted retaliation, and refused to leave the homes they had come to enjoy.

Shadow pleaded with them, but only one other member agreed.

Fuck, I only have three niggas left, me included.

While Shadow made his phone calls, Zaya and Kai sat in the car and listened in silence, the shock keeping them still and petrified. After completing his final call, Shadow began slamming his hands on the steering wheel, swearing and cursing everyone, including God.

"Baby, calm down. You're swerving, and the last thing we need is for us to get pulled over by the cops. They are probably looking for you now, so until we can get to your other spot and dump this car, you should be very careful how you drive."

Exhaling so forcefully, the escaping air vibrated his full lips, he replied, "Ok, you're right."

Shadow leaned back in the driver's seat and began driving with his left hand freeing the right one, and Zaya reached over and held his hand while massaging the back of his neck, trying to calm him down.

When they arrived at his safe house in Waukegan, Midas was sitting on the front porch. The look of horror on his face alarmed Shadow because he knew something else was wrong and it wasn't going to be good news. Jumping out of the car, Shadow rushed over to Midas, and the two of them embraced before Midas began rambling.

"Nigga, I got out just in time. As I was pulling out of the parking garage, the CPD was raiding my shit. I called them other niggas, but they didn't answer. So I drove by there, and they were dragging all them niggas out in body bags. They killed all of them, Shadow!"

"You got to be fucking kidding me?"

"The neighbors said the CPD went in guns blazing. They didn't even give them a chance to surrender. It was like the goal was to kill them."

In deep thought, Shadow responded, "They are cleaning house. It's a hostile takeover, by who, I don't know yet, but what we need to do is re-up to keep the customers happy. That way, it will be harder for whoever is behind this to move in. But if we don't re-up and keep the deliveries on time, they will have to buy from whoever has what they need. So, after we settle in, we need to go see the Russians."

"Nigga, we would need about ten million dollars to even get them pork-smelling muthafuckas out of bed, and neither of us got *that* kind of bread!"

"Let me worry about that! What they did to Cain was fucked up, and we gone deal with that, especially that dirty fucking detective Patrick O'Neil. But right now, the goal is the keep this money flowing. We can't let Cain's empire fall."

"It ain't Cain's no more; it's your empire now." Midas proclaimed.

Overcome with grief, Shadow bowed his head and nodded before he called for Zaya and his brother to join them inside the house.

Later that evening, Shadow contacted the Russians to schedule a pickup, and after setting the date and time, Shadow joined Midas, Zaya, and Kai in the living room. They were all observing the evening news, waiting for the news coverage of Cain's murder and the police raids of all his properties. As the news coverage ended, they all sat in the living room baffled, everyone besides Shadow. He wasn't surprised, and the more his mind began to solve the puzzle of who was behind the takeover, a clear picture slowly came into view.

Everyone turned to Shadow, clearly looking for answers.

"Y'all wondering why zero coverage of the death of the most powerful boss in Chicago? Because that nigga had everyone by the balls, including the Mayor, Governor, and countless Senators and fortune 500 CEOs. Putting his shit on TV would embarrass them, and they not about to let that happen. So, they moved lowkey, wiping the board clean with a total reset. The four of us are the last remaining evidence that Cain ever existed. So they are going to be looking for us, too. Now whoever is behind this is powerful enough to influence the media and the pigs, and there was only one player in this city with that kind of pull, and he's dead. So, we have a new player in the city. I have my suspicions, but until I can prove it, we have to move carefully. Midas, let me holla at you bruh, I need your help with something."

The next morning

Zaya's body felt like it was drifting away from the shore, the current, steady and constant, pulling her further out to sea. Wave after wave of pleasure licked against her clit, Shadow's wet tongue cascading against the sensitive flesh, then wrapping his full lips around it, sucking and pulling her deeper into the abyss. She began to reach above her head, hoping to find a pillow or something to anchor herself, but there was nothing, just her body and Shadow devouring her aggressively. Arching her back, she lifted her legs further in the air and rested them on his shoulders, giving him full access to her, and Shadow didn't hesitate to dive deeper, running his tongue up and down her pussy and then sliding it inside of her and then back out again.

"Ooh, baby," she gasped as she felt him pushed two fingers inside of her and started sucking on her clit. Grabbing ahold of his ears, she braced herself as Shadow began moving his two fingers inside of her and then while pulling them out, lifted them in a "come here" motion so that he can activate her G spot.

The sensation of her stimulated G spot, paired with Shadow sucking on her clit caused her to cry out his name and ask, "What are you trying to do to me?" while looking down at him. Shadow wanted to answer, but his mouth was full of pussy, and this morning he wanted to be a man of few words. She could feel the waves of pleasure turning into violent tsunamis moments away from crashing her to shore. Her hips began to move; her inner muscles contracted around his fingers. At the same time, her pussy flooded out of her, spilling her nectar over Shadow's fingers as he began to speed up the motion of his fingers but continued to slowly suck on her clit.

Letting go of his ears, she began slamming her hands down on the pillowtop mattress, crying out loudly. The rush of her climax broke through her levies, and she flooded Shadows mouth and the bed. Shadow gasped as his mouth was filled with Zaya's cum, and he instinctively swallowed everything that squirted out of her pussy.

"Oh my fucking God!" she screamed as she shook violently, wrapping her arms around herself, attempting to hold herself in the present and not drift away into oblivion. Looking at her while she came, Shadow smiled. Zaya was absolutely stunning when she climaxed. The beauty of her bliss was something he knew he would never tire of watching. But Shadow wasn't here to admire the view; he came to fuck.

It ain't over yet.

He violently pulled her closer to him, spreading her legs, and pushed himself inside of her. His invasion, expanding her pussy while she was still cumming sent her overboard, and she screamed to the top of her lungs when she felt him hit rock bottom. Shadow pushed her legs back above her head, looked directly into her eyes, and began fucking her with the same ferocity he imagined he would kill everyone responsible for Cain's death.

Thirty minutes later, exhausted and gasping for air, the two lovers were sprawled across the bed, arms hanging over the sides, limp and seemingly lifeless.

"Gad damn baby!" Zaya gasped while wiping the sweat from her face. You were on one this morning, weren't you?"

"Hey, that's my pussy now, so I had to make sure it knew who da fuck it was dealing with."

"Mmmmm," she responded, shaking her head while patting her pussy affectionately. "Oh, baby, she knows who she belongs to."

"She better," Shadow responded while rolling over and kissing her on the lips.

"Shadow?"

"What's up?"

"Why didn't you tell Midas about the money?"

"I fucks with Midas the long way; Cain's empire grew because that nigga got game when it comes to selling product. But at the same time, certain information slips out his mouth that shouldn't, and the last thing I need is for the streets to know I'm holding sixty skids of cash. We don't have Cain's protection any longer, so we have to move in smart out here cause we are now at the mercy of the streets, and you and I both know who runs the streets."

"Yeah." Zaya sighed, looking up at the ceiling. "I'm sure my dad already knows Cain is dead, and he's probably looking for your ass, too. So, we got the pigs, my dad's people, and whoever is behind Cain's hit, too. That's a lot, Shadow. Did you ever think about taking the money and just leave Chicago and not look back? That's a lot of money, baby, and we could live a great life down south like Atlanta, Houston, New Orleans, hell, even Puerto Rico! Leave this shit in the rearview."

"Not even for a second."

Smiling from ear to ear, Zaya reached behind Shadow's head and pulled him closer to her, and kissed him.

"That's my baby. You passed the test. I'm yours completely now."

"Really? That was a test?"

"Mmmmhmmm. Had you said you thought about running, I would have still fucked with you, but best believe I

214

would not be trying to hold you down. It would be good until it wasn't, and then it would be over. I don't fuck with runners, Shadow. Never have, and I never will. My dad is right to be nervous around you. Yo ass is dangerous in these streets and in the sheets."

"Oh, you got bars now? So, you telling me had I chose the square life, you wouldn't hold me down?"

"Shit, nigga, this pussy would be for the streets, keep fucking around with me."

Shadow laughed out loud and shook his head.

"I know you not mad? I know a nigga like you ain't gone be satisfied with just my pussy, no matter how wet and tight it is. A phat ass ain't never kept a nigga at home. King niggas have options. I'm not an idiot, but only a King deserves my loyalty. But my loyalty comes with rules and regulations, nigga. If you disrespect me and not keep them other court jester bitches in check, I will show you better than I can tell you. Two can play that game, and babae, women play it betteeeerrrrr!"

"I'm not mad; I respect it. No cap. I wouldn't expect anything less from you."

Shadow then threw his legs over the side of the bed and started to get up.

"Me and Midas gotta go meet up with the connect later this evening, but there's some things I need to handle before I do."

"You and Midas, be careful with those Russian Mafia muthafuckas. I don't trust them."

"Me either, but we don't have a choice. It's either them or no one. If I could, I would buy directly from the source."

"You talking crazy now! You know damn well those cartels don't fuck with niggas. Not directly! That's why they have the Russians being the go-between."

"Yeah, I know. But I still think it can be done. Just because a nigga never made that connection doesn't mean it can't ever happen."

"Didn't you tell me Cain warned you about jumping the line, nigga? Shadow, you hard-headed as fuck! Leave them Mexicans in Mexico and respect the game as it's set up. I believe in you, baby, but right now, we aren't in a position to make those kinds of moves. We are basically on the run, and you have no idea what will happen tonight when you meet up with the connect. So, slow your roll, at least for now. Let us rebuild and then start shaking shit up. Right now, we are just trying to survive the day."

Zaya made sense. And Shadow listened, but at the same time, he knew the Russians eventually would want more. More money, more power, more influence, and with Cain off the board, there wasn't anyone who could tell them no. Deep inside, Shadow knew that eventually, they would have to make drastic moves to stay one step ahead of everyone that's going to be vying for what Cain left behind.

"You right, babe. I'm just thinking out loud. Let me hope in this shower and wash my ass."

"Can I join you?"

"Fuck yeah, you can suck my dick while I wash your hair."

"Nigga you got jokes; you ain't getting my hair wet."

CHAPTER SEVENTEEN

11:30 pm Chicago, Illinois

SHADOW STEPPED OUT OF a black 2010 Chevy Impala and took account of his surroundings. The humidity caused the heat to cling to his skin, making him feel stinky, almost instantly. The police station's parking lot was empty, no Bently sitting in the dark, and no police guards on duty. The only people present were the Russians. Gesturing for him to join them, Shadow made his way inside the police station and made the journey to the large room in the back. Stepping inside the dimly lit room, it was difficult to see past a few feet, which set Shadow's internal alarms off. Usually, the room would be well lit so everyone could see what they were buying, and the cash could be counted effectively.

But on this night, it seemed visual confirmation wasn't paramount. Not a good sign.

"Shadow...isn't it? How are you, my friend?" Yuri said, walking out of the darkness, smoking a large Cuban cigar dragging a trail of smoke behind him.

"I'm good."

"Are you sure?" I know the last twenty-four hours have been very traumatic."

"Comes with the territory."

"Yes, yes it does," Yuri responded, removing the cigar from his mouth and pointing it in Shadow's direction. "It's amazing how resilient you blacks are. No matter how much horror you endure, you still find a way to sing Kum Ba Yah. Or is it Acoom ma a ta ta? Not important, but still, you people are absolutely amazing!"

"So, were you able to secure my order? I know you said that it was last minute, and you may have a hard time gathering what I needed."

"Right, down to business. No more small talk. Well, I was able to secure what you asked, but I don't think you'll be needing the product or the money."

Refusing to play cat and mouse, Shadow knew precisely what was coming next, and he took two steps back and retreated into the darkness. Yuri's bodyguards started shooting in Shadow's direction, but he had already ducked down and used the darkness to his advantage to flank them. Standing directly next to one of the bodyguards as he fired in the direction he last saw Shadow, Shadow lifted his gun at his temple and fired. Before the guard's body hit the floor, he ducked back into the darkness and moved along the room's walls until he was standing directly behind the second bodyguard. Yuri and the other men in the room were firing where they heard Shadow's gun go off.

Shadow opened the other body guard's head from point-blank and then ducked behind a pallet of cash. The Russians began firing at Shadow's last location until Yuri started screaming in Russian.

"Prekratit' ogon'! Vklyuchite svet, vy, blyad', idioty!" (Ceasefire! Turn on the lights, you fuck idiots!)

One of the men ran to turn on the lights. Still hiding behind the pallet of cash, Shadow listened for the Russians footsteps in the darkness and fired in his direction. The Russian fell to the floor, ducking from the gunfire, and retreated in the opposite direction.

"You're not getting out of here alive, Shadow! You'll run out of bullets before I run out of Russians. So, make it easy on yourself, and I promise I will make it quick."

Shadow remained silent while carefully moving behind numerous pallets, using his hands to guide him in the dark.

"My men are on their way to get your brother and that sexy black bitch you're fucking. My men will make sure they enjoy her thoroughly before they put a bullet in her mouth. Now I can't promise I will let them live, but I can make one phone call and tell them to give to them the same deal I'm offering you. A quick death."

Silence...

"Maybe you think we don't know where your safe house is. Trust me; we know where you're hiding. There's no way out of this Shadow. This is how it ends for you, stop fighting the inevitable. Do yourself and those you love a favor."

Silence...

Suddenly, the lights came on, illuminating the entire room and Yuri and his men began searching every inch of the area. After searching every possible hiding place they discovered, Shadow was no longer in the room.

Standing in the middle of the room, Yuri held his gun in his hand and swore loudly.

"Blyad'!" (Fuck!) "Search the entire building. He has to still here!"

Outside in the parking lot, Alexie and Michail stood guard with the door closed behind them to mute the sounds of gunfire coming out of the abandoned police station. Looking down at the parking lot entrance, Alexie noticed a woman sashaying into the parking lot. Her bright yellow summer dress made her dark skin glow in the moonlight. She swayed her hips from side to side as she approached them. Alexie swallowed hard as he cleared his throat and intercepted the strange woman.

"Excuse me, how can I help you?"

"I'm here to see the chief!" she responded, her strong ghetto accent causing her to pronounce here as herr. The sweet smell of strawberry bubblegum invaded Alexie's nose as he looked her over hungrily, licking his lips.

"Is he expecting you?"

Using her hands to showcase her fantastic frame, she rolled her neck and snapped, "Da fuq you think?"

"Well, I'm sorry, but I can't let you in there right now."

"Really? And who are you? Cause you ain't no cop, judging by that weird-ass accent."

Michail watched Alexie and the streetwalker converse, rolling his eyes and shifting his body weight from one foot to the other. After a few more minutes, he decided to walk over to send the hooker on her way.

I don't know what Alexie sees in these she-male monkeys.

As he left his post at the door, two figures dressed in black stepped out of the shadows on the side of the police station. Creeping with their heads lowered, they quickly opened the door, snuck inside the police station, and closed the door behind them. As the door closed, the hinges protested, sending a sharp sound into the night air. Alexie and Michail quickly spun around with their guns drawn. As they turned their backs, the hooker reached down under her sundress and pulled out the weapon equipped with a silencer that was nestled in the holster strapped to her thigh, deactivating the safety; she aimed it at the back of their heads and fired two shots at the base of their skulls. Alexie and Michail's bodies hit the asphalt with a hollowed thump. Ensuring they were dead, Zaya took their guns and quickly ran out of the parking lot and out of sight.

Inside the police station's hallway, Midas silently motioned for Kai to follow him but keep low, and the two of them followed the sound of gunfire until they came to the large office area of the police station. Looking at the smartwatch on his wrist, Midas swiped its screen and studied the "Find My Phone" waypoint and signaled to Kai that Shadow was in the office area to their right. The two of them quickly moved in the direction where they expect Shadow to be waiting for them. Moving in the dark office area, Midas glanced down at his watch again and then made a sharp left, and after taking two steps, he walked into the nozzle of a gun. About to yell, Shadow covered his mouth and shook his head while pointing towards the far right side of the office area. Midas peered above the desk next to him and saw one of the Russians move in front of the beam of light from the emergency lights installed on the police station's ceiling.

Kai moved closer to his brother and silently expressed his frustration with the situation. Shadow could tell his brother would instead just shoot his way out of the police station, but that would be a mistake because he wasn't sure how many other Russian mobsters were hiding in the darkness. Gesturing them to keep low and follow him, Shadow began moving back into the darkness where he was hiding. They moved quickly, like a military unit, Shadow taking the point, Kai in the middle, and Midas holding down the rear, moving with his back to Kai to make sure he could see if anyone was pursuing them. Their formation, coming to them as easy as breathing after their former employer drilled military formations and tactics into them for months.

Finding an unlocked door, Shadow carefully pushed it opened and moved inside. Midas could hear the Russians getting closer, and he reached behind him and tapped Kai's knee to warn him that the danger was getting closer. The tap immediately caused Kai to quicken his step while tapping his brother on the shoulder and then making an X sign on the top of his back. A signal letting him know their situation was dire and they needed to evade or stand their ground. Judging by the small space they were in with only one exit, Shadow knew it was time for them to stand their ground. He quickly pulled Kai to his right and pointed for him to get behind the desk, and he and Midas took crouched positions on either side of the entrance into the private office. The office's door slowly began to open, and Shadow looked above his head to see the nozzle of a gun peek through the door's opening. A few seconds later, the Russian moved his entire body into the office and slowly stepped forward, allowing his partner to follow. Shadow held his breath, refusing to breathe or make a sound that could betray his position behind the door. The seconds moved like an eternity as he waited for the two Russians to have their backs towards them. The first Russian that entered the room tilted his head slightly, trying to strain his hearing. His eyes suddenly widen as he attempted to swing around with his gun aimed at the space behind the office door. A sudden flash and two loud pops rang out as Kai put two bullets into the Russian's spine. Screaming in agony, he leaned back from the pain, and Shadow put two more bullets into his chest. Midas's gun coughed as he fired two shots into the second Russian's chest. The Russian fell forward onto the floor, and Midas put two more bullets into the top of his head.

Kai stood up and put two more bullets into the back of the Russian head he shot and joined his brother and Midas as the three of them ran out of the office in the direction of the hallway.

Yuri heard the multiple gunshots in the backroom and sent three more of his men to see what was going on. Yuri paced back and forth in the storage room, cursing while taking aggressive pulls from his half burned-out cigar.

After a dragging few minutes, Dimitri called Yuri.

"Da?" (Yes?)

"I'm out in the parking lot, and Alexei and Michail are dead. It seems he had backup."

"Let me guess; they are gone, Da?!"

"Yes."

"Call the detective, now! We need access to the traffic and security cameras outside this station. We will use them to track them so we can find out where they are hiding out! They can't be far!"

"Srazu Yuriy!" (**Right away, Yuri!**)

Shadow, Midas, and Kai ran east for five blocks until a blacked-out SUV pulled up with Zaya at the wheel.

"Let's go, now!"

Shadow jumped into the front seat while Midas and Kai hopped into the back and shut the doors behind them. Zaya stomped down on the gas and propelled the SUV forward, burning tires and causing the rubber to scream as it dragged across the asphalt. Reaching down on the floor in front of him, Shadow picked up the AR15 lying on the floor and started checking the clip before pushing it back inside the gun's chamber. Midas and Kai had their automatic rifles in their hands, and both were aiming their guns on either side of the SUV. Zaya glanced down at the handgun in her lap, ensuring the safety was still off before making a sharp turn on 35th street, heading towards the Dan Ryan Expressway.

"Turn here!" Shadow commanded, and Zaya turned the large SUV down a one-way residential street doing close to eighty miles per hour. After driving down two blocks, Shadow yelled, "Turn right, now!"

Following his instructions, Zaya turned the SUV towards the right and nearly collided with a parked car, but she quickly adjusted the steering wheel and increased the speed of the SUV as she headed east again.

"As soon as you get on the other side of the overpass, make a left and get onto the expressway."

The SUV bolted over the overpass; the speed and slight elevation caused the SUV to lift off into the air and come slamming down on the lower side of the overpass. Looking ahead, she noticed the red light and yelled, "What do I do?!"

"Run it!"

She pushed her foot down on the gas and then snatched the steering wheel to the left. The back of the SUV swung wide, causing an oncoming car to swerve to try and avoid colliding with the back of the SUV. Quickly straightening the steering wheel, the SUV responded and corrected its wide turn, and the SUV sped forward. Racing down the on-ramp of the Dan Ryan, Zaya looked in her side-view mirror and noticed two vehicles racing behind them.

"We got company! Light they ass up!" Turning to the back window of the SUV, Midas and Kai opened fired, breaking the rear window while bombarding the front windows of their pursuers. One of the cars swerved and then spun out of control right before hitting the barrier and flipping into the air. The car came down with the sound of a bomb as it crumbled under its own weight. Midas and Kai continued to fire at the remaining vehicle, but the driver began to maneuver their vehicle to avoid the gunfire. The Dan Ryan was crowded with traffic, and Zaya began swerving around the slower cars trying to lose her pursuers. The sound of gunfire caused the motorist on the expressway to drive to the side and run into each other, trying to avoid getting shot in the crossfire.

The chaos on the express intensified the further north the two vehicles traveled at high speeds, leaving carnage behind them.

"We don't have much time before the police lock the Ryan down!" Zaya screamed at Shadow. "We got to get rid of them right now, or we are gonna have more problems than we can handle."

Nodding, Shadow pointed to the shoulder and said," Hit the shoulder! I have an idea!"

Zaya turned the SUV towards the shoulder of the expressway.

"Now, slow down just a bit. Don't let it look like we are trying to let them get closer to us."

Nodding, Zaya took her foot off the gas, counted to five, and then put her foot back on the gas pedal.

Looking in his side-view mirror, Shadow smiled to himself.

Perfect.

Opening the glove compartment, he pulled out a grenade and pulled the pin. Rolling down the window while counting, he hung his hand out of the window and then screamed, "Hit the brakes, now! Hold on!"

Zaya slammed down on the brakes, causing the truck to screech to a halt, and Shadow tossed the grenade onto the ground and screamed, "Punch it!"

Zaya hit the gas again, sending the SUV forward and away from the grenade as it rolled towards their pursuer's car.

"Take the next exit and head back south. We're gonna have to lay low in Kankakee for a while. But hit the expressway on 95th and Stony Island."

"Got it!"

The grenade's explosion lifted the front of the Russian's car, causing it to backflip and land upside in the middle of the expressway.

"Wooooooo!" Kai yelled, watching the car erupt in flames.

Zaya took the next exit and decreased her speed as she joined the traffic on the street and turned towards Lake Shore Drive. From the west side of the expressway, Shadow watched multiple squad cars, and first responders rush towards the scene of the explosion.

An hour and a half later, Zaya pulled into an overgrown lot with a motorhome situated in the middle of the grassy field. She parked the SUV in front of the motorhome and turned the engine off. Exhaling, as if she'd been holding her breathe the entire evening, she let her hands fall from the steering and leaned her head back on the seat's headrest. Reaching over to hold her hand, Shadow looked at her with concerned eyes and asked, "You good?"

"Yeah…yeah…I'm good."

Knowing she wasn't being entirely honest with him, Shadow bowed his head and inhaled deeply.

"Y'all go inside, imma dump this truck, and then I'll be back. Give me about an hour. But we have everything we need in there for now until we can come up with another plan now that we know the Russians were behind Cain's hit."

"That's gonna make the re-up impossible, Shadow!" Midas moaned while holding his head in his hands. "How are we gonna get the product now? Without the Russians, we're fucked!"

"You let me worry about that. Now go inside; I'll be back."

Shadow got out of the SUV, walked around to the driver's side, and opened the door to let Zaya out. Groaning, Zaya climbed out of the SUV and wrapped her arms around him. She held him, refusing to let him go, and whispered in his ear, "I'm coming with you. You shouldn't be out here without someone watching your back."

Knowing that arguing with her would only waste time, Shadow nodded and waited for her to walk around, climb into the passenger seat, and close the door behind her. Hearing her door close caused Midas and Kai to stop their walk to the front door.

"Hey, she's going with you?" Kai complained.

"Go inside; I'll be back. You were a G tonight, Kai. But we got this part. Midas…"

Nodding, Mida understood Shadow's silent instructions to keep an eye on his brother, and he nodded, reassuring his friend he had it under control. Shadow turned the engine and waited for the lights in the trailer home to turn on, letting him know they were good before he backed out of the lot.

Driving down a dark road, Shadow glanced over at a dazed Zaya staring out her window at the woods, moving past her window.

"Hey, I know you said you were good, but you don't look like you good."

"Yeah, I'm good. I just never killed anyone before. You know you talk that shit in the streets about killing niggas or busting a cap in somebody's ass, but when you actually do it. It…just…changes you. My father prepared me for this, so I didn't hesitate to pull the trigger because he set that expectation a long time ago. But it still doesn't prepare you for the feeling afterward."

"Do you regret it?"

"No…no, I don't. I know I would do it again in a heartbeat. But I definitely don't feel like the same Zaya I was yesterday. Turning and looking at Shadow, Zaya pointed at Shadow and continued, "I know Cain was a bad muthafucka in the military if he taught you niggas to ride like you did tonight! Fuck, that shit we pulled on the Dan Ryan…niggas gone be talking about that shit for years!"

"Imma be honest, when Cain was training us, I was pissed because I was like we ain't gone be doing no Call of Duty Modern Warfare type shit delivery to these rich square muthafuckas, so I thought the shit was overkill. Man, I had him all the way fucked up cause had he not trained us the way he did, we would all be dead."

"What about Kai, though? He trained him too?"

"No, I did. Kai begged me to show him everything I learned, and I did because I felt like the way his mouth is, he might need it one day."

Laughing, Zaya responded, "Yeah, that boy talks more shit than any nigga I know."

"Facts!"

Turning down an unpaved road, Shadow drove for another ten minutes until they came to a clearing with a large lake in the middle of it. He drove the SUV close to the edge of the lake, put the SUV in park, and the both of them hopped out. Reaching under the seat, he pulled out a metal pipe and jarred it between the seat and the gas pedal. The engine roared once the metal pipe forced the gas pedal to the floor. Gesturing for Zaya to step back, Shadow reached up and put the gear shift in the drive position, and jumped back right before the truck sprinted forward and rode into the lake. Shadow walked over to Zaya and pulled her close to him. He then stood behind her and wrapped his arms around her as the two of them watched the SUV sink to the bottom of the lake.

CHAPTER EIGHTEEN

Three weeks later...
Chicago, IL
Mayor's office

MAYOR HILL SLAMMED HER hands on her desk and pointed at the large Russian sitting in the chair on the other side of her desk and hissed, "What the fuck are you doing to my city?! Shoot-outs and explosions on the Dan Ryan and an entire police precinct aired the fuck out! A missing captain and two lieutenants and a bunch of dead Russian nationals in my morgue! You promised me that this would be taken care of discretely, that's why I gave you full access to my police department, but apparently, you aren't capable of finding a group of teenagers?!"

Yuri rolled his eyes and looked away from Mayor Hill's fiery gaze.

A woman should know her place.

"These are not your ordinary teenagers from the West Side of Chicago pulling drive-bys and holding their guns to the side. These teenagers killed those dead Russians. At least a couple of them has had a chance to learn from Cain, which in any circumstance makes them formidable. Had you did what we asked and went after the girl's father, we could use him as motivation for her to turn in the Jones brothers and their sidekick."

"I told you, now that Cain is out of the picture, we can't afford not to have King David moving our product on the streets. You have the high-end clientele now, making millions a month. I don't see a penny of that money. My take comes from the streets, so I'm not going to shoot myself in the foot and take out my last pony in the race."

"Well, then why complain? We all have to accept blame."

"No, I will not accept blame for this cluster fuck! You and your men will find them and take care of this, or we will have to reconsider our position on believing you can handling supply and distribution. Because if you don't keep the flow of product moving smoothly, you might have to deal with The Jackal, and I'm sure that's not a job review you want to have with him."

Yuri's eyes began moving back and forth in his head as he considered the ramifications of having The Jackal visiting him personally. Shaking his head, Yuri responded, "No, I wouldn't care for that at all."

"Good, now that we are all on the same page get the fuck out of my office and tie up those loose ends!"

"Very well, Madam Mayor," Yuri said while rising to his feet and slightly bowing in her direction before turning and leaving the Mayor's office.

Kankakee, IL

Shadow threw a disgusted gaze in Zaya's directions as he stormed into the small living area of the trailer home and yelled at the top of his lungs, "No! Hell now! Absolutely fucking not!"

Throwing her hands up and looking at Midas, silently pleading with him to back her, she screamed back, "This is our only play, Shadow! It's been over three weeks, and we haven't been able to re-up nor find an alternative. The Russians got the entire Midwest on lock, and we are wanted fugitives now, by Russians, pigs, and my father's people. And no telling who else is looking to put a bullet in us. The only way we can make this shit go away is if we can start supplying people who can make a phone call and get these muthafuckas off our backs!"

Pacing back and forth, Shadow pointed at Zaya and snapped, "Do you know what you are asking me to do?!"

"Yes, I do!"

"And you don't see nothing wrong with that?"

"It's a risk, but if we can pull it off, baby…we will be back on top. All we need is that one re-up. That's it! After that, we can have your old clientele to negotiate on our behalf, but the longer we wait, the less likely we will be able to regain our position."

"This shit you are talking about sounds crazy as fuck! But you told me my idea of going straight to the source was crazy!"

"And I still feel the same!"

"I'm sure you do! Midas, would you tell her how crazy she sounds?"

Shrugging, Midas responded, "It sounds crazy, but so is this whole situation. They won't expect us from this angle, which could be to our advantage, but sitting in this trailer home ain't getting shit done either. I don't really like it either, but I'm not gonna front and say I don't believe it could work."

Covering his face with both of his hands, Shadow yelled into his hands. He hoped that Midas would disagree with Zaya but secretly knew that Zaya's plan was the only card left they had to play. But it would be putting her directly in harm's way, and if anything were to happen to her, Shadow would tear the city to pieces and murder everyone responsible, no matter who they were or had ties to. But each day they did nothing was another customer taken from them, and soon they wouldn't have anyone left to service, and then they would have to turn to the streets to move whatever product they could get their hands on. Putting them in direct conflict with King David, a conflict Shadow knew they couldn't win in their current state. Closing his eyes, Shadow calmed his breathing and allowed his mind to work and anticipate every possible scenario that could arise from this new hail mary Zaya was proposing. Midas, Zaya, and Kai watched Shadow as he did his signature meditation with eager anticipation.

Opening his eyes, Shadow looked at Zaya and said, "Ok, we'll go with your plan, but any sign of fuck shit. We pulling you out, immediately!"

"I can live with that. Give me the burner. Let me call this nigga!

Hello, Malik! What's up? I need to holla at you, bruh!"

Three hours later, a black Cadillac Escalade pulled into the abandoned Kmart parking lot and pulled next to a white Mercedes CLA. Zaya got out of the Mercedes and climbed into the passenger side of the Escalade, and closed the door behind her. Malik looked at Zaya with eyes filled with concern.

"How are you holding up, Zee?" Malik asked while taking a pull on his blunt and then handing it to Zaya. Accepting his blunt, she took a deep pull on the blunt and handed it back to him.

"I'm good." She responded, her voice strained as she held in the purple smoke attempting to get the full effects of the coming high.

"Your dad ain't been right since you been on the run. He said if you come home, he will protect you."

"Malik, you and I both know my dad is not capable of protecting us from the people hunting me."

"So, what the fuck am I doing here? If your pops knew where I was right now and I didn't force you to come home, he would have me butt ass naked in his basement tied to those pillars."

"Yeah, I know, Malik and I got mad respect for you for putting yourself out there for me. But this isn't a social call. I need to talk business with you."

"Business?! Zee, your ass ain't got nothing I want!"

"Oh, so twelve million dollars ain't what you trying to hold?"

"Shut yo ass up; you ain't got twelve million skittles, let alone dollars. Stop capping, Zee!"

"I don't have twelve million, but Shadow does."

Malik's eyes widen, and his mouth hung open once he began to figure out why he was asked to drive two hours outside of Chicago. The revelation caused him to shake his head violently.

"No, no no, no no no! Fuck no! Hell no! You are trying to get me *fucked up*, fucked up! Shadow a bitch ass nigga for having you ask for him! I thought that nigga had a stronger pedigree, but it seems the nigga made of wet marshmallows. Soft bitch ass nigga!"

"This wasn't his idea," Zaya whispered while lowering her head.

"Say what, now?"

"This is my idea; he really ain't with this."

"If he ain't with it, why are you here?"

"I can be very persuasive."

"Facts! But as much as I want to help you, I can't do that. The risks are too great, and it will look real suspect if I buy twelve million dollars more of the product. They know I know you and Shadow, so it won't be hard to put two and two together, Zee!"

"It's ten million, over time—a little bit here and a little bit there. The extra two million is yours, Malik, if you agree to help us. We just need to get some product moving so Shadow can use his connections with his clientele to use their influence to get these muhfuckas off our back!"

"Them customers of Shadow must have mad pull because after that shit y'all pulled on the Dan Ryan and killing three cops, y'all niggas are public enemy number one."

"Cops?!" Malik, we didn't kill no cops!"

"Fuck, you say? Word on the block is y'all stormed a police station over in Bridgeport and shot the chief and two lieutenants. Them racist cops over there want y'all heads on a pike."

"That's a fucking lie! Malik, you know how my dad feels about killing cops!"

"Yeah. That's why I was fucking thrown when I heard. So, that means y'all got some heavy hitters after you. Fuck Zee! You got yourself tied into some shit that's way beyond the normal street beef. Damn! So you really think if you can start resupplying, some of them can clear some of this shit up?"

"Yes!"

Exhaling forcefully, Malik responded, "Ok, fine, I'll do it, but I want my two million upfront. And then I can only do one hundred thousand per re-up. Nothing more. Anything more, and it will set off all kinds of alarms with them Russian muthafuckas!"

"Thank you, Malik, good looking out," she said while accepted the blunt again and taking an extended pull on it."

"Gad damn, Zee. Give me back my shit! You smoking my shit like you ain't had no weed in decades!"

"Feels like it. I'm fucking stressed! But hey, this is the game, right?"

Taking a pull from his blunt, Malik responded, "Nah, this some other type shit ya'll on."

Letting out an uncomfortable giggle, Zaya responded, "Facts! I will let Shadow know you're down. Here, take this burner; Shadow will hit you and let you know where to pick up the bread! I gotta roll," Zaya said and then reached over and gave Malik a warm hug. Whispering in his ear, she said, "You've always taken care of me. Thank you so much. I'll never forget this."

Refusing to allow her to push his emotional buttons, Malik nodded and said, "Don't hit me with this soft shit. Get yo ass out my truck before someone see us together."

"Asshole!" she chuckled while getting out of the truck. Malik watched her get in the Mercedes and pull off. Sitting in the truck looking over the burner phone she gave him, Malik started shaking his head and thought, *The fuck am I doing?*

CHAPTER NINETEEN

THE SKY SPLIT AND growled like an angry beast as it reigned down its liquid wrath on the northern suburb of North Chicago. Shadow and Midas sat in a white Mercedes E class in the Flannagan Bar and Grill Restaurant's parking lot, periodically looking in the rearview mirror. The impatient duo waited in silence for the third party to arrive for this clandestine meeting. Shadow suddenly noticed a car pull into the parking lot, pause at the entrance and then pull up next to them. The matte black Bently Coupe came to a stop, and Trey flipped his hoodie over his head, jumped out of the car, and ran towards the back of the White Mercedes. Shadow unlocked the doors, and Trey hopped into the back seat, cursing the rain that had instantly drenched his blue and white designer jogging suit.

"It's coming down like a muthafucka!" Trey yelled but refusing to remove his hood from his head. "What's up?! It's been a minute!"

"Yeah, so I know you don't have a lot of time, so let us know what's good," Shadow said, glaring at Trey from the rearview mirror.

"Imma keep it a buck with you niggas cause I got mad respect and love for you. Ain't nothing good, bruh. None of your previous clients want to fuck with you or your product. Even if someone else delivers it."

"What the fuck?!" Midas yelled while turning around and staring down Trey with eyes filled with rage.

Throwing his hands up and leaning back to increase the distance between him and Midas, Trey replied, "Calm the fuck down, bruh! This is beyond me; this ain't my game! I play basketball and these bitches, but I don't have pull in the drug game, my nigga, and I can't sway these powerful men and women to do shit!"

Reaching over and tapping Midas on his shoulder, Shadow gestured for Midas to relax, and Midas exhaled forcefully.

"Trey, we are not asking you to get into anything you ain't comfortable with. But when we told you we had the product, you assured us that your people were ready to rock and roll again. So, we secured the product under the understanding that we would be able to move it. Hundreds of thousands of dollars of product. So, I know my partner Midas can let his emotions get the best of him sometimes, but at the same fucking time, we are talking about a lot of bread, my nigga."

Blinking rapidly, Trey began to process the current situation his big mouth got him in, and his heart rate started to increase.

"Wai...wai...wait!" Trey stuttered as he stared back at Shadow through the rearview mirror with eyes filled with fear. "I know I gave assurances, but they told me that they were on board, then all of a sudden they told me they had decided they would be going in another direction. I don't know why or who they decided to fuck with going forward?"

"Another direction?! Nigga this ain't no job interview type shit! Shadow, bruh, let me handle this shit, please!" Midas snapped while he reached for his gun.

Shaking his head, Shadow warned Midas not to pull out his gun and then turned around to face Trey. Shadow looked directly into Trey's eyes, and each time he tried, Trey turned away from him.

This nigga knows more than he is letting on. Somehow they got this nigga spooked out of his mind, and I wouldn't be surprised if this meeting ended up being a setup. There is only one player in this game right now that could spook a wealthy and privileged muthafucka like Trey. Fucking Russians.

"Calm down, Trey. I understand shit happens. Shit, look at the situation we in right now. So trust me when I tell you, we understand that things don't always go as planned. But, there's something you are leaving out, my nigga. Now, you can play like you don't know what I'm talking about, and then I can step out of this car and take a walk in the rain and leave you two alone, or you can tuck ya nuts and talk to me."

Trey's eyes bolted open when he heard Shadow's threat, and he immediately started rambling, unable to speak in complete sentences and mixing up the information he was trying to share. Annoyed near madness, Shadow roared, "Trey! I said, relax! I can't understand a damn thing you're saying. Tell it, who, what, where, and why. All this gibberish ain't helping no one, especially you. Cause Midas over here is looking at me like he ready to disobey a direct order. Now, start over, take a deep breath and talk to us like you be talking to the media or these bucket head bitches."

Inhaling deeply, Trey calmed down and then began to speak; this time, the information poured out of him in perfect rhythm and order.

"The Russians got some big shit cooking; I'm talking about the federal government big. That nigga, Ronald Nuvanci, is their fucking Manchurian Candidate! He owes the Russian president a shit ton of bread, and they threatened to expose that he's been funneling money from the Middle East from terrorist organizations and investing their money in the US stock market. He's basically helping terrorists turn a profit, and then they use that money to blow up shit!"

"Why the fuck would Nuvanci do some foul shit like that?!" Midas asked. His voice laced with impatience and violent intentions.

"He's broke as fuck and can't pay his creditors, and the only muhfuckas willing to slide him any loans are them rag top niggas. All he got left is his name. His name, Nuvanci, is like the gold standard of elegance in real estate and fashion. You slap that nigga's name on a building or pair of ugly ass shoes, and muhfuckas are willing to pay any asking price just to be seen in it. If the Russians exposed this nigga's real financial situation, that name is dead, and not even the terrorist muhfuckas would want to fuck with him. So with all that money he owes the Russian president and his other activities, he has no choice. He has to run for president. Nuvanci doesn't want to be in the White House; he knows he's not smart enough to run shit but his mouth. But he also knows he hates prison more than looking stupid. But the Russians know his name ain't gone be enough. He needs support!"

"So, they turned to our clientele, the most powerful and wealthiest people in America!" Shadow added. "Get them to galvanize the base, get them to the polls, and vote that raggedy muhfucka in. Damn."

Fucking genius.

"Right!" Trey responded excitedly, pointing at Shadow. "They promised them if they purchased the product from them and them alone, that they will ensure they won't have to deal with niggas and they would protect their image and also offer a lot of perks that only a president and a bought and paid for House and Senate can provide. Nothing you niggas can say or do can top that shit, bruh! Nothing! You know how these rich white muhfuckas are! They hate niggas more than anything, and to get rid of y'all yet keep the party going, is a sweeter deal than any high you niggas can provide!

Nodding, Shadow looked Trey in his eyes and asked, "And what did they offer you?"

"Huh?"

"You heard me nigga. What did they offer you? You are the token nigga, the middle man. No way you would meet us here unless you felt like you would be safe, and there was a reward in it for you. So, imma ask you one more time, what did they offer you?"

Swallowing the fear building in his throat, Trey whispered, "To purchase my own team, the financing to do it, and a low-interest rate on the loan."

"That's an outstanding deal. I don't know anyone that could pass it up."

Midas turned and looked at Shadow as if he'd lost his mind, but he remained silent, waiting to see what the genius had up his sleeve.

"So, where are they?"

"Where is who?"

"Back up, the calvary, the muhfuckas laying in wait to pounce on us as soon as you get the fuck out this whip, nigga. Don't play with me, Trey! I will have Midas put some hot shit in both of your knees. Then let's see how you purchasing a team will work out after we end your career, right here in this fucking parking lot."

"Shadow, I swear to God, I don't know what you're talking abo.."

"Midas, clip this nigga's wings."

"I thought you'd never ask!" Midas pulled out his gun, cocked it, and placed the nozzle on Trey's left knee cap.

"They are going to kill me! Help me, please!

What the fuck? Who dis nigga talking to? Oh, this nigga thinks I'm stupid.

Shadow's eyes became slits of rage as he pointed at Trey's hoodie and gestured for him to lift it up.

Looking like he wanted to cry, Trey slowly lifted his hoodie, exposing a wire.

"Please, please, please don't shoot me! I had…"

Remaining quiet, Shadow placed his index finger over his lips and gestured for Midas to continue his aggressive behavior.

Pressing down on Trey's knee cap with the nozzle of his gun, Midas screamed, "Shadow, what's up?! What you want me to do?!"

Tapping Midas on the shoulder, Shadow gave him a thumbs up and began to speak.

"Put that gun away, Midas. Trey is an NBA champion and a household name. Killing or injuring him would bring so much heat down on us that it would be impossible to walk across the street, let alone try to find a way to move product. We trusted you, nigga, and you played us. Imma tell you right now, Trey, you better hope I never see you again. If I do, I will kill you, fuck the fame and fortune. Now get the fuck out my whip before I change my mind!"

While talking to Trey, Shadow noticed Trey began to nod his head as if he was listening to someone else speaking to him.

Shadow snatched the hood off Trey's head. Turning Trey's head slightly to the right, he immediately noticed a tiny earpiece lodged in his ear. Shadow gestured for Trey to hand him the earpiece, and he quickly complied. Putting the earpiece in his own ear, Shadow began to listen to the Russians at the exact moment they began to give specific instructions on how he needs to leave the parking lot, so he's not caught in the crossfire. Remaining silent, Shadow let them talk until he had all the required information, and he turned to Midas and silently ordered him to pay attention to the right side of the parking lot.

A few minutes later, Trey's black Bently pulled out of the parking lot and made a right onto route 41. After traveling a block, the Bently made a u-turn and sped north on route 41. Shadow's white Mercedes left the parking lot within seconds and made the exact right onto route 41 but didn't make the turn. As the Mercedes raced down route 41, two black SUVs with dark tints pulled alongside the Mercedes. The back windows of the SUVs rolled down, exposing the barrels of automatic assault rifles, and without hesitation, they bombarded the car with bullets. The ear-splitting sound of automatic gunfire filled the air as the bullets tore through the white Mercedes. The car began to swerve and spin out of control before ramming into the concrete medium and bursting into flames.

The SUVs continued to speed down route 41, leaving Shadow's Mercedes on the side of the road, engulfed in flames and black smoke, spewing the smell of burning flesh and the screams of its occupant into the afternoon air.

Three hours later, Trey's Bentley pulled in front of Shadow's trailer hideaway. Draped in a designer blue and white jogging suit, the driver got out of the car and made his way towards the trunk of the car. Looking around to make sure he wasn't being watched, he opened the trunk and reached inside, taking ahold of Midas's hand and helping him climb out of the trunk. Sweating perfusively, Midas stumbled before Shadow braced himself to maintain's Midas's weight.

"You good, bruh?"

"Yeah, but I know imma need some water and something to eat cause it was hot as fuck in that trunk, and I can barely stand."

"I got you, bruh. Kai went to the store and got some food and some Gatorade."

"Kool, but nigga, what are we going to do now?"

"The only thing we can do. Go to the source." Shadow said and started walking Midas towards the trailer.

"Wait, nigga you not talking about going to see The Jackal, are you?"

"That's exactly what I'm talking about!"

Stopping Shadow from taking another step, Midas looked Shadow in his eyes and replied, "Bruh, that's not a good idea. How would you even get there with all the heat on us?"

"The heat we're dealing with is on the low. There aren't any statewide or nationwide warrants for our arrest. This is strictly under the table, and I can use that to my advantage cause they don't expect any of us to hop on a plane and leave the state. They've been underestimating us the entire time."

"But you can't expect them to keep making that mistake, Shadow."

"Yes, I can. Look what they tried to pull today. They thought we wouldn't see through Trey's shady ass because he's a so-called black hero. Man, fuck that nigga. He ain't shit but a nigga that can play a sport. They figured we idolized that nigga and wouldn't try anything, so I played on that. And look where we are, back at the spot without a single bullet fired at us. No telling what they put that nigga through before they figured out he was in that car, though!"

Laughing, Shadow continued to walk Midas into the trailer. Once inside, they walked towards the sound of the television. Hearing them walk into the dingy and dusty living room, Zaya and Kai turned around with faces filled with shock.

"What's up?"

"Wait, you haven't heard?"

"Heard what?" Midas asked while flopping down on the couch and causing a dust cloud to form above his head.

"Trey, that nigga y'all went to go see. He's dead."

"Wait, how?!" Midas yelled while leaning forward, trying to get a closer look at the news broadcast.

"They said he was in a car registered to Cain, and it got shot up and exploded. Witnesses say he was driving a white Mercedes E Class, speeding down route 41. The crazy thing is, Shadow has or had a white Mercedes E Class, but now when I look out the window, I see a black Bentley coup, similar to the one they say is missing that used to belong to Trey. Shadow, you wouldn't happen to be able to shed light on that, would you?" Zaya said while staring directly at Shadow. Shadow was standing in the middle of the living room, arms folded with a triumphant smile on his face while he watched the live news coverage of Trey's violent demise.

Midas turned and looked at Shadow and yelled, "Nigga?! Did you know they would kill him in that car?"

Shrugging, Shadow nodded and replied, "I knew there was a possibility."

"Shadow!?" Zaya gasped. Covering her mouth with her hands.

"What? Am I supposed to be upset that the world lost another bitch ass nigga? Fuck no! I refuse! This nigga went out there to set us up. He was wearing a wire, and when I took that earpiece from him, the Russians told him how to leave to know what car to follow. They told him specifically that they would follow us and kill us once he was at a safe distance. And this nigga was with it. Fuck that nigga! He should die a thousand deaths! If it weren't him, it would've been Midas and me out on 41 roasting in the afternoon sun. I have no regrets! Judge me all you want. We are at war, and in war, even the Knight can get his bag tipped."

"Nigga, Trey was like Michael Jordan or Kobe! That shit is gonna come back on us big time!"

"How, Trey was driving a car in Cain's name, and Russian bullets killed him. We didn't lay a finger on him. But who will have the heat on them is the Russians and Illinois governor for having the number one sports athlete in the world murdered in his state. Now we all know the governor was one of our former customers, so seeing his former supplier's car involved in Trey's murder will definitely get him to get at the Russians and cause some problems between them."

"So, this was you sending a message?"

"Yep. But now that we know we don't have any other choice. I am going to have to go with my first plan. I'm going to leave in the next couple of days. I can't delay this any longer. The longer we wait, the more power we give to those Russian muthafuckas."

Zaya leaped to her feet and began storming around the trailer, swearing at the top of her lungs. Shadow watched her as Kai stood to his feet, pointing at the television and then back at Shadow before saying, "Bro, that shit was fucking brilliant! Fuck that nigga, Trey. But are you sure you want to do this?

I'm with you one hundred percent, and I will pack tonight so we can roll down to Mexico and make that Jackal muhfucka see things our way."

"Slow your roll, Kai. The Jackal ain't no one to play with."

"So, you afraid of that nigga?"

"No, but I do respect his position of power—something you need to start doing. No one gets to where he is and be someone you take lightly. And there's no we. I'm going alone."

"What the fuck?!"

"Stop! I need y'all as far away from this as possible just in case it doesn't go as planned. I need y'all ready to get ghost just in case The Jackal takes offense at me just showing up at his doorstep. From what I've been told, he has a reputation of killing off your entire family and friends."

"I don't like you are going by yourself, but I get it. Now, you're gonna have to do some real work with that one, though." Kai chuckled while nodding in Zaya's direction as she continued to rage around the trailer. Kai, walking over to his brother, placed his hand on his brother's shoulder, sigh while shaking his head.

"You gone have to give her the extra-long and extra-strong D tonight. Other than that, whew, my nigga!" he teased as he walked past Shadow towards the back of the trailer.

Hearing what Kai said, Zaya screamed, "Fuck you, Kai! Everything is a joke to you, right?"

Refusing to engage her and pissing off his brother, Kai shrugged, went into the bathroom, and closed the door. Watching Zaya spaz out in the trailer, Shadow sighed and walked over to her.

Let me calm this girl down before she tears up the last place we have to stay.

Midas began to settle in, and Shadow noticed him relaxing and said, "Nigga, don't get too comfortable. I need you to roll with me. After today's events, an ally will be exposed, and we can't leave him like that. So, we are going to have to ride."

"Ok, I got you, Shadow."

One hundred and fifty miles away, Mayor Hill leaned against the wall in her kitchen, using her forehead as a brace, listening to the governor become unhinged on her cellphone. The sheer number of obscenities and bitches she was called was so numerous; she began to feel like all the words were mixing in together until the entire phone call became a cocktail of insults and threats.

She would periodically respond with "Yes sir," just to assure him she was listening, although her mind was already overloaded and all she heard was his voice sounding like he was speaking to her underwater. Once the phone call was over, Mayor Hill gritted her teeth and began squeezing the cellphone in her hands until her palms became red and the bones in her hand ached. Closing her eyes, the mayor attempted to calm her anxiety, but her phone ringing again dropped her right back into her abyss of panic, and she didn't want to answer, but when she recognized the number, she knew she had no choice.

"Hello, Yuri."

"Good evening, Mayor Hill."

"Don't good evening me, Yuri. I warned you about tying your loose ends, and now one of the most beloved public figures in the world is barbecued in my state all because your men fucked up, and all you have to say to me is "good evening"? Fuck your good and your evening!"

"Mayor Hill, I want to remind you of the financial commitment my president invested in your election campaign. Without him, you would not be mayor of Chicago."

"And as grateful as I am, I did not sign up for your men to start shooting up my state and city! So, tell your president that we are even! After this fuck up and all the cleaning I have to do, he's gonna owe me! Big Time!"

"He owes you nothing!"

"We'll see about that! According to the governor, you and your people are to cease pursuing the remnants of Cain's empire, effective immediately. We need to regroup, and once we do, *we* will take point on the clean-up. You and your organization need to concentrate on more important matters like the upcoming elections. If I see or hear of your people doing otherwise, you will answer someone less understanding than myself or the governor. Am I making myself clear, Yuri?"

"Perfectly."

"Good, now having a fucking horrible night, Yuri!" the Mayor yelled into the phone and ended the call.

Asshole.

Englewood, Chicago IL

King David stood in front of his mounted flat screen television with his arms folded, listening to the news reports of the murder of Trey Wilson. His mind was a hurricane of chaos as he tried to figure out why the Russians would want the basketball star dead. The Russians had already briefed him about their hostile takeover of Cain's empire, and anyone that remains loyal to them would receive massive discounts on their products. Since then, King David's organization had begun to see a significant increase in profits and newly acquired territory. Something he should be celebrating with the heir to his throne, but looking at the empty place on the couch where she would usually sit with him on similar evenings, his hatred towards Shadow grew like a weed. One of his burners reserved for the Russians began to vibrate on the glass coffee table, creating the sound of a giant insect flying up against the glass.

"Hello?"

"Mr. David, how are you doing?"

"I'm good, Yuri. No complaints. How can I help you?"

"Well, my men and I have been doing a quick...you know...audit of our transactions, and we noticed something very strange. Do you have a minute to discuss?"

"Yeah, talk to me." King David said while he muted his television and sat down on the couch to hear what the Russian mobster had to tell him.

Twenty minutes later, Malik walked up the stairs leading into King David's house. One of his security guards followed Malik up the stairs and whispered behind him.

"King David been on the phone for almost a half-hour, and he is in rare form, my nigga. He mad as hell, so be careful!"

"Who he been on the phone with?"

"Hell, should I know nigga?'

"Whatever nigga, good looking out, though."

"Ah, no problem."

Walking into the house, Malik headed towards the living room, and as soon as he was within sight, King David uttered his dreaded phrase, "Hey, let me holla at you, Malik."

As Malik turned towards King David, he could see the front door swing open, and the security detail pour into the house, rushing towards him from the corner of his eyes.

Fuck! Malik thought as he concluded the only reason why he would be a target. *I knew I shouldn't have gotten involved with Zaya and Shadow.*

Counting eight men, Malik shook his head and thought, *should've brought more niggas, they ain't gone be enough,* right before he struck the first man that closed the gap in the throat, instantly shattering his larynx. The man's eyes rolled to the back of his head, and he fell backward onto the floor. Two other men attempted to attack him simultaneously, and Malik took two steps back to dodge their attacks and then landed and devastating hooks to the side of their heads, knocking them unconscious. The next man rushed forward, and Malik ducked under him, lifted him into the air, and then slammed him down to the marble floor. The man's skull cracked like an egg from the force of being thrown onto the floor, a pool of blood spreading around his upper body.

That's four. Four more to go.

Watching the other four men being dispatched with seconds, the remaining four men hesitated, and that's all Malik needed. He rushed his massive and muscular frame forward, ramming into them like a raging bull, knocking them to the floor. He then proceeded to kick and stomp them until each of them was unconscious. Looking around at his handy work for a few seconds, Malik turned towards King David, his broad and muscularly ripped chest expanding and contracting. Looking at him through eyes tainted in red, King David pulled out his gun and aimed it at Malik.

"You've always been the most impressive soldier I've ever had on my team. Also, the most loyal, so I couldn't understand why you would betray me by cutting a side deal with the Russians and using my money to buy extra product so you can build your Empire. So, you want the crown? You're gonna have to take it straight up, nigga. Not by going behind my back."

"I don't want to take your Empire, and I wasn't making moves with the Russians."

"Oh, so that eight hundred thousand worth of dope you bought off them was for what? A birthday party! Nigga, do I look stupid to you?!'

Throwing his hands up, Malik responded, "Chill! I did it for Zaya!"

King David began to stumble when his daughter's name invaded his ears as the full force of the betrayal nearly floored him. Tears started to fill in his eyes, and her name echoed in his head, the soundtrack of his heartbreaking in two in his chest.

Zaya? He whispered, pointing his gun at Malik while his head tilted to one side. "That means she did it for...."

King David's face hardened like black marble right before he pulled the trigger. Without warning, the lights went out, but the heartbroken father didn't stop firing, the light of his speeding bullets creating streams of yellow light in the blinding darkness.

"SHADOOOOOOOOOW!!" King David screamed into the darkness, firing wildly. Malik ducked down on the floor and began crawling towards the back door. He suddenly felt a hand grab ahold of his arm and a Shadow whispering into his ear, "Follow me. I know a way out."

Malik, Shadow, and Midas emerged from a window within a few minutes and raced towards safety. Malik paused for a moment and looked back at the dark mansion, the sound of King David's agony paired with the loud pop of gunfire sending a chill up his spine. Shadow and Midas jogged towards an older model Chevy SUV a few blocks away, but Shadow noticed Malik had stopped following them. He was staring at Shadow like a predator salivating at its coming meal. Reveling in it's inevitable blood-curdling death within seconds.

Noticing his hateful gaze, Shadow closed the distance between them and pointed at the giant, and growled, "If there is anyone you want to blame, it's the Russians. They fucked up, and to try and lessen the blow, they served you up, not me, not Midas, and definitely not Zaya. I paid you for the risk, two million dollars, and for the risk. I'll let you hold on to the rest of that. Think of it as a parting gift from me to you."

"You think money is gonna fix this, lil nigga? Nah, you and me gone have to see each other. Maybe not tonight, but one day we gone have to fade. After that, then maybe we can talk. Fuck outta my way, nigga!" Malik roared while shoving Shadow to the side.

"I guess this is mines, right?" Malik asked while pointing at the older model Chevy SUV.

"Yes, with the rest of the bread in the back. I know you're gonna have to leave town, and there's more than enough money to start over. Even live the life of a square."

"Fuck you, nigga! You and I both know the square life ain't for me. Don't condescend me."

"You right, my bad. Well, we are going to leave you to it." Shadow then reached into his pocket, pulled out a set of keys, and tossed them to Malik. "Oh, and you're welcome."

"For what?"

"Saving your life, nigga?!"

"Whatever." Malik snapped while looking over the keys in his hand. Malik stood next to the SUV and watched Shadow and Midas walk away.

God damn. Even without Cain, these niggas are taking us to school. If given a chance, Shadow could be a better Kingpin than Cain. He didn't have to come get me, but he did, and he brought Midas with him. As much as my ego is hurt, the lil nigga is right.

He saved my life, I just hate admitting that an eighteen-year-old saved my life.

"Hey, Shadow! Good looking on the assist! Watch your back out here in these streets. King David will be coming for your neck."

"We got it, big homie!"

Shaking his head, Malik looked up at the sky and took in a deep breath, inhaling all the pain, stench, violence, and memories of his birthplace and then exhaled it out of him. He felt he would be back one day, but he needed to go elsewhere until then. Checking the bags in the back of the SUV, Malik smiled brightly when the glow of green stared back at him, and he quickly climbed into the driver's seat, started the engine, and drove away.

CHAPTER TWENTY

Two days later
Kankakee, IL

ZAYA WATCHED SHADOW PACK his carry-on bag with her arms folded over her chest. She would periodically suck her teeth and shake her head the more she thought about how stupid and dangerous his plan was. Shadow could feel her watching him, but he refused to acknowledge her angry stare. He didn't need the distraction or the guilt trip she was trying to send him on. This was their last play, and if this didn't work, they would have to leave the Midwest for good, and Shadow wasn't prepared to let those that set Cain up to walk free. Cain had a way of getting under your skin, to push your emotional thresholds to their max. He constantly challenged Shadow with his disrespect and threats, but Cain was there when he didn't have anywhere else to turn to. He gave him purpose and ambition. Of course, he could have found a more legal way to make money, but who's really trying to work for minimum wage anymore. Not when there were hundreds of millions of dollars to be made.

He trained him, gave him keys to the game, forced him to think and learn how to use his mind to force others to use their guns while he kept his holstered. He made him a millionaire before he was eighteen and trusted him with a large portion of his empire. And they took that from him with a single bullet to the back of his head and then tried to murder him alongside him in some dirty alley. No, they would not get away with this. No one. Trey's demise was Shadow's coming out party; once he gets The Jackal to back him, Russians, billionaires, pigs, state and local politicians, even the president of the United States would have to contend with Shadow's wrath. So, Zaya's stare wasn't going to move him. In fact, it made him pack faster.

I gotta get the fuck out of here.

Stuffing the last item into the leather designer backpack, Shadow stood there admiring his packing skills. He then zipped it up, threw it over his shoulder, and began walking out of their bedroom. Zaya stood in front of the door with her hands on her hips. Rolling his eyes, Shadow said, "Baby, move, please."

"No, you're not going anywhere."

"You do know that if I want to get out of this room, I can, right?"

"You can try, but you know I ain't no pushover, Shadow!"

"So, you want to fight? Gone with that bullshit Zee, move the fuck out of my way!" Shadow yelled, trying to force his way past her, but the trailer's master bedroom's door was narrow, and with Zaya's wide hips, Shadow was unable to get past her.

"I said move! I don't have time for this shit!"

"Fuck you, Shadow! I'm not moving!"

"You think this is a game?! These muthafuckas are coming for us. Every day looking for us, and one day they will find us, and I don't want to die in this raggedy-ass trailer in some fucking woods outside of Kankakee! That's not how I pictured any of us going out, and it's not the way I'm going out!"

"I don't give a fuuuuuuuuck! I'm not moving! You hard of hearing or just plain stupid?!"

Gritting his teeth, Shadow pointed at Zaya and stepped into her space, yelling in her face for her to get out of his way. Zaya's eyes widened as she looked at Shadow like he'd lost his mind.

Oh, this nigga thinks I'm a game.

SLAP!!

The sound of Zaya's hand connecting to Shadow's face rocked the trailer's interior, and it seemed like God hit the mute button on the remote as everything went deathly silent.

Without warning, Shadow grabbed Zaya by her arms, lifted her in the air, turned around, and tossed her several feet onto the bed. His show of strength frightened Zaya as her eyes nearly popped out of her head as she watched him handle her like she weighed as much as a bed pillow. Enraged beyond comprehension, Shadow slammed the bedroom door closed and stormed over to the edge of the bed. Seeing the anger in his eyes made Zaya retreat towards the head of the bed, but Shadow was much faster and grabbed ahold of her ankles and snatched her back closer to him.

"Shadow, let me g…!"

Her warning was cut short when he wrapped his hand around her throat and began to squeeze tightly. Pulling her closer to him, he looked her in her eyes, staring through her with eyes red with primal rage.

Still choking her, he growled, "Pull my pants down."

Not hesitating, Zaya began to undo Shadow's pants frantically. She could feel herself getting light-headed as she pulled down his jeans and his boxer briefs.

"Now, get down there and suck this dick as if your life depends on it."

Zaya's eyes watered as she lowered and swallowed his entire dick down her throat. Shadow released his grip around her neck, held the back of her head, and began force-feeding her. Zaya's mouth began to fill with saliva, and it poured down the sides of her mouth as she stayed in rhythm with Shadow's feeding frenzy down her throat. She could feel her pussy warm as her juices started to seep out of her, creating a growing wet spot in her panties. With his dick fully down her throat, she paused and held him in place, His knees nearly buckled under the pressure, and he pulled his dick out of her mouth before she forced him to cum prematurely. Shadow began violently tearing her clothes from her body, and while she stared up at him, he pushed her back on the bed, got down on his knees, and began to devour her pussy.

His tongue explored her with an animalistic vigor, lapping at her clitoris and then running his tongue down inside of her and then back up again. He then took his full lips and attached them to her clit like a starving newborn. Reaching up, he began to twist and pinch her nipples while he sucked and licked on her clit. The paired sensation made her curse so loudly she reached for a pillow to cover her mouth.

Shadow could tell she was almost there, her climax on the brink, and he suddenly stopped eating her pussy, forcefully flipped her over, lifted her amazing ass, and pushed himself inside of her. The pillow wasn't enough to muffle her screams as Shadow fucked her, pushing his entire length inside of her and then almost pulling it out completely and then thrusting back inside again. Zaya, trying to regain control, attempted to match his passion and started to throw her ass back, her dark chocolate mounds of flesh creating an earthquake against his pelvis. Grabbing her hair, Shadow pulled her head back and began pulling her pushing her body, putting her Gspot in the right angle, and Zaya's eyes immediately rolled to the back of her head.

Zaya's screams could be heard outside the trailer, moving across the large clearing where the trailer home sat. After climaxing five times, the fifth one nearly causing her to lose consciousness, she stopped counting her orgasms and gave her body entirely to Shadow as he fucked her as if it would be the last time they'd see each other.

Laying in Shadow's arms, Zaya exhaled while she closed her eyes to cherish the sound of his heartbeat. There was nothing more important at that moment but hearing his heartbeat. Shadow held her close to him, his mind clear and in the moment. He couldn't believe how violently he came, the sensation making him lose his footing and fall forward on top of Zaya. But her amazing ass broke his fall, and they both laughed hysterically at his clumsy climax.

We're still learning, she thought, smiling to herself. *If that shit were on camera, it would go viral for all the wrong reasons.*

Six hours later...

Shadow's smartwatch vibrated on his arm, and he opened his eyes to glance at his watch. 3:00 AM glared back at him, and he quietly climbed out of bed. He stood over Zaya for a few moments, watching her sleep peacefully. He knew it was better this way. They said their goodbyes earlier, fucking again while they took a shower and then laying in bed the rest of the night discussing their plans like ordinary people. No drugs, no violence, no Russian Mafia or foreign plots to influence an election. Just two optimistic adults sharing their dreams of how their lives will be together. Them against the world.

No kiss on the lips.

No kiss on her forehead.

No simple touch on her face to feel the softness of her beauty as she slept.

No whispers of goodbye that only the quiet of the night could hear.

That time had passed. The only thing left was the mission.

Shadow picked up his leather backpack, threw it over his shoulder and walked out of the room and the trailer. His uber was waiting for him outside, and without looking back, he climbed in the back seat and instructed the driver to take him to the airport.

CHAPTER TWENTY ONE

Culiacán, Sinaloa Mexico

THE HUMIDITY SEEMED TO choke the moisture out of Shadow's body, and he constantly wiped his face with his towel, trying to keep the sweat from falling into his eyes. The bus was crowded, without air conditioning, and no one spoke English. His journey from *Federal de Bachigualato International Airport* was difficult, taking him forty-eight hours to find the right directions because no one understood what he was saying or they didn't want any parts of showing a *forastero* or outsider the way to the Cazadores Nocturnos cartel's stronghold, the northwestern city of Culiacán. He had to bribe a Mexican a thousand US dollars to show where the buses going to Culiacán *may* be picking up passengers. It was a stroke of good luck that the information was reliable. Looking out the window, he reveled in the majesty of the mountains in the distance that overlooked the city, casting them in their evergreen shadow, and Shadow wondered if the cartel operated its massive drug manufacturing on the other side of the mountain range that bordered the eastern side of the city.

The bus reached its final destination, and passengers began to get off the bus. Shadow sat patiently, waiting for everyone to get off so he could exit without rubbing against anyone. Everyone on the bus was sweating profusely, and the last thing he wanted was mixing sweat with strangers. As he stepped off the bus, the sun bore down on him with a fiery vengeance that made him swear loudly and look for shade while he used his phone to find a place to sleep. About two miles from the bus station was a small inn that was a known place for the Cazadores cartel members on their way further north to the US, Mexican border. As he walked in the direction of the inn, he noticed the curious stares he would get from pedestrians. His dark skin giving away the fact he wasn't native to the city many called the most dangerous place for foreigners in northern Mexico.

Undeterred by their stares, he continued on his journey, looking around and keeping a record of his landmarks. The city, although small, was a colorful painting of culture, music, and the amazing aroma of native cuisine that seemed to invade his nostrils, causing his stomach to growl with hunger. After an hour of walking through the busy streets of Culiacán, he stepped inside the inn and walked up to the front desk.

"Hi, I would like to rent a room for about two weeks."

"Qué?"

"I…would…like…to….rent….a…room for two weeks," Shadow repeated himself, making sure he said each word slower and pronouncing each syllable.

"*Nosotros no alquilamos a extraños*" **(we don't rent to outsiders.)**

"I don't understand what you're saying," Shadow responded, his frustration being enhanced by the heat and the front desk clerk's antagonizing smirk.

"He said they don't rent to foreigners," a voice said from behind Shadow, and when he spun around, he was staring at a man smiling at him wearing a black and white collared shirt and light blue jeans. His smile was far from welcoming, and the numerous scars on his face added a menacing aura to him. He looked back at Shadow through his bloodshot red eyes, clearly high on something potent. He was studying Shadow, trying to figure out if he was a friend or foe.

"What are you doing in Culiacán, and don't say you're on vacation. No one comes here for that."

Refusing to answer the stranger's question out in the open, Shadow remained silent. He just stared back into the man's eyes, wanting him to see the fearlessness in his eyes. Chuckling at Shadow's attempt at matching his cold stare, the stranger said, "Come, I believe I can help you find what you seek."

He then looked over his shoulder and instructed the innkeeper to give Shadow a room. He led Shadow to the inn's courtyard, where several tables were filled with more patrons drinking and eating, seemingly oblivious to the dark-skinned stranger in their midst.

"Sit," the man instructed as the two of them came to an unoccupied table. "My name is Miguel. So, tell me, how can I help you?"

"I don't know if you can help me," Shadow responded while carefully looking over the courtyard.

"Oh, I am sure I can help you. You're here looking for *El Chacal*, yes?"

"I don't know what you're talking about."

265

"Listen, Zahir; he knows you're here, and he would like to speak with you pronto, señor."

"How do you know…."

"As I said, we can help each other. Now, we can sit here and play games, or you can get up and let me take you to him. He's not a man that likes to be kept waiting."

"You know the Jackal? Mateo Ayala?"

"Why do you think I walked up to you?"

"Cause I'm a black man in a place that doesn't have a lot of black faces in it."

Laughing, the man responded, "Good observation, but *El Chacal* sent me to meet you."

"How did he know I would be here?"

"We've been following you since you landed at the airport, Mr. Jones."

"Why didn't you just come to get me back at the airport?"

"We needed to be sure why you're here and that you are here alone. Now, we need to leave immediately. Grab your bag so we can leave. Please don't make me force you, Mr. Jones." Miguel said while brandishing a gun under the table and pressing its nozzle against Shadow's abdomen.

Sighing, Shadow raised both hands and slowly rose to his feet.

"You see that black van out front?"

"Yes."

"Get in."

The van's sliding door opened with a deep and loud growl, and two men reached out for Shadow and forced him into the back of the van and threw a black cloth bag over his head. The door closed quickly, and Miguel climbed into the front passenger seat and closed the door. He tapped his hand on the side of the van twice, and the van took off down the street. The longer Shadow's head was covered under the bag; he started to feel faint as the chloroform took its effect. His eyes began to flutter until his body leaned over and fell onto the floor of the van.

Miguel turned around and instructed the two men in the back to make sure Shadow was unconscious, and once they confirmed, he told the driver to take them to their hidden location. One of the men from the back called out to Miguel and asked, "How much for this one?"

"Ten million! Call our people in Chicago to get word to his boss, Cain. Tell him we want payment within two weeks, or we will mail him back to him one organ at a time."

The men in the vehicle began to celebrate the successful kidnapping of another high-value target as the van sped towards the mountain range on the city's east side.

Shadow regain consciousness from his head being rocked by a devastating right hook. His eyes slowly adjusted to the dim light around him, and his nose was immediately assaulted by the stench of dirt, death, and decay. A left hook brought his eyesight back fully, and his assailant grabbed him violently by his face and began screaming in Spanish.

"Cuéntenos sobre la organización de los chacales y sus contactos en los Estados Unidos!" **(Tell us about The Jackal's organization and his contacts in the United States)**

"I don't understand what the fuck you're saying!" Shadow yelled back.

His assailant began to pound Shadow's face and stomach. After punishing him for about five minutes, he would stop and ask the same question concerning The Cazadores cartel. Each time they would go through the torturous song and dance, Shadow would scream through his swollen lips that he didn't understand what they were saying. After nearly an hour of a merciless beating, his assailant asked the same line of questions. And Shadow gave him the same response. Ready to continue, the man pulled back his arm to land another punch, but Miguel stepped out of the darkness into the light and stopped his man.

"*Tomar un Descanso,*" (Take a break.)

"Zahir, or would you prefer to be called Shadow?"

"Fuck you, you bitch!"

"Very well, Shadow it is. Please, we can stop this torture if you just tell us everything you know about the Cazadores Nocturnos cartel's contacts in the Midwest. We know you are Cain's second in command, and you've supplied some very powerful people with drugs. Give us their names, and the pain can stop."

"I don't know what you're talking about. I don't know shit, muthafucka!"

"Very well. *Romero, seguir.*" (Romero, continue.)

At Miguel's command, Romero stepped forward and resumed the savage beating of Shadow.

Three days later

Shadow's body felt like he'd been run over by a car several times. His eyes were swollen shut, and when he moved, he could feel a broken rib pushing against the skin on his side. He moved his hands and felt the soft dirt under him. He rolled over and let the cool dirt soothe his aching back. Moaning, he tried to open his mouth, but his lips were swollen and ripped so severely the pain caused by trying to move them nearly caused him to lose consciousness. Suddenly, he heard movement coming out of the darkness, and he tried his best to move, but he couldn't. Whatever it was, it was moving cautiously, circling him, closing the distance with each completed orbit.

Shadow feared it was a wild dog, circling its prey, and Shadow's body wouldn't be able to fight it off when it sank its sharp teeth into his throat.

Closer...

Closer...

Closer...

Something was leaning directly over him, it's warm breath blowing over his face. He wasn't ready to give up. He wanted to fight, but his body would not respond when he tried to lift his arm to cover his throat. Finally accepting his impending fate, Shadow relaxed his body to prepare for his violent death.

Fuck it!

"Relax, señor; I'm a prisoner just like you, so don't fear my friend. I'm not going to hurt you. Rest, you're gonna need your strength. I hate to be a bearer of bad news after what you've endured so far, but if we don't get out of here before our ransom is paid, they are going to kill us. They've never freed a hostage after receiving payment, and neither of us is an exception to the rule," a heavy Mexican accented voice said above him.

Kankakee, IL

Zaya sat on the couch in the living room, holding herself while she rocked back and forth. The tracks of her tears still glistening in the failing light of the day. Midas leaned against the wall looking at the floor. Kai paced the trailer with his gun in his hand, overcome with grief and anger after receiving the ransom demands from Mexico with proof of life. The pictures detailed just how much Shadow had been through, his face unrecognizable.

Ten million dollars, Zaya thought as she recalled telling Shadow to let her know where he was stashing the other forty-eight million Cain left just in case anything went wrong, but he refused. Now, when they needed the money the most to save his life, no one knew where it was.

"We gotta do something! We can't just sit in this fucking dusty ass trailer and let them kill my brother!"

"Kai, how do you suggest we do that? Do we even know where he's being held?" Zaya replied. "Or do you think we can just go down to Mexico and air it out?"

"Whatever it takes!" Kai yelled, waving his gun in the air. "Kill every muthafucka we see until someone starts talking!"

"Yeah, that makes a lot of fucking sense," she snapped. She then got up from the couch, kicked open the trailer's door, and walked outside. Midas watched Zaya walk across the clearing screaming to the top of her lungs at the sky. The pain of her agony seemed to infect the air, nearly bringing Midas and Kai to tears. Looking over at Kai, Midas said, " We gotta do something."

"That's what I'm saying,"

Waving his hand in Kai's direction and shaking his head, Midas replied, "Nah, we not finna do what you are talking bout though." Sighing and standing up straight, Midas pointing outside the door and continued, "Let me go get this girl so we can come up with something that makes sense."

A half-hour later, the trio sat around the kitchen table staring down at a tabletop covered in thirty kilos of white powder. Zaya looked around the table, understanding that in Shadow's absence, she would have to be the one to lead, and although her heart and soul was in turmoil, she needed to suck it up to get Midas and Kai on board with moving such a large amount of product in such a short time.

NAVI' ROBINS

"Everyone knows what they have to do, correct?"

Midas and Kai nodded.

"Good, I'm not one for speeches and shit! Let's get out here and move this shit and not die doing it. Let's make sure Shadow comes home alive, no fucking excuses! Now let's go!"

Zaya stood on the corner of 79th and Yates, waiting for Midas. She'd just unloaded the last kilo and waited impatiently for Midas to come by and pick her up. The three of them had managed to sell every kilo on the street in a few hours with no violence or her father finding out about it. With every kilo being sold, they had raised enough money for Shadow's ransom, and the thought of holding Shadow in her arms again made her smile. But the fire that burned inside her set a blazed with the confidence that she could also be a leader of men on the streets, just like her father, and one day exceeds his accomplishments. Observing her surroundings, the corner pulsated with activity as people went about their day, some making illegal transactions similar to hers, but on a smaller scale. She began to assess in her mind each transaction and created better processes on how each dealer could improve their techniques while making more money.

"Aye, Zaya! Come here girl!"

His voice, like evil decaying the innocence of the world, destroyed her confidence almost immediately. Her body froze, and she felt a cold sweat seep through her pores. Her stomach muscles began to protest as they churned and twisted, causing her to brace herself from gagging and spewing up the infection of his poisonous presence. Turning her head slowly, Zaya's eyebrows collapsed, and her nostrils lifted as if a foul stench had filled the air when she confirmed who had called her name.

Rock.

" Zaya, you hear me calling you. Now, do you want me to get out of this car to come get you?"

Rock leaned over to the front passenger side and opened the door. Inhaling deeply, Zaya looked around one last time, hoping that she would see Midas pulling up, but he was nowhere to be found.

Where the fuck is this nigga? She thought as she slowly made her way towards Rock's black Cadillac Escalade. Accepting no one was coming, Zaya climbed into Rock's SUV and closed the door behind her. Rock watched her with heightened anticipation as she situated her body in the chair. When she was comfortable, Da Rock quickly pulled away from the corner and headed east on 79th street.

"When did you get out?" Zaya asked as she noticed that the SUV was headed towards the lakefront. Looking down at her hands, she noticed they had begun to shake, so she balled her hands into a fist to stop them from trembling.

"A few days ago. Good thing, too! Cause after that shit you and Malik pulled, your daddy needed me to regulate this shit! So, tell me, where is that nigga, Shadow?"

Da Rock then reached down into the driver's side door panel, pulled out his hand gun, and placed it on the dash. Zaya scoffed at Rock's display and replied, "I'm not afraid of that gun."

"Oh, that's because you think your daddy will come to your rescue, but what you don't know is since I've been back, I've been able to convince him to disown you."

"Yeah, right!"

"It was easy after I explained to him that if he didn't show strength, he would lose his soldiers' respect and loyalty. And without his soldiers, yo daddy is a dead man walking, literally."

"If you ever threaten by daddy again…."

"Bitch! Shut the fuck up!" Da Rock growled and aggressively turned the SUV into an empty parking lot. He then brought the SUV to a sudden halt. The force pushed Zaya's body forward, and as she tried to use her hands to stop her mouth from striking above the glove compartment, Da Rock reached for her neck and began to apply pressure while pulling her face closer to him. Bringing her close enough that she could smell the alcohol and marijuana on his breath. His red-stained eyes seemed to burn through her as he stared at her, licking his lips while breathing aggressively in her face. Zaya's eyes began to roll in the back of her head as she felt her lungs run out of oxygen.

"Your daddy is weak! A bitch, just like his daughter. Mmmmm, how I missed that sweet ass of yours, though," Da Rock moaned in her face while licking the side of her face.

Zaya's arms began to swing back and forth, her body fighting for the precious oxygen Da Rock was depriving her. Looking at her reaction, Da Rock scoffed at her weakness and then bit her on the cheek so hard his teeth punctured her flesh, releasing blood into his mouth. Tasting the metallic bliss of her blood, aroused him and he began to suck and lick on the wound like a ravenous vampire. Zaya's body, unable to fight further, became limp, and her arms fell to her side as Da Rock continued to strangle her. Noticing she wasn't fighting any longer, Da Rock flashed a grim smile and then released his grip around her neck and shoved her back to her seat.

Zaya's body immediately rejoiced as she coughed and inhaled air into her lungs while holding her neck. Glaring over in his direction, Zaya screamed, "You fucking freak bitch ass nigga! If you touch me again, I will...."

Da Rock's open hand came from the right and knocked her head against the window with so much force that it cracked and opened a wound on the side of her head. As her blood poured down the window, Da Rock pointed at her and said, "You belong to me, and I will touch you any time I get gad damn ready, bitch! I will threaten that nigga anytime I want, and there's nothing he or anyone else can do about it. After he ran Malik out of town, all he has is you and me, and I both know them niggas on the street don't respect your daddy. They respect me, and all I would have to do is point, and that nigga is dusted. That's why you begged that nigga Shadow to take the fall for me. You knew that if your daddy found out that it was me that butt fucked you when you were thirteen, he would've wanted to go to war. A war that soft nigga would never win, and his loyal and sweet ass daughter couldn't learn to live without her daddy. So you had an innocent boy, who you claimed to be your best friend, to take the blame for your...mmmm....deflowering. Putting him and his family in danger, because you knew had he came at me, I would have washed that nigga and took over all his shit! It was a brilliant move on your part, not what I was expecting."

"Wait, so you did that just to force my daddy into a war with you?"

"Fuck yeah, but I enjoyed every minute of it. But what I didn't anticipate was you being able to convince that boy to take the rap. Now, you out here selling your own father's dope that Malik skimmed on the side, and you probably think you are doing this shit for love, don't you?"

"What do you know about love and loyalty?! You sodomized me so that you can start a war! What kind of fucking monster are you?!"

"The kind of monster that can destroy your fucking world with a single phone call, bitch. I know why you are out here in these streets, risking your life. That lil idiot went and got himself held for ransom in Mexico, and now you are out here raising money for his release."

Zaya's eye's widened as she put her back against the door, attempting to keep her eyes on Da Rock at all times so she could see the next strike before it landed. She then looked around the parking lot to see if anyone was around so she could scream and bring attention to the SUV.

"Who you looking for? Midas? Ha! We caught that nigga and Shadow's little brother down on 63rd. Kai got away, but we got ahold of Midas, and that nigga started singing like Aretha Franklin once we started to tune that nigga up. So, if you're looking for that nigga Midas, he gone be a lil late."

"Fuck you!"

"Oh, we gone get to that soon enough. Mmmmm, did you give that nigga Shadow my pussy? I know you didn't give Midas my pussy. The nigga follows orders too good to be allowed to fuck with a boss bitch like you. But if you want me to keep your lil secret from the kidnappers, you gone have to...mmmm...give me what I want."

"I fucking hate you!" Zaya screamed. The pain of her past abuse at the hands of Da Rock crashing back into her recent memories, breaking down her control barriers. The look of perversion in his eyes caused her to tremble as she started to fumble at the door's lock.

"Calm the fuck down, bitch! I'm not gonna take my pussy right now! I got shit to do, and I need to play the part of the loyal friend just long enough to put a bullet in yo daddy's skull, so he won't see it coming. He's already disowned you at my direction to prevent the men from trying to take over. So, don't try to warn him. He ain't listening anymore. You crossed him for the last time. Now, all that money you made, imma need all of it! We got Midas's portion, we just need yours and Kai!

You have twenty-four hours, and after that, I'm going to start using some of my international minutes," He said, pretending to make a phone call. "Now, get the fuck out of my truck! You already know the drill, so don't play with me! You hear me, bitch?"

Nodding, Zaya quickly jumped out of the SUV and took a few steps back. Da Rock revved up the engine, hit the gas, and sped off, leaving Zaya standing in the abandoned parking lot, defeated and overcome with regret and anger.

276

CHAPTER TWENTY-TWO

Some where Mexico

S HADOW SAT IN A dark corner of the holding pit in silence, unable to muster up the courage to think of a way out of his current predicament. After a few days and help from his nameless cellmate, he felt his body starting to heal, but not enough for him to try and fight his way out. Through the pitch blackness, he heard movement on the other side of the pit, and he trained his ears to pinpoint where it was coming from.

Ok, he's still on the other side of the pit. Good.

Clearing his throat, the nameless man began speaking in his heavy Mexican accent, "So, how did you become a target?"

Shadow refused to answer. Still unable to trust his cellmate even though he helped nurse him back to health.

It could all be a trick to get me to talk. He thought.

"So, you don't trust me, even after all I've done for you?"

Silence. Shadow didn't want to engage him.

"Maybe it's because we don't know each other, eh? We might as well get to it because we only have about forty-eight to seventy-two hours left before its game over. Don't you think we should at least know who we are going to die with?"

"Not really," Shadow grunted.

"So, you've made peace with what's going to happen to you?"

"No, but having a fucking confessional in the dark ain't gone miraculously get us out of here, either."

Laughing, the man responded, "Si, you have a point. I'm just curious. Although you seem like a strong-willed man, you also seem too young to be in this situation."

"Too young?"

"Si, senor. It's in your voice."

"And how would you know that? What are you? Some kind of voice analyzer?"

"No, not exactly. But I've been living in this country long enough to know the difference between those that belong in certain situations and those that don't. And from your voice...you don't belong here."

"Oh, I belong here!"

"Is that so? So, then you know the answers to the questions they have?"

"I don't know shit!"

"So, why are you here?"

"Vacation."

"Vacation?" The man chuckled. "Yeah, I came down here for vacation over twenty years ago, the United States government footing the bill."

"Wait, what? You're not Mexican?"

"No, senor, I am actually from Chicago, born and raised."

"Chicago?! Man fuck type of shit you talking about? You are not from Chicago, no way. Your accent is too strong, bruh. You capping hard for these kidnapping niggas."

Laughing out loud, the man responded, "After over twenty years of speaking nothing but Spanish, how do you expect me to sound?"

"You got a point. So, were you on the run?"

"No, I was a soldier...special forces to be exact. We were dispatched here to take down the cartels that were sending tons of drugs through the borders. I was a patriot, willing to do whatever was necessary to keep my home safe. So, we were sent down here to help the local governments in Mexico to take down the violent cartels."

"We?"

"Yes, me and my brother. We both enlisted together, and we were considered two of the best in our unit. So, instead of sending an entire platoon, they trained my brother and me in advanced espionage tactics and sent us down here to do the work. We hit the ground running, and before we knew it, there was only one left out of the dozens of cartels we took down. Then during our final mission, we found out that they were using us to eliminate all of the competition for the last cartel standing. That is why they told us to leave a specific cartel for last. The US had no intent on winning the war on drugs. They were trying to corner the market and control the flow of drugs into the US by having only one preferred provider. Because South America, especially Mexico's economies, is dependent on narco dollars, they effectively destabilized the Mexican economy by eliminating all but one. Doing so forced Mexico to accept American corporate greed and cheap labor as a means to survive.

But that wasn't the end of the betrayal. After we decided we didn't want to be a part of their plan, they attempted to...retire us. But they missed, so both of us had to change our identities to stay one step ahead of their hit squads. I've played the role of a dead man ever since, living off the grid and using my skills that became extremely valuable in a place like this to survive. But these bastards found out who I am and have reached out to the US secret service. There is a sixty million bounty on my head for proof of life, and they are sending an agent down here to confirm I am who they say I am. Once they find out, I'm a dead man. But I fear they will not stop there and will go after my wife and children next, to close the circle. So, just like you, I need to get out of here before that agent gets here and confirm who I really am."

"Does your family know you've been kidnapped?"

"No, because of what I do, there are times that I am away from them for weeks or even months. So, me not coming home isn't something out of the ordinary. They won't see it coming...."

A solemn silence followed, and Shadow could feel the man's anxiety infecting the air. Both of them needed to get away from their captors, but there was no way they would do it alone. If his story was true, his cellmate was a highly skilled soldier, and Shadow needed his skill set to escape. But there needed to be some form of trust established between them, so Shadow decided to answer the questions the man had previously asked him.

"I came down here looking to set up a meeting with The Jackal."

"You came down here to set up a meeting? So, you came down here without an invitation?"

Shadow sighed after hearing the man's question out loud. The stupidity of his plan being exposed by the amusement in the man's voice.

"I'll take that as a "yes." Your daddy never told you not to come to Mexico without a place to go and someone expecting you to be there?"

"I never met my father."

"No, that can't be possible. I refuse to believe that."

"Believe it or not. That's what it is."

A long silence followed.

"Are you there?"

"Yeah...I'm here. I'm just trying to figure out how someone as ambitious as you didn't know your father. What you did, coming down here to set up a meeting with the most dangerous man in South America, without an invitation, although stupid as fuck, speaks of a kind of ambition that comes from a father. So, maybe you never got a chance to get to know your father, but you at least had a father figure or male role model in your life to encourage that ambition inside of you."

"Yes, I did. But it was my girl that told me my plan is stupid."

"Smart woman. You should keep her close. Well, hopefully, you kept her close because the way things are looking, you won't get to see her again."

"I don't want to accept that."

"Really, so what are you planning on doing about it?"

Suddenly, Shadow went silent. The man in the darkness tried his best to listen for any movement, but he couldn't pick up any sound. Without warning, Shadow appeared next to him and whispered in his ear, "Escaping is what I plan on doing about it. My name is Zahir, but people call me Shadow."

"Nice to meet you, Shadow. My name is Matthew!"

Two hours later

"*¡Oye! Ven aquí rápido. El esta teniendo una convulsion!*" **(Hey, come here quick. He's having a seizure)** Matthew screamed above his head, trying to get the guard's attention. A guard stormed over to the top of the pit and aimed a beam of light from his flashlight down in Matthew's face. Searching around the floor of the hole, his beam caught the outstretched leg of Shadow. Shadow was convulsing violently while foam poured out of his mouth and slid down the side of his face. Becoming increasingly frustrated, the guard waved Matthew off and screamed back, "que se joda, tú lo arreglas. "¡No soy un doctor!" **(Fuck him, you fix him. I'm not a doctor!)**

"*¡Si lo dejas morir, tendrás que explicarle a tu jefe cómo dejaste morir diez millones de dólares en la tierra!*" **("If you let him die, you're gonna need to explain to your boss how you let ten million dollars die in the dirt!")**

"*¡Mierda!*" **(Fuck!)** The guard yelled back before he began to undo the pit's cover. He then threw a rope down into the hole and ordered Matthew to tie it around Shadow's waist so that he could pull him up.

"*¡Apurarse!*" **(Hurry!)** the guard ordered as Matthew completed the knot and pulled onto the rope to let the guard know he can start pulling Shadow up.

"Joder, es pesado!" **(Fuck he's heavy!)**

Pulling Shadow above ground, the guard looked him over as he continued to shake. Terrified that he would be punished if a prisoner died on his watch, the guard momentarily looked away to find someone who could help him, and that was all Matthew needed. Matthew had purposely created an atmosphere of panic, so when the guard threw down the rope, he didn't notice that he had thrown twice as much rope as was needed to pull Shadow up from the pit. More than enough for Matthew to hang onto, and when he pulled Shadow up, he climbed up as well.

With his head turned away from the pit's opening, he didn't see Matthew climb out of the hole and flank him. By the time he returned his gaze, Matthew was already in position to quickly pull out the knife in the guard's blade from its holder and plunge it into his abdomen. Shadow reached up before the man could scream out from the pain, covered his mouth, and pushed him down onto the ground. The overcast gave a perfect cover, keeping the moon's light and the two prisoners hidden as they moved quickly towards the west side of the kidnapper's compound. Shadow promptly looked around as they moved towards the fence, and as he expected, the kidnappers' compound was deep in the jungles on the other side of the mountains that bordered the city of Culiacán. Reaching the fence, Matthew signaled for Shadow to keep watch as he began to create an opening big enough for the two of them to slide through.

Shadow's anxiety heightened each time the clouds betrayed them, allowing the prying eyes of the moon to expose their position. Gritting his teeth when he noticed a guard making his way towards the pit, he rapidly tapped on Matthew's back, trying to get him to understand the severity of their situation.

"Los prisioneros han escapade!" (**The prisoners have escaped!"**) the guard yelled into the night. The compound immediately became engulfed in light as guards began to scurry around looking for their prized possessions.

"Terminado!" Matthew whispered and pulled on Shadow to go through the opening first. Shadow snatched his arm and shook his head.

"You go first! You have a family!"

"If they catch you, they will torture you and make you tell them what I told you in the pit!"

"Then, let's not get caught. Now go!"

Shadow saw movement from the corner of his eye, and before he could warn Matthew, a guard was running up to them, brandishing a large wooden pole. Shadow jumped to his feet to meet the guard head-on while screaming at Matthew, "Go! I'll hold them off!"

Matthew turned around and watched as Shadow rushed forward, ducking under the guard and then hitting him with a devastating uppercut that sent him to the ground. Shadow then lifted his leg and brought it down on the guard's neck, shattering his larynx. Turning towards Matthew, Shadow screamed, "Go! Now!" Matthew's eyes began to water as he glanced at Shadow one last time before he escaped through the opening in the fence and disappeared into the dense bush.

Noticing Matthew had escaped, Shadow turned his attention towards the multiple guards that had surrounded him with their rifles aimed at him. Raising his hands in the air, he got down on his knees and closed his eyes, waiting for the hot metal to pierce his flesh. Miguel walked up to Shadow, pointing in the direction of where Matthew had fled; he asked, "Where is he going? Tell me now, and I won't have my men torture you. We will just put you back in your cell and wait for your ransom to be paid."

Shadow looked into Miguel's eyes and then spat on the ground right next to Miguel's boots. Looking down at the spot where Shadow's spittal landed, Miguel smiled and then pointed at one of his guards and said, *Tómalo y hazlo hablar!*
(Take him and make him talk)

The men tortured Shadow throughout the night. Taking great care not to let him die or lose consciousness as they interrogated him about the whereabouts of Matthew. Miguel made sure they were ruthless because Matthew was a sixty-million-dollar payout, and Miguel refused to be embarrassed by an eighteen-year-old. After hours of constant torture and watching Shadow endure more pain than any man he'd ever interrogated, Miguel decided it was time to end it. Looking out the small window, he noticed the sun peeking over the peak of the mountain range. Taking an aggressive pull from his cigarette, Miguel looked at Shadow's body slumped on the floor and said, put a bag over his head, take him outside, and shoot him."

"*¿Está seguro? El vale diez millones de dolares,*" (Are you sure? He's worth ten million dollars.)

"*¡Vale una mierda! Recibimos una llamada de Chicago hace unos minutos; su jefe está muerto. No llega dinero. Necesitábamos averiguar hacia dónde se dirigía el otro, pero se negó a decírnoslo. Entonces, son setenta millones perdidos a menos que encontremos el otro. Y a juzgar por su desafío, preferiría morir, ¿verdad, Shadow?*"

("He's worth shit! We got a call from Chicago a few minutes ago; his boss is dead. There's no money coming. We needed to find out where the other one was headed, but he refused to tell us. So, that's seventy million lost unless we find the other one. And judging by his defiance, he would rather die, is that right, Shadow?")

Shadow was barely conscious. His body was broken and exhausted. Blood poured out of his mouth, and his body throbbed with pain. But he managed to gather his last remaining strength, lifted his head, and growled, "Fuck you, I ain't telling you shit!"

"Very well," Miguel responded while flicking his cigarette in Shadow's direction. "Get him out of here!"

An evil grin formed on Shadow's face as they lifted him by his arms and began to drag him out of the torture room. Shadow stared into Miguel's eyes, never taking his eyes off of him as they dragged him out of the room.

I will see you in hell.

The early morning sun beamed down on Shadow, warming him and shedding the coldness of the presence of death. He could see the sun beaming through the tiny holes in the cloth, appearing like he was looking up into the stars. The image made him feel at peace with the coming darkness, and he began to tune out the voices of the men around him, taking their positions behind him, counting down.

I'll see you soon, momma. Shadow thought as he kept his eyes open, waiting for the end.

Without warning, the black bag was snatched from his head, the sunlight momentarily blinding him. Blinking rapidly, Shadow's eyes tried to adjust to the sunlight and looked up at the man's silhouette standing in front of him.

"My God, you look just like him!" the man said.

"Look like who," Shadow responded, still trying to clear his vision.

"My brother, your father, Cain," The Jackal responded.

At that moment, Shadow's vision came back to him, and standing in front of him was Matthew, a muscular and uncannily attractive dark-skinned black man, dressed in an expensive light blue designer suit, and next to him armed with an assault rifle was Malik.

"I am the man you came to see, Mateo "The Jackal" Ayala."

286

A black man running a Mexican cartel?! Shadow thought as his mind began to race. Recalling all of his interactions with Cain. Suddenly, everything made sense, from how much attention he gave him, the opportunities, the overprotective behavior, including the night he was about to have unprotected sex with Zaya. It all made sense, and now the pain of losing his mentor and his father cut even deeper. And Shadow had a feeling that his uncle was about to give him all the tools he needs to take back everything they took from them. But the masterful way his father and uncle took over the game that the US tried to murder them for, was nothing his mind could've ever conjured. Now he understood exactly where he got his genius from.

Matthew's sun-kissed face was filled with pride as he looked down at Shadow on his knees. Bloodied and bludgeoned, but still defiant. He was everything his brother Cain had promised and so much more. Nothing could have prepared him for how much Shadow resembled his brother when he was eighteen, and the uncanny resemblance nearly pulled his emotions out of hiding. Clearing his throat, the Jackal reached down and pulled Shadow up from his knees and said,

"Come, we have much to discuss."

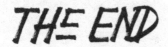

287

Coming Soon

SHADOW OF THE JACKAL
Shadow's Revenge

9 781639 449231